A Time to Choose

Evelyn Wheeler Towler

WestBow
PRESS
A DIVISION OF THOMAS NELSON

WestBow Press books may be ordered through booksellers or by contacting:

WestBow Press
A Division of Thomas Nelson
1663 Liberty Drive
Bloomington, IN 47403
www.westbowpress.com
1-(866) 928-1240

Because of the dynamic nature of the Internet, any web addresses or links contained in this book may have changed since publication and may no longer be valid. The views expressed in this work are solely those of the author and do not necessarily reflect the views of the publisher, and the publisher hereby disclaims any responsibility for them.

Certain stock imagery © Thinkstock.
Any people depicted in stock imagery provided by Thinkstock are models, and such images are being used for illustrative purposes only.

Scripture taken from the King James Version of the Bible.

ISBN: 978-1-4497-1774-2 (sc)
ISBN: 978-1-4497-1775-9 (hc)
ISBN: 978-1-4497-1773-5 (e)

Library of Congress Control Number: 2011929063

Printed in the United States of America

WestBow Press rev. date: 8/08/2011

To Mike –

Thank you for your faithful witness and leadership at LCS. I'm thrilled at what God has done through you and I'm very proud of you.

In memory of

Ellen

Whose spirit soared even though

her body was earthbound

in a wheelchair.

Enjoy the book!

Evelyn Fowler

Proverbs 3:5-6

"Trust in the Lord with all thine heart: and lean not unto thine own understanding. In all thy ways acknowledge Him, and He shall direct thy paths."

Acknowledgments

Without the encouragement and assistance of good friends, I would never have tried to publish! God has been so generous to me in providing those who share my desire to produce challenging Christian fiction for readers of all ages.

There are more of such friends than I can name here, and I am grateful for each one. Among them are Sherry and Randy, who have given me great encouragement and support. I must also mention Fran (age 104!) and her son Scott, and my sister-in-law Betty, who are all great prayer warriors.

Dean Dalton, a longtime friend, took the time to not only read my manuscripts, but to offer me wise and thoughtful suggestions along with his prayer support.

Thanks to Bob Munce for his time and good advice.

I am far from competent on the computer, so strategic assistance came from Sheila, Jim and Sarah, while Jerome and Amanda of Westbow Press offered needed guidance in answering my many questions.

Most important of all, I thank the Lord Jesus Christ, my Creator and Savior, for His faithfulness and without Whom I could have done nothing!

Foreword

For those of us who experienced childhood and youth in the 20's and 30's, and came through the hardships of the Great Depression, *A Time to Choose* will prompt nostalgia for what seems like a distant age.

It is the third book of a trilogy, and while it stands alone, it also completes a journey begun in *Under Sheltering Wings* and *The Road to Home,* all written by my friend, Evelyn Wheeler Towler.

With the insight, experience and skill of a gifted teacher and author, these fictional stories come to life. They reveal the truth that each generation builds on the strengths of previous ones as they find new challenges to be overcome.

From a life invested in the education and training of children and youth from a Biblical perspective, Evelyn shares from a storehouse of wisdom and insight. Whatever the issue, be it family relationships, social change, economic uncertainty, disappointment, romance or one's faith; all come into sharp focus and fulfillment under the gracious Hand of God.

Young or older, you will be enriched as you read of changed lives in these stories. Enjoy!

Dean A. Dalton, Vice President (ret.'76)
Gospel Light Publications

Preface

If you have read *Under Sheltering Wings* and *The Road to Home,* you will greet many of the characters in *A Time to Choose* as old friends. Others you will meet for the first time.

You will now join them in the 1930's, having put the 'Great War' behind them, and a new generation has made its appearance. America in the 30's is grappling with new ideas and is being forced to make choices between traditional beliefs and radical new trends in society. The nation is in the throes of a depression, and there exists a great divide among its people – between the idle, powerful wealthy and the weary soup kitchen dependents. Each individual young person is searching for the right path in which to direct his or her own life, and often the choices are not easy.

While still not aware that the Great War was *not* the 'war to end all wars' (as they had been told), the youth of the thirties are tasting the excitement of new inventions, exploring the unknown skies, and looking for something real to satisfy their souls. They are often bored with life, not knowing that the challenges of the next decade will demand from them every ounce of character that they possess.

So if you are one of those who were young in the thirties, you will enjoy a nostalgic journey. And for those of you for whom the thirties were the 'olden days', you will find that these young people are much like you. I hope you will find yourself in these pages!

Introduction

In *A TIME TO CHOOSE* you will meet the following families:

The WHEATONS
Dr. Rosina Wheaton – President of Birch Lake Academy
Celia Marie and Barbara Wheaton – daughters of Daniel (deceased)
and Dr. Rosina Wheaton
Members of Dr. Wheaton's family – the Huebners
Beth – close friend and nanny to the Wheaton daughters
Grandpa and Grandma Wheaton – lifetime residents of Charlotte,
Michigan

The MARLOWES
Daniel Marlowe – President of Underhill Associates, with home offices
in Charlotte, Michigan
Christy Marlowe – Mother of Daniel and widow of Matthew
Josie Marlowe – Daniel's wife and adopted daughter of Christy and
Matthew
Joseph and Ruthie Marlowe – Matthew's brother and his wife
Eleanor Marlowe – Daughter of Daniel and Josie
Robert Marlowe – Son of Daniel and Josie
Billy O'Conner – Adopted son of Joseph and Ruthie Marlowe

Joshua O'Conner – Son of Billy O'Conner; owner of an aircraft business and youth director in a small church near Charlotte

Julie Anderson – Daughter of Christy and Matthew Marlowe

Sigmund Anderson – Pastor of Redeemer Chapel and husband of Julie

The HOLTS and Friends

John Holt – Owner and craftsman of Holt-Waggoner Metal Works

Louise Holt – John's wife and daughter of Albert and Katherine Waggoner

Penny and Patsy Holt – Twin daughters of John and Louise

Mary Ann and Gordon Walters – Neighbors and lifelong friends of Louise Holt

Kent Walters – Son of Mary Ann and Gordon

Chapter One

Everyone who saw them said the same thing: "They're as alike as two peas in a pod!" In fact they heard it so often that when they were three they turned it into a little chant and could be heard around the house singing, "Two peas in a pod, Two peas in a pod!" Of course they weren't quite sure what the phrase meant, but it made a good song! And one day Penny asked, "Mama, what is a pod?" and Patsy echoed, "What's a pod?" Louise showed them a pod full of peas, but their only response was, "Do we look like those?" and their mother gave up. However, they kept singing their little song. At their age, songs didn't need to make sense!

If one were to judge strictly by looking at them, they *did* seem to be identical twins. The observer could not be blamed if he blinked at first and thought he was seeing double. Little inquisitive faces were framed by bright sunny curls. Their chubby little bodies appeared to be equipped with the machinery of perpetual motion. And where you saw one you always saw the other. The house was never silent after they arrived, and the childish voices were very welcome in a home where any hopes of such sounds had been despaired of long ago.

Louise had longed for children, and she and her husband were equally disappointed when they celebrated their fifth wedding anniversary without any hope of having a family. The delightful surprise of the twins' coming had changed their lives and given their marriage new purpose and meaning.

As far as the twins were concerned, it seemed from the moment they opened their eyes that the air about them was full of excitement. Of course at first this excitement took the form of a new world full of love and snuggles, very satisfying to two little girls who thrived on attention. They soon learned that by laughing and gurgling and always reaching out for more, their wishes were immediately granted. Some might have said they were badly spoiled but to this their doting parents turned a deaf ear. They had waited so long to have children whom they *could* spoil that they completely ignored such criticism. So they showered their love liberally on these two little gifts from heaven. And as Penny and Patsy grew, they came to rule the household with their childish laughter and loving hugs, and their parents were their willing subjects.

In the town of Little Rapids, in southern Michigan, John Holt owned a prosperous business. It had not always been so. A little less than ten years ago, an immigrant in his middle twenties, he had drifted into the small town, saddled with a German name, a deep resentment against a cruel father, and a heavy accent to match his name. But before he hit town, he had already decided to shed one liability – his name – and make a superhuman effort to erase the other. He knew it was possible to learn to talk like an American because his little sister had already proved it could be done. He was confident that without those two strikes against him he could be a success in this great country, now his chosen home.

However, he had little experience at anything except farming and lumbering and he had had enough of both of those. He reasoned that certainly there must be something better to be had with the whole world from which to choose. He would look for an occupation that would not only provide his material needs but would also satisfy his soul. So, hands in pockets and cap perching rakishly on the back of his head, he sauntered down the street whistling softly to himself as his eyes darted from side to side. He had a feeling that there was something here just waiting for him. As he unhurriedly made his way he had no idea what an alluring picture of young manhood he presented, nor did he know that several pairs of feminine eyes watched him curiously. For the owners of those eyes, he was unconsciously turning a heretofore uninteresting village street into a highly attractive thoroughfare.

Suddenly his attention was drawn to a storefront bearing a sign, "Waggoner Metal Works". The display window boasted an intriguing group of toys – all metal and brightly painted. His mind leaped back in time to a small boy who had treasured just such toys and who had, even as a young man, been loathe to leave them behind. Nostalgia almost overwhelmed him as he gazed, spellbound, at the window. He drew closer to examine them even more carefully.

As he stood, eyes glued to the collection, he had no idea that he was being just as minutely examined by a pair of eyes hidden behind the curtain. Time had come to a standstill for him and a prickle at the back of his neck signaled the message he had been hoping for. It seemed to say, "You don't need to look any further. This is where you'll find your future!"

He remembered his grandmother telling him, "Son, God has something good for you. Someday you will find it." Then she would always add, "And when you do, don't forget to tell Glod 'thank you'." His grandmother was convinced that God was in charge of everything and everyone. John was not so sure, but he always smiled and replied, "Yah, Grossmutter, I hear you."

Now her admonition reminded him. "*Danke, God, if you're really there to hear me say it.*" Now he had cleared his conscience. Now he could enjoy his new discovery. But in his elation he somehow still had a feeling of emptiness. Was God really pleased with him? He wished he knew! Maybe there was still something he needed to find. Was it here?

He yanked off his cap, loosing a mop of blonde curls, stuck it in his pocket and opened the shop door. The watching pair of eyes turned out to belong to a young woman of about his age who seemed to be the lone shop keeper. They peered at him out of a piquant face framed by hair as dark as his was bright, and the two young people gazed at each other with a sense of sudden recognition. She was the first to speak.

"Can I help you, sir?" she asked. "Did you come to apply for the job?"

"Job? What job?" Momentarily, he realized he had missed something. "Uh, yes, I *am* looking for a job, but I came in to take a closer look at the toys in the window. May I?" and he reverently picked up the figure of a monkey- like little man who appeared to be dancing a jig. "When I was a child I had a toy just like this, and before today I've never seen another like it. Is it for sale?" For the moment he forgot that the few cents he had in his pocket was his only hope of a meal today.

"Oh, yes, those toys are all for sale. But you know they're hand made and quite expensive. As a matter of fact, they're part of an order which has not been completed yet." With a veiled glance at his well worn shoes and faded shirt, she guessed that he had little money. "Would you like to see some others? I'll get them from the workroom." As she turned to go, he reached out to stop her.

"Did you say the master is looking for an apprentice? Is that the kind of job that is available? Could I talk to him?" Unintentionally, his choice of words rather than his accent revealed his origin.

"Of course. He's back in the shop. If you'll wait here, I'll call him."

She slipped through the shop door with a sense of excitement stirring in her breast. She could not identify the emotion that had engulfed her because she had never experienced it before. But the flash of recognition that had passed so swiftly between the two young people had shaken her. She desperately wanted to have this young man to stay in town, and she knew that her father could make it happen.

"Papa," she called and a giant of a man emerged from the back room in answer to her summons. "Oh, Papa, there you are. There's a young man out front who wants to see you. Perhaps he will be interested in the job you have to offer." The hint of a smile briefly illuminated her eyes. "He looks like he hasn't eaten for a while but is so busy admiring the toys that I'm not sure he knows he's hungry!"

Her father gave her a startled look. "Such a man who is more interested in good workmanship than in his stomach is hard to find!

Ach, yes. He is worth talking to, Daughter." He strode to the door and flung it open. "Come in, young man. Are you looking for a job? Or are you just being curious? But first, tell us your name." He thrust his hand out in friendship, and as John grasped it he realized that for such a beefy man, the hand, though strong, was well formed and sensitive. Much like his own, as a matter of fact.

"Thank you sir. My name is John Holt, and yes, I am interested in a job. To be truthful, I really need one badly. Did you make the toys on the shelves out there?" He jerked his head toward the storefront. "They are just like some I had when I was a child."

"Yah, I make them out here in my shop. I make many objects which are useful and needed by my neighbors, but I make the toys for pleasure – *my* pleasure as well as for the kinder who will play with them." Still grasping John's hand, he introduced himself.

"My name is Albert Waggoner and this is my daughter Louise. Do you know anything about working with metal?"

"Not much, sir. But I could learn. I know how to farm and I've worked as a lumberjack, but I'd like to learn a trade. Would you take me on as your apprentice?" John had felt an instant liking for the huge but gentle man, and could sense the artist in his soul. Suddenly he knew that he could not only work with this man congenially, but that he would find great satisfaction in putting his own abilities to the test, partly to be able to gain his approval.

"Come." Albert gestured to John to follow him. He led him to the back of the large room which was his workshop. "You see here is my hearth, my forge, my molds and my worktable where I plate and paint my toys. You will learn." He pointed to the open yard behind his shop. "There I have an open hearth and anvil where I work as farrior, and many farmers bring their horses to me to be shod." He looked contentedly about his shop. "I have no lack of business."

He turned and looked at the young man for a long moment, appraising him not only for appearance, but appearing to make an effort to read his sincerity. "I like what I see," he announced bluntly. "But you must understand that my work takes a strong body, a will to work hard, and a wish to learn that drives a man to put forth great effort. I cannot use a lazy man in my shop. Do you still wish to work for me?"

John could not contain his enthusiasm. "Please sir, let me have a chance to prove to you that I am the man you are looking for. I know I can do it."

Albert slowly nodded his great head. "I too think you can do it. If you have the necessary knack as well as the desire, you will learn. Now," he continued, " I wish to know about you. Where do you come from, and why have you come to our little town? I do not remember seeing you around here before now."

"I came from Germany six years ago, and settled in the northern part of Michigan. The only jobs available were either in farming or lumbering, and I didn't want to spend my life in either one of those occupations. So I set out to find something which would give me more satisfaction, and perhaps a better future. I believe I have found it here." His eyes again traveled about the shop as if seeing his future, then came to rest on Louise. "Your daughter and yourself have convinced me that this is a town where I would be welcome, and could perhaps make myself useful."

Satisfied, Albert again stuck out his hand. "You will be here early tomorrow morning and we will start. Do you have a place to sleep?"

"No, sir. Is there a rooming house nearby that might put me up?"

"Papa, Mrs. Damon lets rooms and also serves meals for boarders. Perhaps he might find a room there?"

"Yah, that is a good idea. Her house is just two blocks down the street. If you will give me a hand here to finish up a small job, I will take you there and tell her you will be working for me."

And so it was that John Holt became a resident of the town of Little Rapids, and found his place in the world.

From the beginning, the two men were congenial and worked well together. John was quick to learn, and proved quickly that he was anything but lazy. Albert found that he was not only a careful worker, but soon began to see things to do before Albert pointed them out to him. He was also creative, sometimes finding ways to increase the efficiency of the work and greatly pleasing his employer. Best of all, he found great satisfaction in learning the trade, and knew that this was where he belonged.

He was not only attentive to his work, but also very aware of Louise. Their friendship blossomed, and though he attracted the attention of many of the town's marriageable girls, he had no eyes for any but Louise. However, he was very careful in his attentions to her, for she was the only daughter of Albert and his good wife, Katherine, and they were clearly very watchful of her friends. He was a welcome guest in their home. Having had a very proper grandmother who demanded respect from her grandsons, he had learned to handle himself with decorum. Though greatly attracted to her, he patiently awaited the time when he would be sure that his attentions were approved by her parents as well as by Louise, herself.

It took two years to make him comfortable in declaring his intentions. The work in the shop went well, and the relationship between the two men grew in mutual respect. John became a favorite with Katherine as well as Albert, and between John and Louise there was an unspoken understanding. When he finally asked Albert for his daughter's hand, the response warmed his heart.

"Yah, you are like a son already, and her mother and I believe that you will make a good husband for our daughter. It was a good day that brought you to our town and into my shop. Yah," he repeated with great satisfaction, "I believe this is good!" And his wife made her feelings known by an unusual burst of affection as she hugged both John and Louise.

They were married in a beautiful little church where the Waggoner family attended. It had a tall, graceful spire, and inside were beautiful hand embroidered cushions for the altar and the kneeling benches, and the windows were made of lovely stained glass with pictures of Bible characters and stories adorning them. The pastor wore expensive robes and preached well-studied and perfectly worded sermons, but there was little to be learned from them. However, the ceremony was solemn and impressive and John and Louise were happy.

John moved into the spacious two story house as one of the family. In the two years since he had come sauntering down Main Street, he had become known and liked in the small town. The speed and skill with which he learned the trade from Albert was not unnoticed either, and it earned him the respect of his peers. Albert's friends considered him very fortunate to have found an apprentice who so quickly became a real asset to the business as well as to the community.

In a short time, John began building a home just two blocks from the shop. Albert had given the young couple the property as a wedding present, and though he loved his in-laws, John was anxious to establish his own home. Both he and Louise wanted to have a family, and wanted to finish their house in plenty of time to be ready when it came. However, the house was readied, they furnished it with children in mind, and they waited. And they waited some more. For almost two years they waited. Finally with great joy Louise told him that she was pregnant.

Their joy was short-lived. Within three months they mourned the loss of a child when Louise had a miscarriage. The doctor tried to comfort them by telling them to just wait a while and try again. But the years passed and when they had been married for five years, they lost hope.

John tried to comfort Louise but his own bitterness made it awkward. Louise silently mourned, and their communications became strained. John would not blame his wife for their failure, and he was absolutely positive it was not *his* fault. That left only one person to blame – God. If God was really there (which he doubted) He could do something about their empty nursery. But obviously God didn't care about such things, so it was a waste of time to even think about Him.

Soon after their fourth anniversary, tragedy struck the family. Albert, the gentle giant, suffered a sudden heart attack and the family was broken hearted. This event, and the sorrow that it brought, further convinced John that God probably didn't exist. So he turned his attention to the family business affairs, which were now his responsibility.

Since Katherine was now alone in her own big house, Louise and John were glad that they had built their home so close. Then, while they were still adjusting to the loss of their beloved Albert, Louise suddenly found herself again pregnant. Was this the miracle they had been waiting for? Their waiting was a mixture of despair and hope. Then the long awaited miracle happened and the twins made their appearance. They were just what was needed to comfort the bereaved grandmother and to bring life and laughter to the house that had been built for children.

John would never forget the moment he first looked into the faces of the two little girls, both at that moment screwed up in demanding squalls which were music to his ears. Their helplessness tore at his heart, and it seemed to him that his whole being dissolved in such a love for them that he could not help but join his tears to theirs. Then as he held them in his arms, he knew that they would forever be a part of him, as close as life itself. It was a moment that would change his life forever. It was a moment that also forcibly reminded him that God could not so easily be eliminated by simply deciding that He no longer existed. This time John did not have to be reminded to lift a soft *"Danke, God"* toward heaven.

Of course the business now belonged to John and Louise, and John proudly added his name to the sign on the storefront. It now read "Holt-Waggoner Metal Works" and continued to do business as it had when Albert was alive.

Their home was one of the more well to do residences in Little Rapids. The tiny girls were loved and showered with everything money could buy. Dolls and teddy bears occupied the nursery and as they grew, the playroom became filled with toys of every description. Long before they could read, they loved books, and both Louise and Katherine found great delight in reading to them, gradually helping them to recognize letters and sound out words. John almost never came home from a business trip to Charlotte or Lansing without new puzzles, dolls, or toys to surprise his adored babies. Of course he crafted toys for them in the metal shop also, but toys for little girls were a bit out of his line.

Louise took great delight in dressing the twins beautifully and always alike. She and Grandmother Katherine stayed busy making exquisite little dresses and creating comfortable and colorful play clothes for the twins. Of course they were her own little "dolls" and they had enough clothes to dress at least a dozen children.

Their own little kingdom was complete as far as the twins were concerned. They had each other – the most important thing – and they had Mama and Papa with no competition from other siblings. Then there was Grandma Katherine, who was never too busy to rock them or to tell them stories about Grandpa Albert, or about Mama when she was a little girl. And Papa was always good for a ride high on his shoulders, or for a romp in the spacious yard where they had their own swing and seesaw. Since John and Louise were also happy with their own little domain, it was a situation which their acquaintances and friends considered ideal and an example of what a good home should be like.

Respected citizens of the town of Little Rapids were all church goers and the Holt family was no exception. They attended the church in which they were married, and the twins were always in Sunday School. They liked the pastor because his sermons were interesting and demanded nothing of them but their attendance. He often flavored his talks with book reviews of current interest, but with very little spiritual guidance.

So life was good. John made a good living, now had an enviable family, and he was a leading member of society in this town. What more could a man ask?

He couldn't answer that question. He had a deep, nagging awareness that something was missing, but he refused to let it surface. He had decided long ago that even though God might exist, He wasn't really involved in everyday lives, and so there was little use in questioning why there was such an empty place in his soul. He would just ignore it!.

Chapter 2

Only one other family was granted admittance into their tight family circle. Louise had grown up with Mary Ann Walters, and both were delighted when the Holts were able to build their home next door to Mary Ann and her husband, Gordon. The Walters had one child, a son Kent, who was four years old when the twins arrived. From the first time he bent over the cradle and cooed at the tiny babies, he seemed to consider that he belonged with them and he adored them. He was their constant playmate, and was accepted in the family like a brother. He was careful and patient with them, and best of all, from the beginning he understood their language. When the twins began to talk, they learned quickly to understand and respond to their parents, but at times John and Louise were at a loss to understand their baby talk. However, Kent always seemed to know what they were trying to say and would translate for them. Then they would giggle with glee as though the three had a secret between them. It amused the two sets of parents, who were always playing guessing games about what they were saying, but they never won. They were always amazed that Kent was able to understand, but to the twins and Kent, the game belonged to them.

As they grew older, very different personalities began to emerge in the little girls. Their facial expressions became more individual and people quit calling them "two peas in a pod". By the time they started school no one had any trouble telling them apart.

Penny was the aggressive one. She always met life head-on, even running to meet it! Always ready to try anything at least once, she had more than her share of scrapes and bumps, but nothing ever seemed to deter her zest for adventure. After going to see the circus, she tried tight-wire walking on Louise's clothesline in the back yard. Of course she fell off and cracked her head open, necessitating a trip to the doctor. Having her scalp sewn together again was momentarily traumatic, but she soon forgot the pain in her determination to find out what the next adventure would be like. Sadly, she wasn't the only one to suffer through her escapades, because Patsy always wanted to "do it, too"! It took all of Louise and Katherine's efforts to keep the twins from disaster.

Patsy, on the other hand, sat back and waited for life to come to her. She always wanted to keep up with Penny, but seldom ventured very far beyond her comfort zone. She was usually willing to let Penny do the talking for the two of them, but when it came right down to the line, she was apt to do her own thing. However, if Penny got herself into a scrape and needed her, Patsy was there to take part of the blame. Penny was fortunate to have her because she served as a balance wheel – if there had been two Penny's instead of a Penny and a Patsy, there's no telling what might have happened!

So it was with some relief to their parents that their first day of school approached. It was also with some trepidation that Louise and John anticipated that day, for who knew what the twins would do at school? They would be dressed in their most adorable little dresses, their curls would be like little halos, and they would look like little angels. The terrible truth was that they were anything but angelic!

The night before putting them in an unsuspecting teacher's care, the parents determined to have a serious talk with them. Of course they should have been doing this for some time, preparing them for their entrance into the real world, but John and Louise were not the most experienced parents in the world. So when the two little girls climbed into waiting laps as usual, and opened their favorite books to be read, Louise gently took the books from them, closed them and laid them aside. With an arm cuddling one on each side of her, she spoke softly.

"Daddy and I have something to tell you before we read stories tonight. Will you be really quiet and listen to Daddy?"

Looking puzzled, but ready to cooperate, both girls nodded and turned their attention to John.

John began. "Penny and Patsy, I want you to listen very carefully. You are big girls now, big enough to go to school. School is going to be very exciting, because you will learn many wonderful things. But it will be very different from what you are used to, and you won't be able to do things like you do when you're here at home."

Eyes huge and round and wondering, the girls sat without wiggling (a miracle in itself) and watched their father carefully. When their mother spoke, they gave her the same intense attention.

"You see, girls, in school they have rules for you to follow. You know your daddy and I have certain rules that you must follow here at home, but at school the rules are different. Your teacher will expect you to sit quietly in your chairs, and raise your hand when you want to say something, and she will not want you to get up and wander around. All the children have to obey the same rules, because school is not playtime, but a place to learn. You must listen to the teacher and do what she tells you to do."

Penny broke in. "I don't want to go!"

Patsy echoed. "Me, neither!"

Penny again. "I thought school was going to be fun. That's what Kent said."

Now it was John's turn. "School *is* fun – if you follow the rules. But when you don't do as the teacher says, you will probably get scolded and maybe you will be punished. Do you understand? Mama and I will expect the teacher to tell us that you were good girls and did everything she asked you to do. Then we'll be very proud of you."

Penny looked at him reproachfully. "Why do we have to go? I don't like the teacher."

"But you haven't even seen her yet. She's a very nice person, and I'm sure you will love her." Louise sensed a battle coming. She knew the signs.

"We'll just stay home. Won't we, Patsy. We don't want to learn things. We just want to stay here and play." Penny spoke for both the girls, and Patsy nodded her head vigorously.

John sighed and looked at Louise helplessly. "Well, we'll talk about this some more in the morning. Come on girls, time to go to bed now. We want you to be all rested and ready to go in the morning. You'll feel different about it tomorrow." He looked hopefully at Louise. "Won't they, Mama?"

"No." This time the girls spoke in unison. They sat motionless, their little chins set with determination, as they defied their parents. Discipline was rare in this household, and the little "angels" were used to having their way.

"Well," Louise decided to temporarily concede the battle. "Let's read a story before you go to bed. Which one would you like to hear?"

Penny and Patsy looked at each other, then wriggled out from under their mother's arms. "Can we sit in your laps?"

"Of course." John was smiling at this small victory. "We can't read stories any other way."

In the morning it was as if nothing had been said. The twins dressed, ate their breakfasts, proudly picked up their tin lunchboxes, and accompanied their mother to school. Louise was so relieved that she missed the meaningful glances that passed between the two when she wasn't looking. Very often words were unnecessary to the twins' ability to communicate with each other.

Upon their arrival, as they were introduced to the teacher, Louise had her first inkling that all was not right. When Miss Johnson leaned down to greet them, she was met by two sets of hostile eyes and a silence that was not at all shy, but was determined and unfriendly. A little shaken, she offered to show them where to put their lunchboxes before she guided them to their seats. However, they clutched all their possessions to them, including their lunchboxes, and shook their heads in a decided negative. Rather than have a confrontation, she showed them to their seats, where they obediently sat down, still in silence, hanging on to their belongings as if they expected to have them snatched from them. Miss Johnson had other children to greet, so she didn't linger, but Louise watched the little drama with misgivings. Things were not as calm and comfortable as she had thought.

She decided that it would be well to stay a little while to see how things were going to go. She stationed herself in the cloakroom where she could watch the girls without being seen. For a while she had to dodge the arriving parents and pupils, but since the weather was mild, the cloakroom was not crowded and she managed to stay out of sight.

She watched as Miss Johnson expertly got the attention of the class and began to teach them the opening procedures. She noted with wonder how this experienced teacher managed to mold this group of small children into a unit and convince them to follow her lead in singing, bowing their heads for prayer, and saluting the flag. The only ones who did not cooperate were two angelic looking little girls who sat stiff and straight in their chairs, looking straight ahead, clutching their lunchboxes, and not opening their mouths. Her heart sank. Now she felt that last night had been just the beginning of the battle.

A more experienced parent would have just waited for them to enter into the activities, but Louise was not an experienced parent. For the last six years she had bowed to all the whims of Penny and Patsy, and had crossed them only when their physical welfare was at risk. So as she hurried home, she burst into tears, dreading what she would hear from the teacher at the end of the day. She wanted so much to be proud of her willful children, not realizing that they were just putting into practice what they had learned from her. Katherine was sympathetic. She had been through all this before and she knew that everything would be all right. However, it was no use trying to reason with Louise.

John came in from the shop, and they sat down together for a second cup of coffee.

"Well, how did it go?" he wanted to know.

"You wouldn't believe how sweetly they went to school this morning, just like lambs. But when they met the teacher," Louise began to sob. "They looked right through her as if she wasn't even there, and they wouldn't say a word. They wouldn't put their lunchboxes away, they sat straight in their chairs, not even looking around at the other children, and were absolutely silent. You wouldn't even know they were alive, because they didn't move a muscle. They didn't bow their heads for the prayer, wouldn't sing, and refused to stand up when the children saluted the flag. They were just like wooden dolls. John, you just wouldn't believe it," she repeated. "I'm dreading to hear what Miss Johnson has to say when I pick them up this afternoon. I'm afraid they have given her a terrible day – and, oh, John, they're so little to have to be away from home and in a strange place all day!"

John put his hand over hers, then drew her to him, pulled out his big white handkerchief and gently wiped her eyes. "Louise," his voice was tender. "Louise, are you crying because you are worried about their behavior, or are you crying because all of a sudden you realize that they're beginning to grow up? You knew that you couldn't keep them at home forever."

Fresh tears poured from her eyes. "But they're just babies, John! They may get homesick during the day and I won't be there to comfort them!"

"Well, I don't want to be hardhearted, but I can't see Penny crying with homesickness on her first day at school! And if Penny doesn't cry, neither will Patsy." He patted her hand, then took his last swallow of coffee. " I have to get back to work. But if you want me to go with you this afternoon to get them, I can close the shop for a few minutes and ask Mother to sit in the store."

"Oh, would you, John? I'm almost afraid to find out that they defied the teacher on their first day at school - and maybe they won't want to go back tomorrow. Maybe we're not very good parents. Do you think so, John?" Tears were still running down Louise's cheeks.

Her husband set his coffee cup in its saucer and arose. He pulled her to her feet and wrapped his arms around her. "Honey, what we've done is love those two little imps, and you can't raise children without love! I can't believe they're so spoiled that they can't be taught to do the right thing. We may have to change some of *our* ways, but the girls will be all right. You just take my word for it."

After a day of wondering and waiting, it was with a trembling heart that Louise accompanied John to meet the girls after school. She had missed them terribly, and the house had been so silent that she couldn't rest. While eager to hug her babies again, she was almost afraid of what she would find.

She peered timidly into the classroom, expecting to see two wooden little figures still defying this new world into which they had been thrust. Instead, she got the shock of her life. Two little curly headed girls spotted them at the door, and were off like a shot, jumping into their arms and both talking at once. "Daddy, Kent was right. School *is* fun. Come over here and see what we've been building. We've learned to write our names and Miss Johnson said we're two of the best students she has. Isn't that great!" Penny was talking as fast as she could and Patsy was nodding her head and pointing as she hugged her mother's neck.

"And here comes Miss Johnson. She's so nice, Mommy! I just love her!" Patsy finally got a chance to talk.

Louise and John looked at each other in amazement. "I never would have believed it!" Louise whispered.

John grinned with fatherly pride. "I told you they're the best!" he bragged.

The first day at school had been a huge success. Their only complaint was that they hadn't learned to read yet by the end of the day!

And Louise learned a lesson that she had been refusing to acknowledge for a long time. These two little girls had grown to be two little individuals who were going to make their way in life without her! There would be times when they would need her guidance and comfort, and she must be there for them; but she could no longer expect to guide their every step. She must begin to let go of them, and it made her heart ache. Those first six years had rushed by so fast, and her babies were babies no longer!

Chapter 3

John's business was thriving. As the years passed he added new items to his inventory as the technology of the time demanded them. Albert had built up an excellent clientele as a farrior, but John had been the one to see the wisdom of branching out in other directions. He began to build bicycles and to supply parts and services in repairing them. Then he became interested in motor bikes, and again the names of new customers appeared on his account books. Finally, being of a very inventive mind and with the talents to develop his inventions, he began supplying auto parts. He secured contracts from other cities and from large companies, for the name of his state of Michigan was becoming synonymous with motor cars, and his own name was becoming well known in the industry. He enlarged his shop, then built an addition to it, and hired a number of men as his business expanded. His next door neighbor and friend, Gordon Walters, was by now a well established attorney in Little Rapids, and handled John's growing legal needs.

The two families remained close, and Kent continued to be the twins' best friend. For all intents and purposes, he was more than ever like a big brother. Which caused frequent disagreements between him and the girls.

"Penny, the guys on the baseball team like you all right, but they don't want a girl on the team."

"Well, you can make them take me on, can't you? You know I can pitch better than that fat Billy, and I can hit as good as any of the boys. It just isn't fair!" and Penny would toss her head with determination, and the curls (which were now beginning to be more strawberry blonde than golden and were usually caught in a ponytail and tied with a ribbon) would switch angrily from side to side.

The truth was she was right! And not only about baseball, but about most of the activities usually considered to belong to boys only. She was an expert at marbles, and had accumulated an impressive collection before her mother found out that she was playing for keeps. Much to her chagrin, she had to return their marbles to her competitors, and understandably had difficulty after that finding anyone willing to shoot marbles with her. She rode her bicycle with wild abandon, and John and Louise had more than one complaint from pedestrians about the close calls caused by their daughter.

Patsy was no longer the other "pea in the pod". If Penny was a tomboy, she was a little lady. However, as different in behavior as they had become, Patsy was still her sister's sturdy defender, and no one dared accuse one in the presence of the other. But occasionally they still joined forces to create situations that became the talk of the town.

One such occasion presented itself when Penny decided she wanted to join the 4-H club. It was a new club at school, and she considered it a challenge because it involved animals. It was intended as a club for children who lived on surrounding farms, but Penny and Patsy both liked animals and it appealed to them.

Penny especially was an animal lover and soon after they started school, she had begun ignoring her dolls in favor of a pet kitten. Instead of dressing her doll and wheeling it around the block in the doll carriage, the hapless kitten was stuffed into a doll dress and bonnet, and tucked in for the ride. Since the kitten was not always willing to suffer as a replacement for the doll, Penny's hands and arms were almost always scratched and scabby. With the additional decoration of mercurochrome – or iodine if the scratches were serious enough - she looked as bad as any grubby little kid who had been caught in a bramble patch.

What Penny wanted was to have a piglet and raise it to exhibit in the county fair. Patsy was not too enthusiastic about having a *pig*, but was willing to help. Even though their home was not in the country, the Holts had a large back yard, and Penny begged her daddy to build a pen in one corner for her project.

Since John and Louise were positive that their neighbors would not welcome a pig project in the neighborhood, they finally convinced Penny to compromise on a calf. It was a cute little animal, but the girls had not counted on how fast it would grow and how attached they would become to it. They made a pet of it, and one day took it out of the pen so they could play with it.

Sensing the chance for freedom, Mooley suddenly took to his heels, snatching the rope out of Penny's hand. With both girls chasing him, he quickly found the gate and took off down the street. Pigtails flying, and screaming at him to stop, the girls put on quite a show for the quiet neighborhood and nearly embarrassed Louise to death. Mooley made it to the edge of town before he was caught by some young boys who had joyfully joined the chase. He was promptly sold to a farmer of John's acquaintance, and Penny's 4-H career was over.

Though both girls enjoyed the freedom of roaming the town on their bicycles, which they dearly loved, there was one recreation that made them willingly park their wheels. Since both girls had been animal lovers since babyhood, bicycle riding seemed very tame compared to the absolutely incomparable thrill of horseback riding. They were quite the experts, having had the opportunity to ride since they were old enough to sit up straight in a saddle.

One of John's regular customers was the owner of the horse farm on the edge of town. As toddlers, whenever Barney Hood (of Barney's Equestrian Stables), brought his horses to be shod, they could be found crowding as close to the beautiful animals as they were allowed, watching closely everything that took place. However, their main interest was in the horses themselves. They were permitted to pat noses, and occasionally to feed the patiently waiting animals with an apple or a carrot. Barney would put them both on the back of the most gentle mare and hold them as he walked the mare around the fenced in yard. As they got bigger, they took turns riding, and learned to hold the reins and signal their mounts to turn to the right or the left. Always carefully attended by Barney, they gained confidence, and finally were as much at home on a horse's back as they were on their bicycles.

As a result of the business connection between John and Barney, they had a standing invitation to come out to the stables and ride whenever they wished. They each had a favorite horse and loved to brush and groom it. In return, the horses loved the girls and always had a welcome neigh and a nuzzle for them whenever they appeared, for the horses knew they were in for a treat and a satisfying coddling.

It seemed to John and Louise that the years flew by, and suddenly their home was besieged with young men. Some of them were there so much that John wondered if they were moving in! The doorbell rang constantly with one or the other wanting to talk to either Penny or Patsy. One awkward teenager would sit astride his bicycle out on the roadside, just waiting for a glimpse of one of the girls – John was never sure which one!

Worse, the girls were always wanting to go somewhere with one of their pimply suitors. Louise was very firm in demanding to know at all times where they were going and with whom, but none of the "hangers-on" seemed to get discouraged. When the requests for going out in the evening were denied, it seemed just as desirable to shift plans to the Holt living room, and again John would wonder if they would ever leave.

Over the years both girls had enthusiastically practised their piano lessons, somewhat to the surprise of their parents, and in their high school years were much in demand for parties because they could play all the popular songs. Both were popular for other reasons, too. They were full of fun, and Penny, especially, was always ready to try the newest thing suggested by the movies they frequented. Movies were an allowed pastime when the girls first began to date, and it seemed that the novelty never wore off.

As they approached their sixteenth birthday, life was good. They spent hours fixing each other's hair, studying themselves in the mirror and trying out lipsticks and rouge, always being careful to wash their faces clean before they went down to dinner.

John and Louise were inordinately proud of their children. They still had never seriously had to discipline them, even though Penny often came close to rebellion. Patsy was a happy child who never seemed to share Penny's restlessness, though she sympathized and protected her twin sister, often keeping her out of serious trouble. The family was fortunate to have approached this milestone without having had the problems which beset other less fortunate people. There had been no serious illnesses, no divisive discipline crises, no financial problems because the metal works had, in spite of the national depression, provided them with more than a comfortable living. John and Louise were complacent, grateful for a good life, and feeling no need for more religious life than their Sunday habitual church attendance provided them. They always felt good after the Sunday service, having enjoyed an excellent choir rendition and a sermon that assured them that God loved them and was pleased with their faithful attendance and the generous amount which they always placed in the offering plate. They felt that they needed nothing more.

As the big day neared, John and Louise allowed the twins to choose the kind of party they wanted. All of their school friends were invited, and of course Kent was there. They chose to have a picnic in their own huge yard, with a dance following. Their living room opened onto a large sun porch, and with the French doors open, there was plenty of room for such a party. It was a great day. All the guests stuffed themselves with hot dogs and hamburgers, along with everything else imaginable for a picnic meal, topped off by two huge birthday cakes. The fun lasted well into the twilight hours, with either the phonograph playing or one of the girls at the piano. There was even one of the teenage admirers who believed himself to be another Rudy Vallee, and provided live entertainment of a very squeaky and amateurish quality.

After the guests had finally departed, and the house and yard returned to their usual order, everyone was exhausted. But the girls were still too excited to settle down.

"Let's go horseback riding tomorrow, Pat. I don't think I can just stay home and sit around – I'd go crazy! You know, with final exams and all, we haven't been out to ride Whisper and Sweet Girl in over two weeks. Let's go to Barney's tomorrow. It will be a perfect way to finish off our birthday."

"Well, if Dad and Mom will let us. Mom may have something she wants us to do tomorrow." Patsy was much quicker to take responsibility for helping her mother than Penny. Not that Penny didn't care, she just didn't think.

"Hey, Patsy, I just thought of something." Penny had been lounging on the bed, legs crossed and one foot swinging in the air. She catapulted out of bed in her excitement, and landed on Patsy's bed. She drew her knees up and hugged them, as her eyes sparkled. "Let's get Kent to go with us. You know he's home from college for the summer. I think he came home a day early so he could come to our party, but I didn't get to dance with him but one time. If he goes with us, we'll have time to talk."

"That's a good idea. I've missed Kent. It's almost like he doesn't belong to us anymore. I think we need to check out how many girl friends he has at college, and see if we approve of them!" Patsy's eyes sparkled, and the two girls giggled themselves to sleep.

It turned out that Kent was also on a high after the exciting afternoon. First thing in the morning the girls hunted him down and told him of their plan. He quickly agreed to go with them, and the three young people found John to get his permission. As fathers do, he said, "Well, it's okay with me if your mother doesn't mind. But you'll have to ask her."

Louise did have things planned for the day, but realized how excited the girls were, and agreed that they could go if Kent went with them. However, she wanted some help with housecleaning that morning, so it was well after lunch when, with glee, the three mounted their bicycles and headed for the stables which were about a mile and a half out of town.

The horses gave them the expected enthusiastic greeting, and they had an afternoon of their favorite recreation. It was good for all three of them, for it did help them unwind after the exciting celebration the day before. Each of them relived every memorable moment of the picnic, the dance, and their guests at the party. They also fell back easily into their old relationship, and the afternoon became one of those days of glorious youth that one never forgets.

"I think Jimmy Denton likes you, Patsy. How many times did he dance with you? He was hanging around you all day long. He's pretty cute, but kind of dumb, don't you think?" Penny usually compared all the boys to Kent and they seldom measured up.

Patsy bristled. "He's no dumber than that Bruce Baylor who thought he was Rudy Vallee! As a matter of fact, Jimmy had some pretty good jokes, and he was real polite. Bruce is always pestering the girls, pulling their hair and trying to make them mad. I don't know how you stand him!"

"Well, he was pretty nice at the party yesterday. Maybe he's growing up! He carried my plate and got me some more lemonade, and told me about his brother's fancy car. Boy, I wish we had a car like that!"

"What kind of a car does he have?" asked Patsy.

"Well, the way Bruce described it, it's a brand new red roadster, with a rumble seat, and lots of chrome. Lots of power, too. Bruce said it could outrun any car in town."

Kent put in, "Sure hope he has sense enough not to speed around town. In the country it's not so bad, but town's no place to show what a car can do. And from what I've heard about Bruce's brother, he's pretty much of a show-off."

Penny was quiet a minute, then commented, "You're just borrowing trouble, Kent. I'll be glad when Dad will let me drive! I think I'm old enough now that I'm sixteen!"

Kent looked at Penny in amazement. "You just turned sixteen yesterday, but that doesn't mean you're grown up yet! You're not old enough, Penny, and you know it! You're still just a little girl!" He was enjoying teasing her, enjoying the way she always took the bait. But he was unprepared this time for the fire in her eyes and the way she bristled at his words.

The horses were now heading home to the stables. Penny suddenly slapped Whisper on the withers and took off ahead of the others. She circled around, coming back to face Kent with fury.

"Well, Kent, girls grow up faster than boys. You should know that – you've been around Patsy and me enough! Girls have better sense, too!" and she and Whisper flew off toward the stables..

Patsy watched her go and turned apologetically to Kent. "She didn't mean that, Kent. She's always wanted to be older than she is, you know. I guess that's why she's always getting into trouble. She's just sore because she can't have her way." Patsy didn't know whether she was apologizing for Penny, or standing up for her. She was often confused by Penny's outbursts.

Kent burst out laughing. "That's okay. I shouldn't pick on her so much. But she's such a spitfire that I enjoy seeing how far I can go with her. I never pay any attention to her anyway when she talks like that." More amused than anything else, he took off after Penny with Patsy close behind.

By the time they had rubbed down the horses and given them water, it was well into twilight. "Come on, we need to get home before dark," urged Kent. "If I don't get you home on time, your Dad will never let you out again this late in the day."

Soon they were pedaling furiously toward town. The road was narrow, but there was little traffic, and they pretty much had it to themselves. By now they were ready to go home, fall into bed, and sleep from pure exhaustion.

"You girls ride on ahead, single file, and stay way to the side of the road. I'll ride behind and watch for cars coming behind us. And be sure you turn your bike headlights on," called Kent as they rode out onto the main road.

They were a silent trio as they hurried toward home. The twilight was fast waning and it wouldn't be long until darkness would fall. It was the end of a perfect day, and all three were more tired than they realized. The only thought in each of their minds was just to get the lights of home in sight.

However, the " perfect day" had yet one more surprise for them. A very unexpected one, and one which would change the direction of each of the three young lives forever.

Chapter 4

The day had also been one of rest and relaxation for Pastor Sigmund Anderson and his wife Julie. Sig had arisen early and had spent two hours in his study, putting finishing touches to his sermon for the next day's services. He always tried to keep Saturday afternoon and evening free – barring an emergency call from one of his parishioners – so that he would be fresh and at his best for the Sunday morning services. He felt a tremendous responsibility in handling the Word of God. He wanted to be sure that he gave a faithful discourse which would be true to the Bible and would help his listeners to grow spiritually. As he closed his Bible at eight o'clock and leaned back in his office chair, he thought of some of the various individuals who would be depending on his message from the Word to help them through the hard times in which they found themselves. There was Granny Thompson, who had just lost her lover of 65 years, and was terribly lonely. Even though she knew that they would meet again in Heaven, not having him by her side now left her quite desolate, for there was no one who could take his place.

Then there was the young couple, the Eddingtons, whose baby was in critical condition in the Little Rapids Hospital. Sig's immediate urge was that he must see them this afternoon, and determined that if Julie agreed (which he knew she would do), they would break their rule of relaxing on Saturday, and would go and sit awhile with James and

Adele. They would have to cross town to reach the hospital, but that would be a nice ride, even though their errand was serious.

And then there were three teenagers, who just a week ago had made their decisions to follow Jesus. They needed teaching and encouragement, and he must be sure that his message was simple enough for them to understand, while giving them courage to stand up for their belief in a school where Christian young people were in the minority. Yes, his responsibilities were great, but much prayer had gone into the preparation of his sermon, and he was depending on the Lord to give him the right words to say while allowing him to communicate to his flock how much God loved them. He sighed, offered up a short prayer for wisdom, then closed his Bible and stood up just as Julie called "Breakfast is on the table, Sweetheart. Come while it's hot!" As he entered the kitchen, she held up her face for a good-morning kiss, and his sigh became one of satisfaction that all the activities of the day were under the direction of the Lord.

Obviously, Pastor Sigmund and his wife were deeply in love. God had brought them together first at Moody Bible Institute in Chicago from which Sig had volunteered for service against Kaiser Wilhelm's rapacious armies. Julie had completed a nursing course and also traveled overseas, joining other young women (both English and American) who felt they must support their brothers and lovers in the battle for freedom. Both had experienced the hell of the European battlefields, and as soon as they reached home soil again, they had married. Obeying the call of God that had drawn them together during their years at Moody, they had accepted the small pastorate at Little Rapids, happy to be close to Julie's hometown of Charlotte. Their fifteen months in the little church had been a time of forging deep ties of love and fellowship between the congregation and their pastor.

Sig and Julie had recently spent two weeks of their vacation time with her family. Sig remembered vividly the last Sunday service before they left. They were leaving their congregation in the capable hands of a former schoolmate from Moody. Strange, but it felt to him the way he believed a parent would feel at the first separation between father and son. He and Julie had become so enmeshed in the lives of their church members, that parting – even for so brief a time - had been an emotional event for all of them.

In that service, the congregation had sung lustily and with great enthusiasm.

"Amazing grace, how sweet the sound
That saved a wretch like me!
I once was lost, but now am found
Was blind, but now I see!"

Pastor Sig had sat with bowed head listening to the timeless words of Isaac Newton's majestic hymn. It was that very grace that had brought him and Julie to this place. Having survived the Great War - Sigmund emerging from the trenches with battle scars from wounds that had threatened his very life, and Julie with nightmarish memories of horrors in the field hospitals - they were now very mindful of "what might have been". God's grace was very real to them.

Sig remembered how emotional he had felt as he took his place at the pulpit that day. He had stood for a moment in silence, still lost in the immensity of the truth that he and his people had just sung.

Not a sound interrupted that long moment as the people waited for his message. This close group, who in truth obeyed the command to "Love one another", had grown from just a handful of dedicated souls who were meeting together when the Andersons first arrived, to a church now packed with more than a hundred people who worshipped regularly at services. They were effective witnesses in the community and staunch supporters of their pastor and his wife. Even though the pulpit would be filled for the next two Sundays by the excellent substitute from Moody, they would miss their spiritual leader – as he would miss them!

All had given rapt attention, he remembered, as he broke the Bread of Life to them. The only sound was (as usual) the slight rustling of Bible pages as he announced the verses he would read with them.

"My beloved brothers and sisters in the Lord," he began, "we are each instructed in the Scripture that in everything we do, we are to do it to the glory of the Lord. You have had a good witness in the town of Little Rapids. The presence of many of you is a testimony to the faithfulness of others. As we are each members of the Body of Christ, serving in our own special capacity, we are always subject to our Head, the Lord Jesus Christ. As your human shepherd, I also am subject to the will of the Great Shepherd, who leads me as I lead you.

"So my message to you is this. Your instructions as to how you should live come not from me, but always from the Lord through me. You have in your Bibles the same set of guidelines that I possess. So this morning I want to remind you of some of the spiritual basics which, if you commit yourself daily to Him for cleansing and instruction, will keep you in the center of His will." Then he instructed them to turn to the fifth chapter of I Thessalonians where Paul had recorded a number of commandments to Christians. He pointed out to them that they were to keep these commandments not because they must, but because they loved their Savior and Lord and wanted only to please Him.

The scratching of pencils and the rustle of Bible leaves had given testimony to the fact that the listeners were busily storing up the Word in their minds and hearts. It was their guidebook by which they must live every day of their lives, and they wanted to be sure it was tucked away securely in their minds and hearts.

As he came to the close of the service, Sigmund had had some personal remarks to make.

"Mrs. Anderson and I will be only a short distance from you. We are going to spend our vacation weeks with Julie's mother, Christy, who still, at this time of year, has a difficult time emotionally. This is the time of year when the Lord took both her beloved Matthew and her son Jamie home to be with Him. Julie's brother Danny and his family also live in Charlotte and other family members live close by, so it will be a time of family reunion for us."

He continued. "Elder John will be able to get in touch with me at any time in case of emergency. Please pray for us as we will be praying for you."

After the benediction the ladies of the church had spread a banquet of homemade goodies on long tables under the ancient spreading trees.

By mid afternoon Sigmund and Julie were on their way to a time of rest and family renewal. But having been refreshed, they were now back with their people and concerned with their needs.

He was unusually silent and thoughtful all through breakfast, and as Julie poured him another cup of hot coffee, she gently chided him. "A penny for your thoughts, my love. I feel like I'm having breakfast all alone." She bent down and kissed the top of his head.

He reached up and pulled her face down to his. "I'm sorry, honey. I was thinking about the service the day we left for vacation. I don't think I've ever experienced more love and closeness among our people than I felt that day. You know, we have been privileged as few pastors are, to be able to serve a church like this one."

"I know." Julie sat down, pushed her plate aside, and set her coffee cup in its saucer. She put her elbow on the table, rested her chin in her hand, and looked at him pensively. "Even though I was excited about going home, I hated to leave here."

"But it was good that we had some time away. Do you remember how much fun it was to just be the two of us together again, with no interruptions and no one needing us? Though I love to be needed and to minister to my people, I love having time with just my wife!" He came around the table and stood behind her, wrapping his arms around her and kissing the back of her neck until she giggled.

"Hey, it's not just the solitary two of us in the privacy of the car now! What would Elder John think if he should walk in and find you making love to me this early in the morning?" Julie giggled as he continued nuzzling her nape.

Sigmund straightened up, laughing. "It just might do him good. I love the old man but I wonder how he ever managed to get up courage to get married! His stiffness isn't all old age, I'm afraid!"

Now it was Julie remembering the vacation trip. As their roomy, well loaded touring car had sped along the road to home, she had leaned back against the cushions with a happy sigh and a smile of anticipation.

"You know, Darling, I love our work and our little church, but it's good to be going home again. Did you feel like this when we visited Sweden last year?"

Sigmund had chuckled, a sound she loved to hear. "It seemed to me like a trip into another world, if you must know. Of course Dad was still there, and I almost expected Mother to walk in the door, but I guess I had been away too long and seen too much. With all the changes there, things didn't even seem to be familiar." Then he paused, and added slowly, "Of course if Mom had been there it might have been very different."

"Do you know that when I was in France I dreamed about home almost every night?" asked Julie.

"I'm not really surprised because I did too – whenever I got a chance to get a few winks. Sleep was our only escape in the trenches, and I guess we all reverted back to the happiest times we could remember. And you know," he reminded her," I thought you were only a dream when I woke up from surgery and saw you there."

She had been silent, suddenly sobered by her own memories. "I just remember how happy I was to find you, even if you were just barely alive." Still remembering, she had added quietly, "However, I had a hard time convincing you of that!"

Wistfully he had probed for an assurance he needed to hear again and again. "Are you still sure you don't mind having a man who will never be whole?"

"You know I'd rather have you than any other man, even if you were blind and in a wheelchair!" she had cried, quickly closing the distance between them on the car seat. Laying her head on his shoulder she had whispered, not for the first time – nor the last, "After all this time, do you still have a doubt?"

He had given her a sidewise grin. "Not really. But I can never hear it too often!"

Now across the breakfast table, she knew it was time to say it again. "Have I told you lately how much I love you?"

He grinned at her, pursing his lips as if kissing her at a distance. "Now that you've invoked Elder John, I don't dare demonstrate how much I return that love! But the Lord has been very good to us, hasn't He, Honey?"

"Oh, yes, and part of His goodness is still having Mom to go home to! I'd love to see her right now! I hope she knows we're talking about her! Do you remember how, when she knows we're coming, she watches out the front window? We never can even get out of the car before she's out there hugging and kissing us." Julie smiled as she added, "She always gets so excited about things."

"That's what makes it so much fun to go home," returned Sig. "I can imagine that life was never dull for your parents."

Julie smiled at her memories. "I'm glad you got to know Dad. Mom was always thinking of something exciting to do but Dad was our comfort and stability. I'm not surprised Mom always has a hard time on the anniversary of his death. She knows she'll see him again in heaven, but she still misses him so much here." Then in a small voice she added, "And so do I!"

"I know, Honey."

Drinking the last of their coffee in companionable silence, they sat anticipating their day of rest that stretched before them.

Working in their little yard was always a means of relaxation for Sigmund, and he happily pulled weeds and edged around his pampered flower garden, whistling and enjoying the warmth of the day. After lunch, they set out to check on the Eddington baby. They found a pair of ecstatic parents who had had an encouraging report from the doctor, and who were making plans to take their little one home. Since they were there at the hospital, Sig and Julie took the opportunity to make a couple of additional calls on church members who were ill. By the time they started home, it was twilight.

"Sig, let's go home by way of Barney's Stables. I always love to see the horses and their riders. We ought to go out there and ride more often. I think it would be a good change for both of us. How long has it been since we've been horseback riding?"

"A long time, Sweetheart. Much too long, especially since we have stables so close to us. Let's come out next week then keep doing it at least every two weeks. Think we could schedule that?"

"All we have to do is make up our minds to do it. Look, see those three riders over there? They're having a wonderful time. They're good, too. And I believe they're just kids."

"You're right. I like to see them start young like that. They're good enough that the horse and rider almost look like one. That takes skill."

They watched until the three horses were out of sight, then Sig drove down the narrow road that led into the nearby forest.

"Let's drive down Little River Road. It's so pretty with the spring green on the trees and all nature coming to life again after the long winter." Julie took a deep breath of the invigorating, fragrant air. "Let's just poke along and enjoy the end of a perfect day."

"Sounds good to me. In the morning I always think it's the best time of the day with the world just waking up, but in the evening it's so restful to both soul and body." Sig was driving slowly, taking in the beauty all around him.

They stopped for a few minutes by the river to watch the water as it whirled in the rapids. Time seemed to stop for them. They were mesmerized by the beauty and the sound of the rushing water. Finally, reluctantly, Sig started the car and they moved slowly toward home.

Suddenly Julie came to attention. "Look, Sig." She spotted three bicycles being pedaled furiously along ahead of them. "Sig, be careful. You never know what kids on bicycles are going to do!"

"I'm watching, Honey. It's beginning to get too dark for safety. They do have headlights but no taillights. I think I'll just coast along behind them and make sure they're not in any danger."

"I don't recognize them, do you? Wait! Yes, I do too! They're the three kids that we were watching back at the stables. I don't think I know them, though. They certainly aren't any of our youth group. I wish they were – they look like nice kids!"

Sig stayed far enough behind them so he wouldn't make them nervous, but so he could still see them clearly. It wasn't long before they were approaching town.

Suddenly there was a roar behind them, and it became deafeningly loud. Watching out of his rear view mirror, Sig saw a red roadster approaching them at a frightening speed.

"Sig, he's going too fast!" Julie cried. "Roll up the windows quick, or we'll be eating his dust!"

"I'm not as worried about eating his dust as I am about those bikers. I wonder if he can see them!"

At that moment the red streak passed them, then suddenly swerved, evidently seeing the riders for the first time. At the same time Patsy, apparently confused by the noise and the dust, momentarily lost her balance, and her bicycle wobbled into the path of the car. Brakes squealed, the car skidded, then shot off again, seemingly unaware – or uncaring - that it had left a wrecked bicycle, and worse, a crumpled body lying by the side of the road.

Chapter 5

Sig jammed on brakes, and he and Julie jumped from the car, racing to join the boy and the girl who had thrown their own bicycles to the ground and were bending over the pitiful little body. Julie shouted at them, "Don't touch her – don't touch her! We need to see how badly she's hurt before we try to move her!"

The girl was sobbing and her tearstained face was twisted with fear. The boy was quiet, but his hand, though shaking, was gently stroking the unconscious girl's hair. When he looked up, Sig and Julie saw that he, too, was weeping quietly.

Sig gently lifted the frantic girl aside, and Julie knelt by the motionless body. She checked for a pulse, then nodded and smiled. "She's alive, bless her heart, and it's probably a good thing she's unconscious. Sig, would you bring me that blanket from the back seat of the car, then you and – what's your name, Son?" She turned to face the handsome boy with the tortured face.

"I'm Kent Walters and these are the Holt twins, Penny and Patsy. Oh, thank you for stopping. I don't know what I would have done if you hadn't been here!"

"All right, Kent. I'm glad we were close, too. I think you and my husband should go into town, get an ambulance, and let the girls' parents know what's happened. I'll stay here with…" she paused and looked at

Penny, who choked out her name. "I'll stay here with Penny and we'll take care of Patsy until you get back. And, Sig – please hurry!"

"You bet! Come on Kent. We'll swing by the hospital and send the ambulance out, then we'll go pick up the parents." And the touring car took off toward town.

Julie tucked the blanket around Patsy, and kept her fingers on her pulse. Penny continued to sob, and Julie talked quietly, hoping to calm her before she made herself sick. "You hold her hand, Penny, so she'll know you're here, and we'll just pray while we wait. Okay?"

Between sobs, Penny whispered, "I don't know how to pray except for 'Now I lay me down to sleep'" She thought a minute then added, "I know the Lord's prayer too, but what good would it do?"

Julie replied very quietly, "Then you just hold her hand, and I'll pray. You see, God is the best doctor there is, and since he made our bodies, he knows how to fix them when they get broken. Lord Jesus, you know all about our trouble, and you know how badly Patsy is hurt. Just be with us, dear Lord, and touch Patsy and comfort Penny. Thank you, Lord."

Penny was watching her with wide, tearstained eyes. This was like nothing she had ever heard before. Talking to Jesus like He was right here beside them! She couldn't understand it all but suddenly she did feel comforted. She brushed at her eyes with her hand, streaking her face with dirt, but she was no longer sobbing. She began to stroke Patsy's face as Kent had been doing, and she talked softly to her twin, wanting her to know she was not alone.

"Open your eyes, Patsy. You're going to be all right. Kent and the nice man have gone to get help, and this lady prayed to God for us. Patsy, you *ARE* going to be all right, I just know it! Please open your eyes!" Her voice shook and the sobs began again.

Suddenly Patsy's eyelids fluttered. She opened her eyes for a moment, but didn't seem to be seeing anything. As her eyes closed again, there was the sound of a motor car and the ambulance drew up beside them.

Julie stood back with her arms around Penny, who was still shaking from the shock. The ambulance attendants took Patsy's pulse, then her blood pressure. The doctor examined her quickly and expertly, then spoke quietly to the attendants, who lifted a shaped board from the ambulance and carefully laid Patsy on it. They strapped her securely so she wouldn't fall off, then skillfully and gently placed her on the cot inside the ambulance. The doctor turned and spoke to Julie.

"Ma'am, I'm afraid this little girl is seriously injured, but I can't give you any real answers until I get a chance to examine her thoroughly. You did well to keep her warm and not move her. We'll take her to the Little Rapids General Hospital, and get her immediately into x-ray. We'll meet you there." He started toward the ambulance, then turned around. "I believe the gentleman who sent us is coming back for you?"

Julie nodded assent. "Yes, he is. But first he's picking up the girl's parents, so we should all be at the hospital in a few minutes. Thank you, Doctor, for being so prompt in coming. We'll meet you at the hospital as soon as we possibly can."

The ambulance had no more than driven away when Sig and Kent arrived, with John and Louise in the back seat. Penny was beside them in what seemed a single movement, throwing herself into her mother's arms, and sobbing uncontrollably.

Julie joined Sig and Kent in the front seat, and in low tones repeated the doctor's words.

They arrived at the hospital just as the attendants were lifting Patsy from the ambulance. Then came the waiting. It seemed interminable. Kent went to telephone his parents while Sig and Julie offered what comfort they could to John and Louise. Penny sat tightly pressed within her father's firm and loving arm, with her mother on her other side holding her hand. She still sobbed from time to time as she took great gulps of air, trying valiantly to get control of herself.

"Let us introduce ourselves, Mr. and Mrs. Holt. I'm Julie Anderson, and this is my husband, Pastor Sigmund Anderson of Redeemer Chapel. We're so glad we were nearby when the accident happened, and we've been praying for your girls and for you. It's so good to know that God is near, and can comfort us when we find ourselves in such desperate circumstances."

John answered in hushed tones. "We certainly appreciate your help. But I don't think God will want to do much for us. We haven't paid much attention to him for a long time." He paused, pulled out a big white handkerchief, and wiped his eyes. Then he blew his nose and wiped his eyes again. "I'm sorry, but these two girls are all we have, and I'm so afraid of what the doctor is going to tell us." His voice trailed off, and he continued to wipe his eyes. Penny tried to dry her eyes with her father's sleeve as she continued to lean against his arm.

Louise let the tears roll. "I had a feeling that something had happened. They are always home on time. Maybe we shouldn't have let them go out there this afternoon – but Kent was with them and we thought ..."

Julie broke in. "There was nothing Kent – or anyone else - could have done. We were driving very slowly behind them, and Kent was riding behind the two girls, obviously protecting them as best he could. A red roadster came hurtling out of nowhere, going so fast that there was no way the children could have gotten out of the way if they had seen him coming – which they didn't." She paused, obviously shaken herself as she recalled the tragic details of the accident. "And the driver didn't even stop!" To Julie, as well as to her listeners, the failure to stop was unforgiveable.

John sat forward at the words "red roadster". He asked, "Could you see who was driving?"

Sig shook his head sorrowfully. "No. It happened so fast and he stirred up so much dust that we couldn't see anything except that it was a red roadster." He looked at John with a question in his eyes. "Do you have a suspicion as to who it might be? Do you know someone who has a red roadster?"

Suddenly Penny came to life. "*I* know who has one! Bruce Baylor was bragging yesterday that his brother had a new red roadster. I bet it was *him*! Oh, I could kill that smart alec!"

"Now Penny, you don't *know* it was the Baylor boy. But I'll certainly find out!" With purpose in his voice, John continued. "I'll have the police check on him right away. He mustn't be allowed to endanger children like that – or adults, for that matter. He should be stopped – if he's really the one who was driving!"

Sig and Julie nodded in agreement. Louise was still so overcome with fear and grief that she was hardly following the conversation. She sat with her head down, still weeping quietly.

Julie reached over and patted her hand. "Mrs. Holt, would you mind if we prayed with you? You know, the only way we can face this terrible accident with courage is if we lay it in the Lord's hands. He can not only comfort you, but if it's His will, he can bring Patsy back to health again."

John shook his head. A darkness seemed to settle over his face and his eyes took on a hard expression.

"I know you mean well, Mrs. Anderson, but it wouldn't do any good. God is not pleased with us and for good reason. We've got no right to ask Him for anything."

Louise looked stricken as though hope suddenly went out of her and left her empty. In her heart she knew what John meant and that he was right.

Sig was not one to give up easily. "My friends, God loves you and is always ready to listen. We can never get away from God's love."

John leaned forward, rested his elbows on his knees and covered his face with his hands. He remembered Grossmutter using almost those exact words. But no one really understood how far he had wandered from God. And they didn't know the hate he carried in his heart – hate that had driven him from his boyhood home and which he had nurtured ever since. He had kept it imprisoned in a dark place. The only problem was that it wouldn't stay there and now here was a companion for it – the driver of the red car.

He didn't *want* to hate, but it had become a part of him by now, and he really didn't think he could ever find God again at all.

Therefore, it was these good samaritans who had helped the children so much – *they* were the ones who would be doing the praying, not him. John shrugged his shoulders and finally nodded his head. After all, it couldn't hurt, he reluctantly conceded in his wounded spirit. For his precious daughter he would try anything that might help.

As Louise turned her red-rimmed eyes toward the pastor's wife, Julie now thought she detected a look of slight hope in them. She sent up a silent "Thank you, Lord". Louise and John both nodded assent, and Sig led them in a simple prayer, thanking God that Patsy's life had been spared, and praying for comfort for the family. Afterward, the group sat quietly until the door opened and the doctor entered the room.

Observing the sad group with compassion, he put as much encouragement in his voice as he possibly could. "Mr. and Mrs. Holt, your daughter is still unconscious, so she won't know you when you go in to see her. However, that is probably a good thing for now. If she were conscious she would be in a great deal of pain. But I think it would help if you could just hold her hand, and let her feel that you're there."

"How badly is she hurt, Doctor? Will she get well?" The words were hushed and tentative, and Julie could feel the pain in John's voice as he asked the question that was in all their minds.

"Patsy has a badly crushed leg, and her head sustained a severe blow. One wrist is sprained but not broken. She has cuts and bruises which will be painful but not life threatening. We were fearful of injury to her neck and back, but that seems to be minimal." He paused a moment, then summed up, "She's in for a long recovery, but I believe she'll make it. We can't tell yet what the long-range damage will be."

He stood up and shook hands with each of them. "Now, if you'll follow me, you can see her for just a few minutes. I suggest that one of you stay with her, and the others go home and get some rest. Then you can take turns staying with her, so that someone will be sure to be here when she regains consciousness." He turned and led the way from the waiting area to the room where Patsy lay white and still, swathed in bandages.

Kent, having completed the call to his parents, had rejoined the group unnoticed, and heard the doctor's words. He followed them down the hall to Patsy's room, and stood in the door staring at the sad little form on the bed. He was not only angry at the driver of the roadster, but he was angry with himself. He had been with the girls to protect them, and he had failed – miserably. He felt that he could never forgive himself, and dejectedly he returned to the waiting area and sat with his head in his hands, fighting to keep back the tears. He had heard the strangers talk about God, but he was angry with God, too. After all, He had let it happen – and to Patsy, of all people. Patsy was so gentle, so sweet, never hurt anyone and always had compassion for those who were hurting. She didn't deserve to be treated like this. He felt like shaking his fist in God's face, but instead found himself silently crying out to Him, pleading with Him for Patsy's life and recovery.

Suddenly, he stood up with a cynical kind of mirth boiling within him. Here he was, praying to a God that he wasn't even sure existed! This horrible event must be affecting his mind! He shook his head to rid it of these unwelcome emotions, and made his way back to the sick room.

Chapter 6

Mary Ann Walters lay so still in the bed that she seemed to be asleep. But her eyes were wide open, staring into the dark, as she reviewed in her mind the events of the evening. The house was so quiet that she could hear Kent's even footsteps, pacing back and forth across the floor above her. She turned on the light to check the time and was shocked to find that it was after two o'clock. Would the boy never go to bed? She wondered if he were ill. After all, yesterday had ended with a terrible shock, and he had seemed very quiet and withdrawn all evening. She had thought it no more than natural after what he had been through, but he would make himself sick if he didn't get some sleep. She also knew that they would all be needed to take turns being with Patsy around the clock and that Kent would insist on taking his turn.

She slid out of bed as quietly as possible, being careful not to rouse Kent's father. She felt for her robe on the chair where she had dropped it, slipped it on and silently opened the door, closing it just as quietly behind her. As she mounted the stairs, she wondered about Louise, who had taken the first watch of the night. What a terrible thing it was for her to have to go through. And Penny. She had been beside herself, but she was confident that John would be able to handle her. He and Penny seemed to have a very special father-daughter relationship and he would know just what to do.

And she and Kent had a very special mother-son relationship. So when she softly knocked, it was with no surprise that he opened the door and saw her standing there. She held out her arms, and all six feet of her boy fell into them. He put his head on her shoulder and without embarrassment finally let the tears fall.

"It's alright, Son. We all know there was nothing you could have done to prevent this terrible thing." She knew by instinct just what was bothering him.

"I could have insisted that we start home earlier." Kent pulled his sleeve across his eyes, wiping at the tears that streamed down his face. "We shouldn't have stayed so late. It was beginning to get dark and we hurried, but it was just too late when we left the stables." He had given up his pacing, and now his legs would no longer hold him up. He sank into the soft, overstuffed chair beside his bed, and shook his head in despair. "It was my fault, Mom. I just have to face it!"

"It was *not* your fault, Kent. Stop blaming yourself. You and I both know that the twins, especially Penny, would not have left the stables until they were good and ready! Nobody has ever been able to *make* them do anything!" Now Mary Ann was sitting on the arm of his chair, smoothing his hair back from his forehead. "Now stop this foolishness before you make yourself sick!" She cradled his head in her arms, and for a moment they rocked together, taking comfort from each other.

"Mom, something bothers me. That lady, Mrs. Anderson, kept talking about God. Did she actually believe that praying would help? She seemed very sincere and nice, but does anyone really believe that God cares about what happens to us – if there is a God, that is?"

Mary Ann sat up straight in shock. "Kent, what are you saying? Of course there's a God. You know that. You went to Sunday School and we took you to church all your life, and you wonder if there's a God? Where in the world did you get such an idea?"

Kent shrugged his shoulders and looked a little sheepish. "Well, Mom, my professors at the college all say that the Bible is just a myth, and that men invented the idea of God because they needed something to worship – like some people made idols, you know. They say that no one really believes in Him any more – it just makes them comfortable to believe in a God who is strong and can protect them."

Mary Ann was almost speechless. "And this is what they've been teaching you? We sent you to college to get an education! And they've been brainwashing you instead!" She shook her head in disbelief. "I can't believe we've been so naive!"

"But what I want to know is what makes people so sure that there *is* a God and that He knows and cares what happens to us. My professors are supposed to know and they laugh about people who believe that, but the Andersons insist that they know what they're talking about. And I think they really believe they're right. When Pastor Anderson prayed, it was like God was there beside him. listening to every word he said. How am I supposed to know who's right, Mom? Do *you* know?"

Mary Ann was busy asking herself that same question. Finally she answered, "Yes, Son, I know there is a God and that He loves us. But I can't tell you *how* I know. I just know." She thought a minute, then added, "I think it's all in the Bible, but I don't know where to look. I did learn the books of the Bible when I was a little girl, and I learned a few verses. I only remember one verse, though, and I think I can recite it correctly. You learned it too, I'm certain. If you remember it, say it with me." And she immediately began to recite John 3:16. Kent heard the first few words, then the verse began to come back to him, and mother and son found themselves sitting together in the middle of the night, reciting God's message of salvation to the world.

"For God so loved the world, that He gave his only begotten Son, that whosoever believeth on Him should not perish, but have everlasting life." Somehow they found comfort in saying the words, but the sad fact was that neither of them really understood the meaning – or the importance - of what they were repeating.

"When I see Mrs. Anderson again, I'll ask her to explain the verse to me," promised Mary Ann.

And Kent silently promised himself that he also would have some questions to ask Pastor Anderson as soon as he had the chance.

The chance would come sooner than he expected.

Mary Ann tucked her son into bed as she had when he was just a little boy, kissed his forehead and turned off the light. She padded softly down the stairs and curled up on the sofa with a light blanket over her. For the remaining few hours of darkness, she slept like a baby, awakening only when daylight crept through the lace curtains of her makeshift bedroom. She made her way to the kitchen and put the coffee on to brew. She had just poured herself a steaming cup when Kent joined her at the table. A few minutes later Gordon clattered down the stairs, having been reminded the moment he awoke that this would be a fateful day. When they arrived at the hospital, it was just slightly past eight o'clock, and the first person they saw was Pastor Anderson sitting in the waiting room.

Shaking hands all around, the Pastor was the first to speak. "I'm guessing that none of us slept too much last night. I know you're as anxious for an update on Patsy as I am. I'm going to find the doctor, or at least the nurse. Why don't you go to Patsy's room and I'll meet you there."

Louise was sitting by Patsy's bed, holding her daughter's hand and stroking it gently. Patsy still lay without moving, her eyes closed, and Louise looked wan and tired. Mary Ann stood behind her, and as she rubbed her neck Louise began to relax.

"Louise, let me stay with Patsy for awhile and you go home and rest. I promise that I'll call you the minute she makes a movement."

Louise nodded. "All right. I'm so tired I can hardly hold my head up. She's been like this all night, even though at times I've gently shaken her and I've talked to her a lot. The doctor said that it may be a few hours yet before she comes back to us." Her eyes filled with tears. "She groans every once in a while, so I believe she's hurting, but the doctor has set her leg and he gave her something for pain, so maybe that's why she hasn't regained consciousness yet." She stretched and surrendered her seat by the bed to her best friend.

Gordon took her arm. "Come on, Louise, I'll take you home. By the time you've rested awhile, maybe Patsy will wake up. I'll come back and Mary Ann and I will watch her carefully."

As Gordon and Louise left the room, Pastor Anderson came in. He laid his hand on Patsy's head, closed his eyes and again said a prayer just as naturally as if Jesus were standing right there beside him. Now Kent was sure that he had to talk to the pastor – right away.

Sig sat down a few minutes and talked to Mary Ann, telling her much the same thing as Louise had reported. As he left the room, Kent fell into step with him.

"Pastor, are you in a hurry, or would you have time to answer some questions for me?" Kent's voice was urgent.

Sig saw the same tortured eyes that he had encountered the day before. This boy needed help, and Sig wanted with all his heart to be able to relieve his anxieties. "Let's sit down over in the lounge, Kent. I have all the time in the world. What can I do for you?"

Kent didn't answer until they had found the coffee pot, and each had settled into a comfortable chair with a heartwarming cup of coffee in hand. He slouched in his chair, held his cup with both hands, and looked into it as if he were trying to read some answers there. Finally he looked at Sig and asked, "Pastor, when you pray, it seems like you know God so well that you're just making conversation with Him. Do you really believe that God is real?" His troubled face revealed his great confusion.

Sig considered the handsome, downcast face with compassion. Here was a soul not only hurting, but searching for truth, and his heart went out to the boy.

"Yes, Kent, I do. He is *very* real. He's my best friend, and He's also my Savior. Since I am His child, I know He hears me when I pray and that He will answer me."

After a moment of silence, in which Kent mentally digested that very positive answer, he asked. "But how do you *know* that? My professors say that if we can't feel or see something – if we can't experience it with one or more of our five senses – then it's *not* real. We can't experience God with our senses, can we? Can *you*?"

This time Sig took his time answering. "Kent, the Bible doesn't even try to prove that God is real, because all that we see and have speaks to us of the God who created all things – including us. We don't have to prove that there is a God. But we do have to accept by faith that He exists before anything else makes sense to us. When we do accept His reality by faith, then He can make His presence known to us. He's with me all the time, and I can talk to him at any moment wherever I am. This is true for any of His children. He has promised to hear and He always keeps His promises."

Thoughtfully Kent asked, "Then you believe there *is* a God and that the Bible is true. At college they tell me that God is just a fantasy, and the Bible a bunch of fairy tales. How do I know they're wrong and you're right?" Quickly he added, "No offense, Sir. But I really need to know."

"Then let me ask you a question, Son. How do *they* know that God is a fantasy? Have they given you any proof that *they're* right?"

"No, sir. But they laugh about the idea of anyone believing in God, and say that people only need Him as a crutch in order to get along in the world. They say that people who believe in God are weak."

"Well, what do they suggest people do if they *don't* believe in God? You know, I'll be the first to admit that I'm weak. I couldn't get along without Him. Are they strong enough to do so?"

"I don't know." Kent shook his head, and it dropped on his chest. Somehow he couldn't meet the pastor's eyes, and he felt terribly alone and empty. "I know that when Patsy was hurt yesterday, I didn't know where to turn, and I was afraid. I knew there was nothing *I* could do for her and I felt like all three of us were deserted and alone – until you came to our rescue. But you couldn't make her well either. I knew that and it made me feel even worse. What are we going to do?" He finally raised agonized eyes to meet the gaze of the pastor.

"Well, there's really only one thing *to* do. That is to ask Jesus to come into your heart so that you'll never be alone again. That's all it takes, and God is just waiting to have you ask." He was silent for a few moments, waiting to see if he would have a response from the boy. When there was none, he continued.

"You see, the Lord Jesus, who is the Son of God, died on the cross for your sins and mine. But He didn't stay dead. He arose after three days and went back to Heaven. He's there now, on His throne by the side of God His Father, listening for prayers like yours and ready to come into your heart when you ask."

"Excuse me, Sir, but that *does* sound like a fairytale. How can I know that's really true, when I don't even know for sure there's a God? You see, I just don't understand. I do remember hearing about Jesus on the cross when I was a little boy in Sunday School, but I didn't really understand it then, and I still don't. How could He even know about me? That was so long ago – if it really happened!" The boy looked and sounded completely confused and perplexed. But of one thing Sig was certain – he was searching for answers and wanted to be persuaded.

"Kent, let me emphasize again that there are some things that don't have to be proved. They have to be believed. There are lots of things we don't understand in this world, but we have to take them by faith. I don't see the wind, but I can feel it blowing. I don't understand how a tree grows from a little acorn, but I can see the tree, so I know it happens. We can't see God, and we don't understand how He could love us, but we know He does because we have life, which could only come from Him. The Bible tells us, 'By grace are you saved through *faith*.'" Again Kent was silent, obviously thinking seriously about the pastor's words.

"Kent, I want you to do something for me. Do you have a Bible?"

The boy shrugged his shoulders. "I suppose there's one at home somewhere."

"Well, I have a little Gospel of John in my pocket, and I'm going to give it to you. In it you will find some verses written in red. I don't want you to read *just* those verses, however. I want you to start reading at the beginning, but pay special attention to those verses, because they are the words that Jesus said. Will you read it?"

Kent nodded. "Yes, sir, I will. Can we talk again?"

"Yes, very definitely – and soon. And Kent, if you have other questions, write them down as you think of them, and I'll try to answer them for you. But remember, the first thing to do is ask the Lord Jesus into your heart. After that, you'll find that you understand things as you never have before."

The pastor and the young man arose, shook hands cordially, and Kent felt that he had not only found a friend, but that this friend could maybe help him fill that empty, alone feeling which seemed always to be inside of him. He could hardly wait to get into the small book and find out what it had to say to him.

Chapter 7

*K*ent didn't know it yet, but soon he would make the acquaintance of a young man who would play a big part in changing his life. As he was eagerly reading the little book that Pastor Anderson had given him, Joshua Brownlee O'Conner was busy examining the engine of his new Cessna single engine aircraft. He needed to know every detail of it, just as he had known how his old biplane was put together. He was very proud of his new, shining closed cabin plane, and wanted to be positive that he could service it and even repair it himself if anything should go wrong.

With his father, Billy O'Conner, Josh operated a small airport and maintenance area on the outskirts of Charlotte. Billy had started the business many years ago as a bicycle repair shop, and, as John Holt had done, had added motorcycle parts and repair, and finally automobiles had become his specialty. He not only sold them but had added a garage for keeping them in good operating condition. The airport and hangar were Josh's responsibility. He was well fitted for the job for he had been around the shop all his life, and loved moving vehicles. He was just a child during the Great War, but had been fascinated with the newly invented aircraft, and seemed from an early age to have a sixth sense concerning flying machines.

His first one he built himself, and barnstormed around the countryside, selling rides to brave souls who were willing to risk their lives in his home-made craft. Now he had sold that biplane for a considerable sum, and had invested in the little Cessna he was now exploring and polishing with tender hands.

At twenty-six years of age, he had a flourishing business, not only in the airport but in transporting clients from city to city. They were all quite short flights, but because of his safety record and his reputation of total honesty and trustworthiness, he was a very busy young man.

His father, Billy, had already made an enviable business reputation for himself before Josh came into the business. Orphaned as a boy, Billy had been rescued from poverty and the hard life of the street by Matthew Marlowe, a wealthy Charlotte businessman who had found him in Lansing. When Billy's mother died, he had been adopted by Matthew's brother Joseph and his wife Ruthie, who then raised him as their own son. Already given a strong moral heritage by a Christian mother, Billy grew to accept the standards and principles of the family into which he had been adopted, and became a respected businessman.

When Billy grew up, he married a very lovely girl in Charlotte, but their happiness had been cut unmercifully short. She had died when Josh was born, and Uncle Joseph and Aunt Ruthie had this time helped their adopted son raise his own motherless baby. With the extended family provided by the Marlowe clan, Josh had grown up with more love and mothering than most boys could ever dream of having.

The Marlowes had always been a close knit family. As he worked, Josh found himself thinking of how fortunate he was to be a part of it. Most of the time he just took it for granted that he belonged, but today his mind seemed to be subconsciously calling the roll of those he loved. He remembered fondly his Uncle Matthew, gone now. However Aunt Christy, Matthew's widow, was still living in the old brick family home. As it was just adjacent to the airport, Josh was a frequent visitor there and was always sure of a warm welcome. Then there was Uncle Danny, who was like a younger brother to Billy, and who lived with his wife Josie and their family, just across the street from Aunt Christy in Josie's family home. Danny's brother, Jamie, had died in a motorcycle accident when he was just a teenager, but Jamie's twin, Julie, now lived in nearby

Little Rapids with her husband, Pastor Sigmund Anderson. Both were survivors of the Great War, in which Julie had been a Red Cross nurse, and Sigmund a veteran with many scars. They had no children, but Danny and Josie had a daughter, Eleanor, and a son, Robert. Robert, a gifted musician, was now studying piano at Peabody Conservatory. Eleanor, a headstrong, rebellious girl, gave Danny and Josie many anxious moments. Josh, who loved his cousins as he would have loved a brother and sister, was in the habit of trying to look after Eleanor and keep her from getting into serious trouble - which sometimes took some doing! *"Sometimes I wonder why I keep trying – but I can't just let her ruin herself – and the family!"* And that reflection brought to mind her latest escapade and his part in it.

*****

The family was getting ready to go to a church picnic, planned especially for Robert's visit home. Eleanor really wanted to go, but she considered herself a *"sophisticated"* twenty year old, and being a "part of the crowd" was important to her. And she *did* have a date with Arnold. Robert and Josh were enthusiastic members of the youth group in the little white church that the family attended, but Eleanor had no interest in such things.

However, because of Robert she felt a little guilty for not going to the picnic. But, having made up her mind, she gave one long last look in the mirror, smoothed her bangs and checked her makeup to be sure it was on just right. Then she opened the dresser drawer and pulled the little flask from its hiding place. It was empty and she didn't intend to fill it but Arnold would want to see that she was carrying it. She swung her hips, making her short skirt swirl, and started out to meet her date.

She heard the family leaving out the front door, so she waited a minute till all was quiet again. Then she crept out through the kitchen and down the back steps.

Flashing through her mind as she ran down the hill to meet Arnold was a big unbidden question. *Why am I doing this? I don't even like Arnold much and I sure don't like the places he takes me. I just don't fit in but I'm really kind of scared to tell him so. Maybe I'll do it tonight – if I can get up enough nerve! I almost wish I had gone to the picnic with Josh and Robert. After all, Robert is only home for a few days – but I know Arnold would be furious!*

Arnold leaned across and swung the passenger door open so she could slide in. He gave her an admiring look and pulled her into a hug, planting a wet sloppy kiss on her cheek. With a wiggle she managed to avoid a direct kiss on the lips, always distasteful to her but a familiarity that Arnold seemed to think was his due.

"Hi, Baby. You sure look good enough to eat tonight! Got your flask with you?"

She knew he'd ask that. He had paid a tidy little sum for that bauble, and he wanted it appreciated.

"Of course." Eleanor moved as far toward the passenger door as she could get.

"Oh, come on, Baby! Move over here by your Arnold. I'm lonesome so far away!"

"You're not my Arnold, and I'm not your baby. Let's get started to wherever we're going."

"You're not very cozy tonight, Miss Priss. What's eatin' you?"

"Well, to be truthful, my family's having a party, and I'd kind of like to be there. However, I made you a promise and I'm keeping it!"

"You better be glad you're keepin' it!" A threatening note in his voice made her shiver. "I wouldn't like my girl standin' me up." He made a grab at her leg. "C'mon, Honey, sit by me. What's so great about an old family party when we can go out with the gang? Families are stuffy anyway!"

Eleanor slapped at the hand groping her leg. "Get your hands off of me, Arnold. If you don't this will be our last date. I don't belong to you and you know it."

"Well, la-de-dah. Aren't we getting huffy! Okay, hands to myself but I don't want to hear any more about no family party."

When they arrived at the Roarin'Roadhouse, the party was in full swing. Arnold found them seats at a table where liquor was flowing freely.

Robert had seen Eleanor slip out the back door, and had noticed a yellow roadster awaiting her at the foot of the hill. However, having just arrived home, he didn't know that his father had forbidden her to go out with Arnold, so didn't pay much attention to what he saw. However, when Josh asked where she was, Robert told what he had seen.

"She was meeting her date at the foot of the hill. He was sure driving a nifty yellow roadster!"

Josh had responded in alarm. "Uncle Danny told her she couldn't go out with Arnold. She's going to be in trouble!" Then he added with a worried tone, "I think I know where they may be going. Come on, Robert, maybe we can get there first. There's going to be a raid there tonight! I have a friend who's a cop, and he let it slip today. We can't let her get caught in it!"

The boys rushed out to Josh's flivver and were soon racing across town toward the speakeasy near the railroad tracks. Josh pressed the accelerator to the floor and the flivver bounded ahead. Pushing the speed limit, he hoped he could reach the roadhouse before the cops did. If he could get Eleanor to come away quietly with him, he could spare her and the whole family the embarrassment of an arrest. The entire police blotter would appear in the newspaper and he wanted to keep her name off of it. If only they could make it in time!

Dodging slow-moving vehicles and using all the shortcuts he knew, Josh handled the runabout as he handled his plane "flying low" and avoiding all possible delays. Finally he pulled up behind a concealing clump of small trees half a block from the back entrance of the building. Jazzy music was blaring out on the night air, and loud voices drifted through the open windows, interrupted by frequent gusts of raucous laughter. The long Michigan twilight was just beginning to fade into darkness.

Josh left the engine running and as he slipped out of the car he whispered to Robert, "Slide over here behind the wheel, and be ready to move as soon as I come back. If I'm lucky I'll only be a few minutes." Robert nodded, and watched Josh disappear in the darkness.

Josh slipped close to a door that stood slightly ajar. He peered cautiously inside, taking time to carefully observe all corners of the room before stepping in. He noted the location of the bar, the front entry, and scanned the faces of the merry-makers, recognizing many of the town's tougher crowd as well as sons and daughters of elite Charlotte families.

By good fortune (or more likely the special arrangement of the Good Shepherd Himself, thought Josh) Eleanor was sitting with a couple at a table just inside the door by which he stood. Arnold was nowhere in sight – probably at the bar or in the men's room was Josh's guess. During a burst of the loudest laughter from the bar, he slipped inside and touched Eleanor on the shoulder. She jumped in surprise and whirled around to face him.

Putting a finger to his lips, he leaned down and spoke directly into her ear. "Eleanor, I've come to get you. There's a crisis and you need to come home."

He was relieved to see a look of alarm rather than resistance play across her face. He knew if she refused to come with him, the game was up.

She jumped to her feet. "Oh, my goodness!" Then to her table mate, "Cissy, I have to go. We have an emergency at home." She grabbed Josh's arm and he heaved a sigh of relief.

"Let's go out this door, Nell. My car is just a few steps down the road," and grabbing her hand, he pulled her with him into the darkness.

Without questioning him further, she was in the passenger seat as he vaulted into the seat behind her. "Let's go, Robert. Don't waste any time." Robert wheeled quickly into the street and around the corner just as three police cars came to a squealing halt in front of the roadhouse.

"Robert, what are you doing here? Josh, what's wrong at home? Why did you come for me?" she finally asked, holding on for dear life as the flivver tires squealed around a corner. "Did something terrible happen?"

"I think so. Actually, you just saw it happen. The police were raiding the club just as we were pulling away. You would have been arrested and taken to jail if we hadn't gotten out that very minute!"

"Then nothing's wrong at home?"

"*You* said that. I didn't. But something would have been *very* wrong at home if we hadn't gotten out of there when we did. Can you imagine what would have happened if your name had shown up on the police blotter when the newspaper came out?"

She was silent for a long moment. "Oh, Josh, that would have been terrible!" A sob escaped her as she lay limply back in the seat. Robert glanced at her, and commented in a true brotherly fashion, "Oh, dry up, Eleanor. You know how bad Dad and Mom would have felt. Why didn't you think of that earlier?"

Eleanor bit her lip, guilt bitter in her mouth. "Josh, how did you know about it and how did you know where to find me?"

"Well, the last question isn't hard to answer. Where else does Arnold hang out? Fortunately Robert saw Arnold waiting for you at the foot of the hill." He gave a wry smile and added, "Thought I better play Sir Galahad and rescue the fair maiden!"

******

Now, thinking back on that recent wild ride, Josh shook his head, discouraged about the way his cousin was behaving. As he often did, he said a little prayer right on the spot. *"Dear Lord, please find me a girl who's just the opposite of Eleanor! I love her but I sure wouldn't want to have to spend the rest of my life with her!"* Though they fought like cats and dogs, Josh was only too aware that Eleanor considered that he belonged to her.

Though he didn't know it yet, by the time this very week would be over, Josh was to find the answer to his prayer!

Chapter 8

*B*efore Robert had come home, there had been a hayride planned in the regular schedule of the youth group. The picnic had been an extra, just for Robert, so the hayride was still to take place as planned. On the evening of the hayride, Josh went around from group to group as the young people gathered, laughing and joking especially with the younger ones, for whom he was a counselor. Though some of the young people of the church considered themselves (as Eleanor did) too sophisticated for such recreation, there were others who could and did get excited about a simple outing that was just plain fun. And often their enthusiasm made their self-centered and haughty peers think twice about turning down their invitation. And as a result the turnout for the hayride included several new faces.

Josh not only had great concern but also great sympathy for the many kids who were only interested in pushing their luck. The more dangerous their fun, the better they liked it. He knew they were heading for disaster, for they seldom listened to their parents or to the youth counselors. He often came in contact with such immature – and often very rich – little playboys in his business, so he was familiar with the problem. Their "toys" were the latest automobiles or the raciest motorcycles that money could buy while they were often at the age when they should have still been riding their bicycles. So he had made the plans for this hayride of such a magnitude that he hoped would attract even the most self-styled "sophisticates" in the group.

Josh himself had come to know God at a summer camp when he was a teenager. The camp was sponsored by his church, but run by a summer gospel team from the Moody Bible Institute in Chicago. He had known about Moody because Aunt Julie had attended there. And he was just the age to idolize anyone (male and female) who was a veteran of the Great War, so when she and Sig had offered to pay for his week there, he jumped at the chance. He had found the team of camp counselors to be just as down to earth and attractive as his Aunt Julie was, and the experience had been good.

That summer he had come to realize that he needed something but he didn't know what it was. He knew that there was a huge emptiness within him, and he had always supposed that it was because he didn't have a mother. All the kids he knew had mothers, and though Grandma Ruthie was very special to him, he couldn't help but wonder what it would be like to have a real mother. He had never let Dad or his grandma know how he felt because he didn't want to hurt their feelings.

Then one day one of the camp counselors, not too many years older than Josh, had led a devotional in which he confided to his little group that he was an orphan. And he had told them about a friend who had pointed out a Bible verse in which God promised that boys like him who lacked one or both parents were special to Him. Josh had talked to the counselor for a long time, and had finally asked Jesus to come into his heart. Suddenly that empty feeling was gone and he knew that he would never be alone again. He guessed this must have been something like what his dad felt when the Marlowes had rescued him. Now he wanted to do everything he could to help other lost and confused youth to find the same wonderful peace of mind and heart that he now possessed.

So he would make this hayride so attractive that kids would not want to miss it. There was to be an exciting team of horses – stallions that would fascinate the boys and thrill the girls with their strength and beauty, and he made arrangements for two oversize hay wagons. He asked a talented member of his group to bring his guitar so they could "sing along" favorite songs while riding the country roads.

Then he arranged a huge campfire down by the lake. Grandma Ruthie offered to organize the church ladies to provide the food. Of course there were hot dogs and marshmallows to roast over the fire, fat homemade buns and big dishes of potato salad and baked beans, and of course the (always favorite) German chocolate cake that one of the ladies was famous for. This, along with lots of cold tea to wash it down, was always the menu the kids asked for. Josh knew that until their hunger was satisfied, the teen-agers would never listen to his message as the campfire died down.

He also knew that the hayride would produce no worthwhile results if there were not a lot of prayer to support it. That was the job of not only the Christian kids in his group but also of the praying people of the church, and they had taken their job seriously..

So now all was prepared and the big evening was here. He sensed the excitement of the kids as he moved from group to group.

Just as they were loading, a car drove into the church parking lot. Josh turned to greet his old friend, Mr.Wheaton, who owned the big creamery in town. He had been a member of this little church for many years and everyone knew and loved him. As the car doors opened, two lovely young girls climbed out. Mr. Wheaton motioned Josh to come over.

"Josh, I want you to meet my two granddaughters. They're here for a few days visit, and I thought they would enjoy the hayride. Do you have room for them?"

Josh took one look at the lovely girl who managed to look graceful even climbing out the back seat of a car. She met his eyes, smiled at him, and he was struck completely dumb. He felt like the breath had been knocked out of him. Never in his twenty-six years had he met anyone who had that effect on him. Not that he had never dreamed about it happening!

"This is Celia Marie, my oldest granddaughter, and over here is Bardy, her sister. I know you'll take good care of them for me, won't you, Josh?"

Josh managed to nod his head and smile, and gradually sanity returned. "Of course. We're glad to have you both! We're just loading up, and I have a place for you right here." He handed Bardy up to a space beside one of the girls in his group, just about her own age, then escorted Celia Marie to the leading wagon. "I know we have another seat on this wagon, and as soon as I get things moving, I'll come and sit with you. Here, Tom, would you help Miss Wheaton up?" and he motioned to one of the senior boys who, with great enthusiasm, hurried back to give her a hand.

He went through the motions of checking on everyone, seeing that they were comfortable and making sure that nothing - and no one -was left behind. He fleetingly wondered how he was able to remember everything, for he was conscious of operating in a daze. As the wagons started moving, he swung up on the lead wagon and found his way to the seat beside Celia Marie. Tom was very reluctant to make room for him, but Josh was determined to have that seat.

"It's great that you picked this week to visit your grandparents, Miss Wheaton." He smiled at her and received a beautiful smile in return. "How long will you be here?"

"I think at least a week. My mother will be driving down next weekend, and hopefully she'll be able to stay a few days. If not, we'll go back immediately." Her voice had a husky quality which was as appealing as her blue eyes, honey colored hair and gorgeous smile. Josh wondered if he would ever be the same again!

"Well, I hope you'll be coming again soon. In the meantime, we'll try to make this hayride the highlight of your visit."

He was as good as his word, and by the time a weary, happy group tumbled out of the hayracks later that evening, the two had become good friends. Josh was elated at how quickly they had become at ease with each other, and how exciting it had been to have her near him. Tom had gotten in the way a few times, but he soon understood that he was the odd man out and found another girl who was eager to have his company.

Celia Marie was so lost in thought that she scarcely heard anything Bardy said as they rode home in Grandpa Wheaton's car. She rattled on endlessly, so Celia Marie wouldn't have had much chance to talk even if she had wanted to. Grandpa Wheaton noticed her silence, but Bardy demanded his attention.

However, when her grandmother asked her if she had had a good time, her response was an amazed, "Grandma, I know you won't believe this, but I think I'm in love!" Grandma Wheaton's mouth fell open in consternation, and as she started to speak, Celia Marie held up her hand and said, "Please, Grandma. I don't think I want to talk about it. Let's wait until morning. Then I promise to tell you all about it." And there was nothing an impatient and flustered Grandma could do but wait!

From that point on, things moved swiftly. The two young people had such a short time to get acquainted that they spent most of their waking hours together. Celia Marie inspected Josh's airplane, and both she and Bardy had the wonderful experience of flying high above the earth – though Grandma watched with her shaking hands pressed against her mouth, hardly daring to breathe until they were safely on the ground again. She heard all about Josh's family and was introduced to most of them. In turn Josh heard about Birch Lake College where her mother was the president, and also the story of how her mother came to America from Germany when she was just a little girl. He heard about the sad loss of her beloved father, Dan, and how her mother had moved herself and the two girls to Ann Arbor so she could study for her doctor's degree in education. Soon they felt that they really knew each other, and both were absolutely sure that there would never be anyone else on earth for either of them.

They had one weekend to spend together before she would have to go back to Birch Lake. Josh thought he knew just how to spend it.

"Joshua! Oh, it's good to hear your voice! Is everything okay in Charlotte?" There was no mistaking the delight in Julie's voice as she answered the telephone which had been ringing madly off the wall of the little parsonage.

"You bet. Everything's fine and even better than fine, Aunt Julie! I have a surprise for you, and I wondered if you and Uncle Sig would mind if I came over to see you on Sunday and brought a friend with me."

"You know you're welcome any time, my dear. Will you be here in time for the morning service? And who's your friend?"

"Yes to the first question and you'll have to wait and find out the answer to the second when we get there! That's the surprise! Want me to bring anything along for dinner?"

"Josh! You know better than that! Of course not. But what do you want me to fix? Anything special?"

"Only the usual! A Sunday dinner such as only you and Aunt Christy can fix. I love you, Aunt Julie and give my love to Uncle Sig. See you Sunday. Bye!" and the click of the receiver on the other end signaled the end of the conversation.

Julie hung up quickly and ran into the study where Sig was deep in his book. "Honey, guess what. Josh is bringing a friend with him and will be here for the service Sunday morning. They're going to stay for dinner afterward – and for as long after that as I can keep them! He says the guest will be a surprise – I can't imagine who it will be. It wouldn't be Mom or he would have told me."

"Now Julie, are you going to be guessing from now until they get here? Let's see, that will take up at least two whole days, won't it? Do you think you can stand it that long?"

"Oh, quit teasing me, Sig. Josh doesn't get over here that often – I have a right to be excited!"

Josh was a very important and dear member of the family, and the Andersons loved him with all their hearts. They considered him a very special gift from God. He was the 'son they had never had' for Julie and Sig would not be having any children of their own. Sig's battle wounds had left him permanently disabled, and Josh had filled an empty place in both their hearts. She was therefore as excited at his coming visit as she would have been had he been her own son.

But Sig had something on his mind, and he seemed frustratingly absent minded the rest of the day. Finally, Julie could contain herself no longer. She invaded his study, appropriated his lap, and turned out the desk lamp. "Now, Sig, I'm tired of talking to myself. I know you have something on your mind, because if you didn't, you would be as excited about Josh's coming as I am. Does it have something to do with those beautiful twins and that handsome young man? Have you heard something you haven't told me?"

Sig held her close, then lifted her off his lap and moved them both to the couch. "Julie, I can't get Kent off my mind. He blames himself for not taking better care of Patsy, but worse than that, he's been infected with these devilish ideas that are being taught in so many colleges these days. He doubts that God even exists, so he has nothing to hang on to when a real crisis takes place – like this accident. He needs something solid to steady him, but he can't let loose of those ideas that have been taught to him by godless professors." He shook his head sadly. "I talked to him and gave him a gospel of John. He promised to read it, and I hope I'll be able to talk to him again soon, but in the meantime he's constantly on my mind and heart."

Julie, now as serious and concerned as Sig, nodded with understanding. "I know. I realized that Penny knew nothing about God except for a couple of memorized prayers, and I suppose Patsy is just as ignorant as Penny." She thought a moment, then added, "I guess that leads us to believe that their parents are as lost as they are. I think, Sig, that we walked right into a mission field the other day and now it's our responsibility to do something about it."

As a matter of fact, Kent was at that moment keeping his promise to Sig. He was sitting by Patsy's bed, taking his turn in the long vigil, anxiously awaiting some sign of life other than the even rise and fall of her chest. But she continued to lay, otherwise motionless, on the bed. Occasionally a soft moan, which always wrenched his heart, brought him upright, and he would search her face eagerly for some sort of expression to tell him she was coming back to consciousness, but she continued in that deep sleep which the doctor had called a coma.

However, he was making use of the long hours by perusing the small book that Sig had given him. At first it made little sense to him, but before long he found himself reading avidly, caught up in the narrative. Then a flash of memory brought to mind a little Sunday School picture that he remembered from his childhood. It had shown a long-haired, unshaven, rough looking man clothed only in some sort of short animal skin, pointing to a handsome young man, and quoted as saying, "Behold the Lamb of God, who taketh away the sins of the world." For a moment he turned from the book, looked off into space, and wondered where *that* had come from! Turning back to the page that he had been reading, he found to his amazement those very words, and he hurriedly read on. Now he rubbed his arms and felt the goose bumps arising. There was something here that he didn't understand. But he felt, deep in his gut, that he was on to something big. Nobody in college had ever mentioned this story that he was now reading. They had just ridiculed the Bible as nonsense. This wasn't nonsense, of that he was certain. If he could only grasp it, he had a feeling that here was truth, even though the professors had told him that there were no absolutes in life. Well, maybe, just maybe, this little book would prove them wrong.

In the next couple of days, he finished the book, and started it all over again. This was an unbelievable story, but he wanted so much to believe it! By Sunday morning, his mind was made up. He was going to go to that little church where Pastor Anderson would be preaching. Maybe he would hear something more to help him understand, or maybe he would get a chance to talk to the man who had given him this strange little book.

But it wasn't Sig who helped him move toward a vital decision in his search for – he really didn't know *what* he was searching for! This time it was a young man who was introduced to him by Mrs. Anderson as her nephew, Josh. When he entered the church, Julie had spotted him, and she hurried to him with a blaze of welcome in her smile. She led him to their pew, and he sat between her and Josh, who greeted him with unusual warmth. He somehow had the feeling that they were waiting for him.

The service was strange to him. Whenever he had attended his own church, (and he had not done that for several years past), the service had been very formal. There had been a great deal of ritual and he had never been quite sure what it was all about. Here in *this* place he experienced an immediate feeling of warmth and welcome, even though the pews were hard and everything was very plain. Instead of all the windows being of expensive stained glass, there was only one small colored one right behind the pulpit. It depicted a man (whom Kent guessed to be Jesus) kneeling and looking up toward heaven. He stared at it, strangely moved. He felt an unaccustomed sensation of peace, seeming to in some way have a connection to that pictured man.

He looked around and noticed that just about everyone had some kind of a book of their own, and he saw that Josh had one too. He leaned over to see its title and discovered that it was a Bible. Julie was sharing her hymnbook with him, and when Sig began to preach, she opened her Bible and held it where he could see it too.

He noted that though both had their own Bibles, Josh shared his hymnbook with a lovely girl who sat beside him and who had been introduced to him as Celia Marie, Josh's girl friend. It was his guess, from the way they looked at each other, that she was more than just a friend, and something within him approved, for they seemed to suit each other.

Kent loved to sing, and he had a pleasing baritone voice, but many of these songs he had not heard before. However, there was one in which the words reminded him of what he had read in the little red Gospel of John.

"On a hill far away, stood an old rugged cross,

The emblem of suffering and shame,

And I love that old cross, where the dearest and best

For a world of lost sinners was slain."

He remembered the story in the book about the kind Man who had been hung on a cross by some soldiers, and how the mob had shouted for his death. He had wondered why the people hated Him so much, for He had healed and fed them, and helped them in so many ways. He had felt a great sorrow as the images of what he was reading had formed in his mind, but he also remembered the joy he felt when, at the end of the book, the Man had come back to life. And again he had a vague memory of hearing that story before, and of being told that this Man was God. Could it be real? Sig would insist that the story was true. He was sure of that. But would this fellow, not much older than he – would he laugh at it or would he agree with Sig? Kent felt that it was very important for him to find out.

So as soon as the 'Amen' had been said and they had been greeted by Sig, (both receiving a bear hug from him as they exited the church), Kent turned to Josh with his all-important question. "Josh, Pastor Anderson gave me a little book to read and it told the story of a man who claimed to be God, and who was killed on a cross. The book said He came back to life and the Pastor said He is in Heaven now. Do you believe all that? I remember hearing about Him when I was a little boy, but nobody in the college I attend believes that God even exists! How do you feel about it? Would you mind telling me?"

Josh was more than willing to answer Kent's burning question. Many years ago, when he was still a small boy, he had heard about Jesus at the knee of his adopted grandmother, Ruthie, and it had prepared him, when he went to camp, to be ready to say "Yes" to the Lord. So it was with joy that he responded, "Hey, Kent, I'd love to tell you. I believe in Him with all my heart, and I couldn't live without Him. When you know Him, everything in life is different, because He is in charge of things! He has a plan for everyone's life, you know, and when you let Him work it out for you, this world is a different place! You know, if you haven't asked Him to be your Savior, you ought to do it right away. Why don't you talk to Uncle Sig about it this very afternoon?"

"Thanks, Josh, but I have to think about it a little more. But I do have one more question for you, if you don't mind. You said God has a plan for everyone's life. If He does, why do some people have accidents and get hurt? Are things like that in His plan? I can't understand that."

"Sometimes things are real hard to understand, Kent. All I know is that God created us and He loves us. And He has promised those who believe in Him that 'all things (will) work together for good to them that love God.' He doesn't promise that everything will be easy or the way we want it, but He does promise that somehow things will work out for our good. To me that tells me everything I need to know!"

"I never heard that before, Josh. I mean I never heard that God cares about each one of us personally." Kent thought for a moment, then nodded his head. "But Josh, there's something else that's been bothering me. My professors say that Darwin proved that all life came from a single-celled animal, and that human beings came to be like we are now by the process of evolution. It sounds kind of screwy to me, but I guess that's science. But if God created us as you say, I don't see how that could be." He paused, then brushing a hand across his eyes, he continued, "And if He loves us like you say, why does He *even let* bad things happen to us? You see, I have a good friend who had an accident a couple of days ago. She's in the hospital in a coma, and even if she lives, she may be crippled for the rest of her life. I just don't understand God letting that happen to her. That doesn't sound to me like anything that could be for her good! "

Josh, reading the agony in Kent's eyes, put his hand on the boy's shoulder with a comforting squeeze. "Kent, I don't know all the answers, but I do know that God loves you. Please talk to Uncle Sig, and ask him to help you understand."

As Kent made his way to the hospital, the thought occurred to him that Josh was inexplicably different from the fellows he knew at college, and he wondered why? Sometimes his college pals acted as if they never had a serious thought. They were good friends of his, and he loved the fun times they had together, but Patsy's accident had caused him to think seriously about life and about the future. He suddenly felt reluctant to ever return to the dormitory. He hated to leave Patsy in the first place, and in the second place he had a feeling that none of his friends would understand that he was not the same Kent that they knew and that he would never be the same again. They wouldn't understand how he felt even if he tried to tell them.

Kent spent his afternoon sitting beside Patsy, again with the little book in his hand. He had much to think about, and he knew that the answers to *his* questions would be ones that Patsy would want to hear too, when – and if - she woke up again. He was glad that he didn't have to return to college right away. He had to find a way to talk to Pastor Anderson again soon. He must have some answers or he would go crazy, and if Patsy woke up, it was very important that he share with her what he learned.

Chapter 9

Penny was also thinking about things that she had never considered before. The accident had shaken her badly, and her mother worried about her. She was not her usual sunny self, but was moody and almost cross. She was finding it hard to spend time with her friends, for they were always asking her questions about Patsy and she didn't have any answers. That was really her big problem. She didn't know what was going to happen! And she wasn't used to living without Patsy at her side. They would share daring escapades together, but Penny's impetuous nature would always be balanced by Patsy's own more thoughtful, considered judgements. As is common with twins, without Patsy she felt like she was only half alive!

And she couldn't bear to think that Patsy might die and leave her alone forever. She was sure that she would die, too. She knew she didn't know how to live without Patsy and - she didn't know how to die either! She had never had to think about such a thing before! It was a dilemma that intruded upon her dreams that filled the endless hours when she was sitting by Patsy's bed. She sat and watched Patsy – but it seemed to her that her twin *wasn't really* there at all! Momentarily forgetting, she would start to tell her something – and suddenly remember that she was not hearing and of course would not be able to answer. Then she would put her head into her hands and great silent sobs would get in the way of her breathing, and she realized that there just wasn't anything to look forward to – alone!

As with Kent, the spontaneous prayers that just seemed to flow out of their new friends, the Andersons, had made a tremendous impression on her. Life was so different now, and she felt the need of such comfort as she had never felt it before. Her mother and father didn't seem to be much better off than she was, though they tried to be cheerful and hopeful – especially when she was around. Though she loved her parents dearly, she usually didn't pay too much attention to the needs of anyone but herself (and of course, Patsy's), but she sensed their despair and just now felt very close to them.

However, being Penny, her reaction to the Andersons was not at all like Kent's. She felt a deep resentment toward them. It wasn't fair for them to have such a friend in God that they could talk so easily to Him, when her own family knew so little about Him. Of course she had gone to church with her parents since she was a child, and so had Patsy, but she only knew God as a great far-away Supreme Being, who would probably be too busy to listen to a common ordinary person like her. She wondered if the Andersons and the Holts believed in the same God! It puzzled her greatly.

Her way of coping with the present disastrous situation was to simply ignore the reality of it and expect everything to turn out all right. When she sat by Patsy's inert form, that determination would fade, but Penny simply refused to face the possibility that – Patsy could *die!* No!. Patsy would not – *could* not die! She would not have it, and if she refused to believe it, it wouldn't happen! She clung to that idea, for she had nothing else.

Jimmy Denton, whom she knew had a crush on Patsy, sought out Penny on Sunday evening, and she allowed him to walk to town with her. She really didn't have any destination, but intended to just sit in the ice cream store with a soda and daydream for a while. She was lonesome at home, but dreaded having to go to the hospital and see Patsy lying there without being able to talk to her. The soda fountain was a popular hangout, and for once she felt the need of being with people. She knew that Jimmy was honestly upset about the accident, and was really kind of glad to see him, but she didn't expect at all what he had to tell her.

"Penny, have you heard that the police questioned Bruce's brother Jason about the accident? I heard that they examined his car, too, and found some damage on the right front fender. It looks pretty definite that he was the one who hit Patsy."

Penny looked at him in astonishment. "How did you find out? Dad must not know – at least he hasn't said anything about it. Have the police arrested him?"

"No, it's just the grape vine working overtime. I don't think they've made any announcement about it. I hear that Jason has denied everything, but it looks like there's a lot of evidence there. No, they haven't arrested him, but I hope they do and that he gets the book thrown at him!" Jimmy's voice suddenly turned hard, and Penny shivered at the rage she felt in him. She immediately decided he was a kindred spirit. That same rage had been gnawing at her ever since that fateful evening.

"He's sure got it coming to him. Poor Patsy may never wake up, and if she does she may be crippled for life! He ought to be made to suffer, too, even though *that* won't help *her* any. He must be a rotten kid!"

"That's for sure. But he's not much of a kid. He's at least two years older than Bruce. Penny, tell your dad and mom that all of Patsy's friends are pulling for her, will you? She's a swell girl, and everybody really feels bad about it."

Penny turned to him, and surprised him with a quick kiss on the cheek. "Thanks, Jimmy. I'll tell Patsy, too, when she wakes up." She paused, a tear trailing unnoticed down her own cheek. "She *has* to wake up, you know!"

Now Penny couldn't wait to get home. She *had* to find her father, and relay Jimmy's message without delay. She found him in the back yard, pounding furiously on the big anvil, flattening a horseshoe under his hammer into a useless piece of iron.

"Dad, Dad! Have the police talked to you?"

John laid down his hammer, and tossed the tongs aside. "Penny, what are you talking about?"

"Jimmy said that the police have found damage on the fender of Jason Baylor's new car, and they think he's the one who hit Patsy. He denies it, but everyone thinks he did it, even if he won't own up to it!" Penny was out of breath with excitement.

"No, they haven't called me. Probably are trying to make certain he's guilty before they bring charges against him." John looked grim. "I'd like to have a talk with that boy!"

"What'll they do to him, Dad? I hope it's bad! I hope they take his car away from him for one thing."

"My thinking exactly, Honey. If he's guilty, he shouldn't be allowed to endanger anyone else. I'm going in and clean up, then I'll head right down to the police station." He started toward the house, then with the door half open, turned back to Penny as he remembered something.

"Honey, I'm supposed to go to the hospital in a few minutes and relieve your mother. Will you go instead and tell her where I've gone?"

"Sure, Dad. I want to see if Patsy shows any signs of waking up yet. You'll come to the hospital and tell us what you find out, won't you?"

"I'll be there as soon as possible." And John hurried off, his mind busy inventing every punishment he could think of for the boy who had caused his little Patsy to suffer.

At the hospital, Penny hurried up to her twin's room. She quietly opened the door and slipped inside. Then she stopped in amazement. Her sister was propped up in bed, leaning against the pillows. Her eyes were open and fixed on her mother who was sitting beside her, tears rolling down her face unheeded. The nurse stood on the other side of the bed, her fingers on Patsy's wrist, and Penny thought she saw tears in her eyes, too. Penny stood in the door, looking from one to the other, overcome with sudden, intense joy. As soon as she saw her, the nurse moved aside and motioned her to take her place.

Penny leaned over and carefully put her arms around her twin and laid her own wet cheek against Patsy's. "Oh, Patsy, you're back! I was so afraid you weren't going to wake up, and I nearly died! Oh, Patsy, I've missed you so much!"

Patsy lifted her good arm and held Penny tight. "Penny, I don't remember what happened. Why am I here?"

Louise, without taking her eyes off her daughter, explained, "She only woke up a minute ago. We haven't had time to talk, and the nurse said to be sure not to tire her. But, Honey, you need to know that you had an accident while you were riding your bicycle back from Barney's. You've been here in the hospital for three days, asleep. But we've been with you every minute, Dear, and the doctor says that you're going to get well. Oh, Patsy, we're so glad to have you back!" She leaned over and kissed her daughter, and for a long moment the two curly heads and Louise's 'salt and pepper' hair were clustered together in a loving embrace.

In a moment Patsy's eyes closed again and the nurse signaled the others to let her sleep. "She will be sleeping normally now," she told them, "and she needs the rest. I'll tell the doctor that she has awakened, and he'll be here in a few minutes." She rustled busily out of the room, anxious to be the bearer of such good news to the doctor.

"Oh, Mom, I'm so happy. A few minutes ago I was sure she would never wake up!" Penny was careful to whisper.

"God has been good, Sweetheart. He has brought her back to us." Louise was still.dabbing at her eyes, and wiping the tears from her face.

Penny looked at her mother with resentment in her eyes. "God wasn't very good to let Patsy get hurt! Why do you say He's good to let her wake up? Seems to me that He probably doesn't care at all!"

"Oh, Sweetheart, don't say things like that. Of course He cares. We need to thank Him for letting her live. She could so easily have been killed!"

"Well, He could have kept the accident from happening at all!" Penny snapped, momentarily forgetting to lower her voice. She clapped her hand over her mouth but Patsy didn't stir.

However, Penny clearly had her mind made up, and her mother was appalled. She had had no idea that her daughter would doubt God's goodness. After all, she had always been taken to church and Sunday

School, and though she had never discussed such things with the twins, Louise thought they had been well taught.

Then Penny remembered her news. She whispered, "Mom, Dad said to tell you he'd be here as soon as he can make it. The police believe that Jason Baylor was the one driving the car that hit Patsy, and Dad has gone to the police station to talk to them. While Patsy's sleeping, I'll go and telephone Kent. He'll want to come over right away, I know."

"All right, Sweetheart. I'll just sit here quietly until your father comes." Louise didn't say the words aloud but she thought, "*While I wait I'll be asking God for forgiveness that I didn't teach my daughters about Him. I certainly have a lot to talk to Him about!*" And for the first time in many years, Louise Holt did some serious praying.

After dinner at the Andersons, it was time for talk. Josh, of course, before the Sunday service, had introduced Celia Marie as his future bride, much to the delight of his aunt and uncle. However, they were happy to hear both Josh and Celia Marie add, "the Lord willing" when speaking of their plans for marriage. Of course, they had to hear all about how the two had met at the hayride, and how they had met because Josh and the Wheatons, Celia Marie's grandparents, all attended the same church in Charlotte. It had been love at first sight, for before the hayride was over, they both knew that this was not to be an ordinary friendship.

"But we're going to wait, Aunt Julie, for at least a year. I want to fly up to Birch Lake and meet the rest of Celee's family, and probably her mother will need a while to plan the wedding."

"Besides," added Celia Marie, "This has happened real fast. We both need some time to find out all about each other, and I know Mother wouldn't agree to us getting married right away."

Josh again. "Of course we'd like to announce our engagement soon, but we'll have to see what Celee's mother says and" he added, "I want my family to get to know her better, too. They already love her, and it helps that the Marlowes have known the Wheatons for years. They've known my dad for a long time, too, so we don't have any problems there." The Wheatons had actually known Billy when he married, and had wept with the family when he was left with a child to bring up without a mother. They had watched Josh grow up, and knew him well.

Celee grinned and put in, "And my little sister, Bardy, thinks there's no one like him." She squeezed Josh's hand under the table. "Bardy was thrilled with her plane ride, and believes that no one else in the world has a more exciting brother-in-law than Josh! Other people travel by automobile, but Josh flies his own airplane! Talk about hero worship! She can hardly wait for him to visit Birch Lake and land on the athletic field where all the students and faculty can see!" She smiled at Josh with her heart in her eyes. "And I agree with her! What more could a girl ask in a brother-in-law!"

Sig and Julie had to know all about Celia Marie's family, and both were very impressed with what they were told. Julie was especially interested in hearing that Celee's mother, Rosi, had authored some children's books, and looked forward eagerly to meeting her. But at the moment, it was enough to see that Celia Marie was easily fitting into the family, and that she and Josh seemed to be very deeply in love.

As the afternoon waned, and twilight began to fall, the telephone on the wall jangled for attention. Sig excused himself to answer it, expecting that one of his parishioners probably needed to talk to him. Instead, he gave a great shout, quickly signed off, and rushed out to the porch. His face was alight with excitement.

"Sig, what in the world? You look like you're going to explode!"

"Honey, guess what! That was John Holt on the phone, and Patsy is awake! The Lord has brought her back to them! Though we won't be allowed to see her but for a few moments, he wants us to come over to the hospital this evening." He turned to his guests. "We have an incredible story to tell you. How about riding over to the hospital with us and we'll tell you on the way."

As the story unfolded, Josh began to make connections with the questions Kent had asked him that morning. So that was what was bothering the boy! Maybe now that Patsy had awakened, Kent would be more receptive to what first Sig, and then Josh, had tried to tell him.

The excitement was infectious, and it was a hilarious group that piled out of the car at the hospital.

Celia Marie and Josh hung back, not wanting to intrude on the family celebration. For a few minutes they sat in the waiting room, and Josh told Celee what Kent had discussed with him. Then Kent himself walked in.

"Wow, I can hardly believe it! I thought Patsy might never wake up, but she seems to be perfectly fine – except that she doesn't remember what happened to her! What a relief – especially for Penny and her mom and dad! And I can't remember when I was ever so excited. It seemed like everything was off track and now things are on schedule again!" He laughed. "Maybe that sounds funny, but until she woke up, nothing seemed to be right." Then he sobered. "But we still don't know if she'll ever walk again."

Josh put his hand on Kent's shoulder. "One thing at a time, Kent. Don't borrow trouble. We'll just keep praying. God's hearing us, I know, and He's taking care of Patsy."

Kent looked at his new friend with peace in his eyes. "I know beyond the shadow of a doubt that God did something here. I did a lot of thinking after church, and was suddenly aware that I no longer believed all that stuff they tried to tell me at school. I told God I believed in Him and loved His Son as soon as I read in the little book how much He loves me – and everyone! You helped me a lot, Josh, by urging me to get things settled right away." Then he looked at Josh with wonder in his eyes. "And you know what? Right after that Patsy woke up! I know it was God!"

Josh could hardly contain himself. He grabbed Kent's hand, then reached out to him with a big bear hug. "That's great, fella. Now we're brothers in Christ. Oh, Kent, this is just the beginning for you and for Patsy, because I'm positive that God has that plan that we were talking about –not only for you but for all your family. God is so good!"

Kent nodded, still with that quiet peaceful smile on his face. He could hardly wait to tell Patsy about his discovery, and read that little red book of John with her. "You know, Josh, I believed it all even before she woke up, because I never knew such a Man as that book tells about. I loved Him just by reading about Him, and I told Him so. And you know what else?" Kent looked from Josh to Celee as they held their breath, waiting. "I don't have any doubts anymore, none at all. I can believe that God created us, and that He knows all about us – and that He really cares about Patsy and me and all of us. Suddenly it all makes sense to me and I can see that those things I was taught just don't add up. I've never felt like this before, Josh. I feel like I'm lighter than air, and I'm not worrying about a thing because somehow I know that He's going to take care of everything. What I want now is to tell Patsy and my parents, and Penny and *her* parents all about it because I want them to know Him too. Can you believe that?"

"You bet I can, and I can tell you that it's the first day of your new life and things will never be the same again!" Josh put his arm around Celee, whose smile was as bright as the sunlight. "Isn't that right, Sweetheart?"

"Oh, yes, and I'm so very, very glad, Kent! This makes our day even more wonderful and special – and it has been a very special day for us! This makes it perfect!"

"And I can't wait until you get a chance to tell Aunt Julie and Uncle Sig! Boy, what a great day all around!" Josh knew they would remember this day forever.

Chapter 10

The Wheatons were getting ready for company. The big surprise that Celia Marie had sprung on them had sprouted new plans for the day that her mother and Beth would arrive. Not only would there be a special dinner, second only to Grandma Wheaton's famous Thanksgiving spread, but there would be at the table prospective new family members. Of course Josh was invited – and had accepted very promptly! – and also Billy, along with Joseph and Ruthie, would be there.

Celia Marie was still in a daze, excusable under the circumstances, and Josh wasn't much better. It really didn't matter who was around, they had eyes only for each other, and Bardy was getting a little tired of it. Still, she guessed Grandma was right. When people were in love, they really weren't responsible for their actions!

The two girls were busy helping Grandma get ready for this very special dinner. They expected their mother and Beth to arrive soon after lunch, for they had spent the night with friends about half-way down the road to Charlotte. They hoped that Mom had been able to arrange for a few days absence, and of course they intended to stretch that time out for as long as she would allow.

"Grandma, I polished the silver and I have the table set. Shall I go out and pick some flowers for a centerpiece?"

"Please do, Bardy. There are some beautiful lilies in the garden, and you might pick some smaller ones to arrange around them. Just choose what you like, dear. I know you'll do a lovely job."

It was a beautiful day, and Bardy loved nothing better than being outdoors. She was daydreaming over her assignment when she saw her sister come out the front door..

"Celee, come tell me what flowers you want for a table centerpiece. After all, this dinner is for you, and you should choose."

Celia Marie jumped off the porch and came running to join Bardy. "Oh, Bardy, how beautiful! You really don't need any help, those lilies are gorgeous!" She reached over and touched one of the delicate blossoms. "Oh, everything is going to be so perfect tonight! I can't wait to see Mom when she meets Josh. I just know they'll love each other at once!"

"She will, Celee, she will. Everybody just loves Josh. You're so lucky to have found each other!"

Celee shook her head. "Not lucky, Bardy. You know Mom says that God has a plan for everyone's life, and I think meeting Josh was in God's plan for both Josh and me. We told Aunt Julie and Uncle Sig that we are going to wait at least a year, though, to be sure we're doing the right thing." Then she added with confidence, "but I don't have any doubts about it at all!"

Bardy gathered up the flowers and laid them carefully on the edge of the porch. "Celee, I know Josh calls the Andersons 'aunt' and 'uncle', but are they really? Grandma said something about Josh being adopted."

"Not Josh. Josh's dad, Billy, was adopted by Mr. and Mrs. Joseph Marlowe when he was about fourteen years old. Josh's mother died when he was born, and Mrs. Marlowe (his grandmother) raised him. That's why Josh and his dad are part of the Marlowe family." She stopped and thought a minute, wanting to get the family connections straight. "You see, Mr. Joseph Marlowe, Billy's adopted dad, was a brother to Matthew Marlowe and that kind of made Billy like a brother to the Marlowe kids. Aunt Julie is a sister to Danny Marlowe, and they are the children of Matthew Marlowe." Celee grinned at the puzzled look on her sister's face. "Kind of complicated, isn't it? It's a wonder I have it straight – or at least I *think* I do."

"And I heard Grandma say that Danny's wife, Josie, was adopted into their family too." She and Celee shared a good laugh. "I guess we'd have just about as much trouble explaining Beth to anyone outside the family, too, wouldn't we? I kind of forget that she isn't really related to us. She's been one of us ever since I can remember."

Celee sobered down. "I guess there are a lot of people in this world who aren't nearly as fortunate as we are, Bardie, and it's a good thing that families like the Marlowes and the Beckmans are around to take care of them. Even though we lost our Daddy, we still had someone to love us and care for us. Beth didn't have anyone, so I'm glad that her mother sent her to Aunt Babette. Otherwise we wouldn't have her, and I don't know what we'd do without her."

"Me, either." Bardy stood back and critically inspected her flower arrangement. "What do you think?"

"Perfect!" Celee called to her Grandma who was busily creating her kitchen miracles. "What's next, Grandma? Do you need us out there to help you?"

Grandma bustled into the dining room, rubbing her hands on her apron and with a smudge of flour adorning her nose. "No, my dears, I think I have everything under control. There's not much more that we can do ahead of time. Find something to do while you watch for your mother and Beth to arrive. I'm sure it won't be long now." And she disappeared back into the kitchen, pulling her apron off as she went. "I'm going to try to take a nap myself, but I think I'm probably too excited to sleep!"

There was another family conference going on over in the brick house on Lawrence Avenue, the Marlowe home where Grandmother Christy lived. Matthew, her beloved husband of many years, had passed away some years before, but Christy still lived in the house where they had spent so many years together. She often found herself wanting to consult him in times of family crises, such as the one with which she found herself just now. His even temper and good judgement had always been there to balance her impetuous nature. However, as always, she prayed for wisdom with which to meet the needs of her granddaughter Eleanor, who seemed to have inherited from her that same restlessness and need for direction.

She didn't remember having such problems with Danny, who was much like his father, nor with Julie, who always seemed to know how to handle life's challenges. Jamie had been their child who pushed his limits, and he had died doing just that. She still shuddered as she remembered the shock of being told that he had not survived the motorcycle accident. She had never been the same, though time had mercifully tempered the grief that had overcome her.

But now here was Eleanor, Danny's and Josie's eldest, in the throes of another kind of shock. And she, Christy, didn't know how to help her. This kind of a problem was one she had never experienced. She had had many beaux, but none that she had taken seriously until she met Matthew Marlowe, so she had never had her heart broken in disappointed love. Now Eleanor was crying that her world was destroyed because Josh had fallen in love with another girl, and she was feeling extremely sorry for herself. Of course she didn't see it herself (she was far too selfish), but she was making life miserable for everyone around her. Danny and Josie couldn't seem to cope with her (a dilemma they had encountered frequently ever since she was born). All her life she had felt that Josh belonged to her, and she had depended on him to get her out of her frequent scrapes, just taking it for granted that he would be there for her. Now with the announcement of his engagement to Celia Marie, she felt forsaken, and suddenly realized that she was in love with him. Her reaction was predictable – she was spoiled and not being able to have her own way, she was taking it out on all the family.

She had called Christy an hour ago. "Grandma, do you mind if I come over? I really need to talk to you!" Since she called, Christy had been sitting in her rocking chair, rocking slowly and wondering just what she would say to Eleanor. As she rocked, she absently stroked Chester, the yellow tom cat who was possessively occupying her lap.

He was making the most of her quiet waiting, periodically nudging her hand with an insistent little nose whenever her fingers ceased their soft massage behind his ears. She smiled at him, enjoying the comforting warmth of his body. He had kept her company ever since Danny had brought him to her as a kitten.

That had been just after Matthew left her to go home to heaven. Chester seemed to know that his only mission in life was to be her companion, and that she was his very own person. He wanted no other. He was polite to other family members but he adored her only.

Suddenly the door opened and there was a quick step in the hall. *"That's the way I used to burst into the house,"* reflected Christy, smiling to herself. *"But I was usually late – and never apologetic about it!"*

"Grandmother, are you here?"

"Come in, Dear. I'm in the parlor." Christy thought that Eleanor didn't sound too brokenhearted. Maybe this wasn't going to be so bad after all. "I'm glad you called. I don't see you very often anymore. You must be staying very busy."

"Not really, Grandmother. There isn't much to do that's interesting. I play tennis with some of my friends, and we go to a lot of movies, but I'm really bored." She draped herself on the comfortable old sofa, and propped her head on her hand, half turning so she could see her grandmother. Her boredom showed clearly in both her body language and her face.

"Grandmother, what did you do to keep busy when you were young? Daddy won't let me go out with Arnold any more, not that I really want to. I don't like the places he takes me and the people he runs around with – and I really don't like him!" She sighed, "but at least it was something to *do*! Now there's nothing happening – nothing exciting, that is."

"Well, I'm afraid I agree with your father. I'm glad you're *not* running around with that crowd any more, even if you have to endure boredom!" Christy smiled as she scratched Chester under his chin, eliciting a loud purr. "And I think you show good taste in not liking the places he goes. I'm proud of you for that."

"But what else is there to do?" A whine now crept into Eleanor's voice, and Christy decided it was time for some straight talk.

"It depends upon what you *want* to do. If you want to waste your life with just playing, then fill up your time with movies and games. If you want to amount to something, then find a way to be useful to other people. You might start with going to the church youth group and getting involved in their activities."

"Oh, Grandmother! You *know* I can't do *that*! I would be running into Josh all the time because that's where he hangs out in all his spare time."

"Are you going to be avoiding Josh for the rest of your life?" Christy couldn't help it. She had to cut right to the problem.

Eleanor jerked her head up to see her grandmother watching her with a stern look, not often seen by her grandchildren. "You don't have to tell me, Eleanor. I know that you think you're in love with Josh, and you're jealous because he's in love with another girl. Well, a Marlowe doesn't sulk about things that can't be helped. And this can't be helped. You've had a disappointment, but it's not the end of your life. What you're doing is not only making yourself sick about it, but you're making everyone who loves you unhappy, and you're making Josh and Celia Marie very uncomfortable. You ought to be ashamed of yourself, you know."

Eleanor couldn't believe her ears. She had thought that Grandmother Christy would sympathize with her. That's what she had come for – she wanted a shoulder to cry on! Instead she was getting a sound scolding from a very severe disciplinarian. The shock silenced any excuses that were ready to be made.

"And let me tell you this," her grandmother continued, "if anyone had reason to feel sorry for himself and just quit living, it was your grandfather. When his mother and father and brother and sister died of typhoid fever, he wasn't much older than you are, but he went on living and took care of his brother and sisters and made something of his life. You can do the same, but not if you just sit down and cry when you don't get your way. You do like he did and find some way to help someone else, and forget about feeling sorry for yourself."

Suddenly Christy realized how hard she was being on Eleanor, who had been reduced to silence, still with the shocked look on her face. "Honey, you can do it. You're a Marlowe, and maybe you need to learn to trust God like the rest of the Marlowes have! Just look at your Aunt Julie and Uncle Sig. They've overcome tremendous difficulties. Your Mother and Father have faced lives of tremendous loss. Josie lost her parents when she was just a little girl, and Danny lost his brother in a terrible accident. They didn't cave in and just quit now, did they? And you won't either. I believe you have more character than that, and I'm expecting to see you snap out of this and get busy. Go volunteer at the hospital, or help take care of children at the daycare center, but do something for somebody other than yourself." Then she added, "Maybe you *should* go to some of Josh's youth meetings. I think you would find there what you need to help you be the person that you can be."

Suddenly Eleanor was seeing herself in a new light. Was this the way her family saw her – as a spoiled, selfish brat? No wonder Josh wasn't in love with her. All she had demanded from him was that he be her caretaker – and even her little brother Robert was able to see that. She remembered his disgusted attitude toward her the night the two boys had rescued her from being caught by the police at the nightclub. And she was supposed to be *his* big sister! In a flash of understanding she realized that their roles had been reversed, and that both Josh and Robert had a right to be disappointed in her. It now occurred to her to wonder if it was too late to redeem herself in the eyes of her family.

"Grandmother…" she hesitated, not knowing how to put her feelings into words. "Grandmother, have I made all the family hate me? I never realized before …"

"No, of course not, child. No one hates you. Your family loves you very much. They've just been waiting for you to grow up." Christy paused, wondering if now was the time to tell her granddaughter some of her own early history. She decided that perhaps now was the perfect time.

"You see, honey, I understand you better than you think. When I was your age my family didn't know what to do with me, either. I was restless, unhappy with the restrictions my parents put upon me, and – if I must admit it – a little wild. As a matter of fact, I really didn't grow up until I met your grandfather. That's when I knew that it was up to me to make my life worth something – that I could make a difference in this world, if I would just face the reality that everyone else was not put here just to make me happy. And Eleanor, that's when I first understood what happiness really is. It's the joy of making someone *else* happy, and I had never known that before."

Christy sat quietly, stroking Chester and watching Eleanor. The girl was deep in thought, somehow conscious that this moment was crucial in her life. The silence lengthened until, giving a deep sigh, Eleanor spoke.

"Grandma, I didn't know. I don't want everybody to always be tiptoeing around me, afraid of what I might say or do. And I *have* been like that. I see it now. Do you suppose I can change?"

Christy's voice was now tender. She knew this was only a start for Eleanor; that she wouldn't change overnight, and would face many discouraging days. "Of course you can change, child. Maybe not all at once, because you've developed some very bad habits. But if you really *want* to change, you can, and everyone will help you – especially God, if you ask Him. You'll see. We all love you, and want you to be happy. You can count on your family, my dear. The Marlowes always stick together."

Eleanor nodded, but had one more question. "Grandmother, Josh… Will I ever be able to face Josh without being embarrassed? Do you think he knows that I love him? Will he want to be around me?"

"Well, dear, that *is* a ticklish situation. But maybe if you try to make friends with Celia Marie and let them both know that you wish them well, the embarrassment will just fade away. Do you think you could do that? It will take some courage, but I believe you can do it."

Eleanor nodded slowly. "Celia Marie is a nice girl. I already like her. I just resented her because Josh wanted her instead of me." She took a deep breath. "Grandmother, I'm glad you talked straight to me. Knowing you understand will make it easier, I think."

Christy lifted Chester gently to the floor, and pushed herself out of the rocking chair. Funny how hard it was to get out of a chair lately. And it always took her a few steps before her legs were willing to work properly. *"I guess this is just part of getting old, and I don't like it. If Eleanor only knew how hard it is for me to accept the fact that I can't get up and run around like I used to, maybe she'd realize that she isn't the only one who has to rearrange her attitudes from time to time! Matthew, I wish you were here to talk to! But I guess I did all right by our grandchild this time!"* She was glad she had baked that cake this morning. She made her way to the kitchen to get a tray of goodies. After a conversation like this, she needed some comfort food and she was sure that Eleanor did too.

Dr. Rosi Wheaton and Beth arrived in Charlotte about four o'clock, anxious to see their two girls again, and, as always, looking forward to a good visit with the elder Wheatons. After greetings all around, and after their luggage had been deposited in the spacious guest room upstairs, Rosi settled herself in the soft armchair in the girls' room, ready for a long talk. Beth occupied the rocking chair and the girls were perched on the bed, each hugging a pillow. Since childhood, and especially since Daddy Dan died, this had been the usual pattern for their long heart to heart talks.

"Mama, I have the most wonderful news in the world to tell you." Celia Marie could contain herself no longer. "I'm in love!"

Rosi smiled at her eldest daughter. She had guessed as much from the moment they had arrived. She hadn't worked with young people for years without recognizing the symptoms!

"Then, my dear, I need to hear all about him. I think that's what this conference is all about. Am I right?"

Bardi flopped over on the bed with an exaggerated sigh. "Oh, Mom, you'll hear about him all right. Over and over and over…"

"That's enough, Bardy. Let Celia Marie talk. You can listen once more." She turned to Beth. "Can you believe it, Beth? Our little girl, all grown up and in love!"

"I can't wait. Tell us about him, Celee." Beth was leaning forward, her eyes sparkling with anticipation. "I'm sure he must be a wonderful person."

Celia Marie didn't need another invitation. "Oh, he is! His name is Josh – well, it's Joshua O'Conner. He lives with his father and his grandparents here in Charlotte, and Grandma and Grandpa have known him since he was a baby. So you know he's allright, Mom, because Grandma and Grandpa just love him to death!"

"Well, that's a good start anyway. Go on, Celia."

"He works with his father in an automotive parts store on the edge of town, and he has a business of his own, too, flying his own airplane and taking passengers – mostly businessmen- on short business trips. The best thing is that he works with the youth group at Grandpa's church, and that's where I met him, at a hayride he arranged for the young people. He's awful smart, Mom, but he's so sweet! You'll just love him, I know!"

"I'm sure I will. What does he look like, Celia, and how old is he?"

"You'll see him tonight, Mom. He and his father and grandparents are coming to dinner. He's tall, with brown curly hair, and a kind face. He's twenty six, and I know you're going to say he's too old for me!" Celia Marie hurried to get that item cleared. "But he's not! He says he's been waiting for the right girl to come along, and he's sure – and I'm sure, Mom – that we're meant for each other. Just wait until you meet him!"

Bardy rolled her eyes and dramatically hugged her pillow. "Yeah, Mom, just wait!" She suddenly sat up and in all seriousness said, "Mom, he *is* a great guy. I'm doing a lot of kidding, but I really like him. He's different from any other guys I've ever met. He's serious and polite and kind, but he's also loads of fun. The kids he works with think he's the best ever, and you know that kids aren't very often fooled! Grandpa says his reputation at the church and around town is tops."

"Well, Celee, I like what I'm hearing, and I'm anxious to meet him. You say his father and grandparents will be here too?"

"Yes, Mom, and I need to tell you something else. His grandparents are Marlowes, and they adopted his father when he was about fourteen years old. He grew up with the Marlowe kids, and they're like his family. You know who the Marlowes are, don't you?"

"I've heard the name for many years. Matthew Marlowe was quite famous, but I think he's dead now, isn't he?"

"Yes, but Grandmother Marlowe is still alive, and Josh calls her Aunt Christy. His grandfather's name is Joseph, and he and Matthew brought up their sisters after their parents died of typhoid fever. It's a very sad story. But his father's story is sad, too, in a way, except that it turned out all right. Matthew and Joseph found Billy all alone in Lansing after his mother had died, and he was only fourteen years old. Joseph and his wife, Ruthie, adopted him and brought him up like their own son. They're swell people, too. You'll meet them tonight."

As Rosi unpacked her bags and made herself ready for the much anticipated dinner of the evening, her mind was busy. As she had listened to Celia Marie talk about her Josh , and had watched the emotions of young love play across her face, she had been taken back to the early days of her acquaintance with Dan, the love of her own life. She remembered the quick response of their attraction to each other, and how soon she was sure that she could trust him implicitly. She sensed that same assurance in Celia Marie. How often she had prayed that her girls would find the same sweet experience in their own lives, and somehow she felt that her prayer had now been answered for her eldest. Of course it was too soon to be sure, and her introduction to Josh this evening would be crucial. Rosi had learned that in some unknown way, her first impressions were not only very important but usually were borne out by time to be accurate.

The past crowded in on her, flooding her mind as she hung up dresses, bathed and completed her toilette. Finally, ready except for slipping on her dress and being very comfortable in her robe, she settled herself back into the easy chair beside her bed and surrendered to those insistent memories. As she leaned her head back and closed her eyes, she could see the young Dan and Rosi, hand in hand, strolling the shady lanes of Pellston. Then she saw them as they were seated in Brother Mosher's study, listening intently as he counseled them, and finally she felt, rather than saw them, standing together in Babette's parlor, looking into each other's eyes and promising to love and cherish each other, for better or for worse.

There had been great happiness in their union, a marriage that had fulfilled the dreams of both the young girl and her mate. The good years had brought into the world their two precious daughters, and the blessing of having Beth come to live with them. She had had the friendship of the wonderful woman whom she had succeeded as president of Birch Lake Academy, and the young family had been surrounded by the love of her own family. She would never forget the wisdom and loving care she had received from Grossmutter and her own little Mutter, nor the protection and guidance that her older sister, Babette, and her husband Jesse, had given her in her growing-up years. Then there was dear Celia, (for whom Celia Marie was named) who had taught her, a little German girl, how to live with the customs of America, her adopted land. Oh, there were so many wonderful people whom God had brought into her life, climaxing with Dan, without whom she would never have been complete.

Now unaware of time, her mind sped on to the hard times, to the excruciating pain of losing Dan in the horrible flu epidemic. But even as she relived the terror of those days, she again felt the presence of the Lord Jesus, comforting and sustaining her. She couldn't have made it without Him, and she remembered Babette's assurance that she was always protected by God's sheltering wings. That had been true, she now knew, from the time she was born. And it was still true. And it would be true for her girls. She had no doubt of that, and didn't know that she was smiling until she felt someone gently shaking her. She opened her eyes as Celia Marie bent over her, concern on her face.

"Mom, I was worried about you. It's getting late, and Josh and his family will be here in just a few minutes. But when I saw you were smiling in your sleep, I knew you were okay. What were you dreaming about?"

"Darling, I guess I was tired and I'm sorry I worried you. But I was thinking about how good God has been to us over the years, and I was reliving the blessed memories I have of your father." She jumped out of the chair and peeled off her robe as she continued, "Celee, please get me that light blue dress with the roll collar. I'm all ready except for slipping it on and combing my hair. I'm glad you came in – you can help me get my hair just right!"

"Sure, Mom, you'll be the most beautiful lady at the table!" and together they were soon descending the stairway to greet their guests.

Chapter 11

As the Wheatons and the O'Conners were deep into making plans for a joyous occasion, Daniel Marlowe was faced with a different kind of challenge. He was searching for a solution to a serious problem, and it was beginning to tell on his disposition. Normally a cheerful, outgoing personality, he was beginning to show an unnatural impatience with his family, his employees, and the world in general. His usual optimistic attitude toward life was seemingly turning sour. His wife, Josie, in whom he had always confided, was feeling shut out.

One day, over lunch with her mother in law – who was also her adopted mother – she was not her usual talkative self.

Christy finally laid down her fork, sat back in her chair, and folded her napkin. As she laid it on the table, she turned to Josie and said, in very "no-nonsense" tones (with which her family was very familiar), "All right, Josie. What's bothering you? And don't tell me 'nothing' because I know better. Just remember, you were one of my children before you were my daughter-in-law, and I can read you like a book."

Josie gave a sigh of relief. She had wanted to talk it over with Christy, but her sense of loyalty to Dan was too great. However, now she knew it was time to share her concerns with the only person she knew in whom she could confide.

"Mother, have you noticed a change in Dan lately? Sometimes he won't talk at all, and when he does, he seems so absent-minded he can't carry on a conversation. He usually will tell me when something is worrying him, but he's been completely shutting me out, and I *know* something is wrong." With a pleading look and tears springing in her eyes, she added, "Mother, I just don't seem to know him any more!"

Christy nodded slowly. "Yes, I've noticed the change in him. And, no, I don't know what's causing it. He hasn't been over to see me for a couple of weeks, which is very unusual, as you know, and the last time he was here, he only stayed a few minutes to see if I needed anything. Yes, Josie, I've been concerned, too."

"What can we do, Mother? He just won't talk to me. Do you think you could talk to him?"

"Well, I can certainly try. I've tried never to advise him unless he asked for it, but maybe it's time I did a little prying. After all, I *am* his mother, and I do have a few privileges, I believe." She sat quietly for a few minutes, deep in thought, then pushed her chair back from the table.

"Josie, I want you to stop worrying and try to act as if you haven't noticed anything unusual. Give me a few days and we'll see if we can get to the bottom of this."

At home that evening with a purring Chester occupying her lap, Christy rocked and did some serious praying. This was something she knew she couldn't handle without help.

The next day she telephoned her son at the office, a thing she seldom did.

"Miss Winton, this is Mrs. Marlowe. Would you tell my son I need to talk to him?"

"O, good morning, Mrs. Marlowe. Mr. Marlowe is out of the office just now. Could I have him call you back?"

"Yes, thank you. And please tell him it's urgent."

Within the hour, Dan was on the phone. "What's the matter, Mom? What's wrong?"

"Danny, nothing is wrong with me, but I need to talk to you. Could you come by this afternoon for tea? I baked your favorite cookies, by the way, so don't turn me down!"

"I would never turn you down, Mom, cookies or no cookies! You know that! But you also know I can't turn those cookies down! I'll be there about four."

Promptly at four he rang the bell, and as usual, without waiting for her to come to the door, he burst into the living room where she sat rocking in her favorite chair. He kissed her, looked at her quizzically, then pulled a footstool up close to her chair. He took her hand, settled down to listen, then spoke. "All right, Mom. I know there's something wrong, or you wouldn't have called me to come over. Let's have it."

Christy laid his hand aside, put Chester on the floor, and reached for the plate of cookies. "These come first, Danny. Pour us each a cup of tea. I talk better when I'm nibbling on something."

Dan laughed and did her bidding. Finally, he repeated, "Now, Mom, what's this all about?"

"Danny, since you've grown up, have I ever tried to meddle in your affairs, or tried to tell you what to do?"

Dan stared at her in amazement, then shook his head slowly. "No, Mom. I've always come to *you* and asked for advice when I needed it, but you've never interfered in my affairs in any way. Why are you asking such a question?"

"Well, for the first time I'm going to pry into your business. Something is worrying you, and you haven't been yourself for several weeks. I need to know what your problem is. I probably won't be able to help you solve it, but neither will I agree to have you continuing to punish yourself without knowing what it is that's bothering you. So, Son, let's have it. If your father were here, he would be the one asking this question, and I know you would confide in him. But since he isn't here, it's left up to me, and I need some answers!"

Very deliberately, Dan set his cup on the coffee table, and took a seat across the table from her. He sat silent for a few long minutes, then smiled a bit sheepishly and commented, "I never could keep anything from you, could I? But, Mom, you're right. This is *my* problem, and there's nothing you can do to help. But I'm glad you asked, because it will be a relief to talk about it to someone.

"I remember how Dad always talked things over with Grandpa Underhill and they always worked out their problems together. And when Dad was still here, he and I did the same thing. But with them both gone, and the business entirely in my hands, I don't have anyone – close – to discuss problems with. Dave Pomfret, my chief assistant, is a very capable guy, but this is a family business, and of course I just don't have the same relationship with him that I had with Dad.

"So, to answer your question, yes, I am worried. I have been thinking a lot about what's going to happen to the business when *I'm* gone but (he held up his hand to ward off Christy's protest) I'm not planning to *be* gone for a long, long time!" He laughed at the look on her face. "Lighten up, Mom, some things take long-range planning. You know that! Anyway, to get back to my problem! Since Robert isn't interested in anything but music (and believe me, I'm glad he's found his place in life and I wouldn't have it any other way) I've been trying to figure out what I should do about training someone to take over when I retire. I've been watching Dave very carefully. He's a nice boy but he doesn't have the drive and the leadership qualities that I'm looking for. It has to be someone with abilities like Dad's and who shares his moral convictions. This business and its future are my responsibility and mine alone, and I'm looking for answers.

"So, Mom, you asked and I've told you." He leaned back in his chair and sighed with undeniable relief. "And it feels good to be able to share my problems with someone else!"

Both of them sat quietly for a time, deep in thought. Chester reclaimed his place on Christy's lap, and she scratched him gently between the ears, eliciting from him a loud, contented purr. Dan picked up another cookie, then another, poured them each another cup of the cooling tea, and waited.

Finally Christy spoke. "Danny, you have only one son, and, as you say, he's not inclined toward business. But you have another child. Have you considered Eleanor?"

Dan leaned forward in disbelief. "Mom, what are you thinking? Eleanor can't even get her act together, much less be helpful in the business. And" almost under his breath, he added, "She's a girl. Girls aren't interested in business affairs."

"Son, I have a strong conviction that the reason Eleanor can't get her act together, as you phrase it, is because she has no goal in life. And, as to that last comment you made, I'll ignore that for the moment! But, Son, the very characteristics that caused her to give you trouble as she was growing up are the very same ones that, directed towards a positive goal in life, would make her a success in anything she does. Besides, you remember that I believe in miracles and you should too. Ever since we recovered you alive from the kidnappers when you were a little boy, I've known that God works in very wonderful ways to supply our needs and answer our prayers. He could do a miracle in turning my granddaughter's life into something good in the same way that he preserved you to fulfil His plan for *your* life."

Dan still looked at her as if she were talking an entirely different language and he couldn't understand her. "Mom, I can't believe what you're suggesting. Not yet at least. I'll give it some thought, but…" He paused, then asked, "Do you have any reason to believe that she would be interested at all? She would have to go to college, and study business management and perhaps business law, and somehow I can't see Eleanor doing that. Can you?"

Christy nodded. "Yes, Son, I can. She paid me a visit not too long ago, and we had a long talk. I believe she's tired of playing around, and really wants to do something worth while with her life." She paused, looking Dan straight in the eye. "Now, back to that inane statement you made about her being a girl. Please tell me why that should make any difference? Women are constantly proving that gender doesn't matter when it comes to intellectual and leadership abilities. Even in things like aviation – just look at Amelia Earhart! Don't write her off, Dan – your daughter has a lot to offer. But she needs to be challenged." Now she had her son's riveted attention. "Daniel, I recommend that you give my suggestion a lot of thought, and if I were you I'd feel her out and see how she reacts. I could be wrong, but I think you might be surprised in what you find out about your daughter."

Dan was silent as he gazed at his mother with new respect. She returned his searching look with eyes that never faltered. Finally, he rose, bent and petted Chester, and kissed his mother tenderly. "Well, Mom, you certainly have given me something to think about. And I promise you that I'll talk to Eleanor right away. If she's willing – or even interested – in pursuing further education, we'll take it from there. You know" he turned back to face her again. "You know that she has always turned up her nose at going to college. But if her attitude has really changed, perhaps something will work out. Now, are you sure you don't need anything before I go? No problems with the house here or anything?"

"No, Danny, I'm fine. I just hope that you can find a solution to this problem and quit worrying about it. And try discussing it with Josie. After all, as you said, it's a *family* problem!"

Dan nodded, smiled at her again with his old, carefree smile, and closed the door behind him. As he made his way home, he shook his head again in disbelief and thought to himself, *"I guess Mom will always be full of surprises. She sure rocked me with one this afternoon! No wonder Dad always consulted her about everything. Maybe I should do this more often!"*

****

At almost the same moment, Kent was hurrying to the hospital, anxious to see Patsy again.

"Patsy, I have the most wonderful thing to tell you!" Kent could hardly wait to share with her his exciting discovery. She had been back with them, out of her coma for a whole day, but the doctor had warned them about tiring her. He said she needed a lot of rest, and was not to be excited or upset. So, though Kent felt that what he had to tell her would only encourage and please her, he had been patiently waiting until they could have time alone, and he could be sure that she was strong enough to hear his story.

"Are you feeling okay?" he questioned her anxiously. "Do you feel like listening to something I've discovered?"

Patsy smiled up at him with her old smile, gladdening his heart. "Of course, Kent. Please talk to me and tell me anything you want to. You know I'm always interested in anything that interests you."

"That's right, you are. I guess that's one reason I missed you so much while you were in that coma, because you've always listened to me. And I was so scared and lonesome for you. I wondered if you would ever come back to me. Oh, Patsy, I'm so glad you did!"

She smiled at him again. "I'm waiting, Kent. You're so excited that it must be something very special you want to tell me."

Kent took a deep breath, and realized that he didn't know where to start. Well, she knew now about the accident, so it wouldn't hurt to talk about it. He plunged in.

"Patsy, when you were hit by that car and we thought maybe you were killed, I felt like I would die too. It was like I didn't have anything left to live for if I didn't have you. And I felt like I was in a deep hole and couldn't get out of it, and it was dark and I was scared.

"Then a car stopped behind us and a man and woman came rushing up to help. The woman knew exactly what to do until we could get a doctor, and I was so thankful they were there. But I was so afraid you were going to die and I didn't want to leave you, but I had to go with the man in his car to show him where your folks lived and then to get the doctor. As we were rushing along (fast because we didn't know how badly you were hurt) this man started talking to God just like He was sitting in the car with us. He asked God for help and he asked Him to look after you and Penny and his wife until the ambulance could get there, and then he thanked God as if he was positive that God would do what he had asked Him to do. Then I found out that he was a preacher, and that he was used to talking to God like that, and he actually believed that God would do what he asked. I had never heard anything like that in my life before."

Patsy interrupted by saying softly, "I guess it was a good thing he knew how to talk to God. From what I've heard from Mother and Penny, I *was* almost killed."

Kent was quiet for a moment as he thought about this. "Yes, that's true," he finally continued, "and I didn't have any idea what to do, and neither did Penny. But Penny said the woman prayed like that too, and was just as sure as her husband was that God was hearing her and would answer. Have you ever prayed about things that way, Patsy?"

"No." Patsy turned her head on the pillow. "No, the only way I know to pray is with the prayers we memorized as kids. I didn't know you could just talk to God like regular conversation."

"I didn't either. Somehow hearing it made me feel better, but I didn't understand it. You know at college nobody believes there even is a God, much less prays to Him." Kent took a deep breath, then continued.

"When I asked this preacher, Pastor Anderson, about it, he told me that he *absolutely knew* that there is a God, and he gave me a little book to read. While I was sitting here, waiting for you to wake up, I began reading the book, and I got so interested in the story that I read it over twice. I remembered hearing something like it in Sunday School, when I was a kid, about a Man who was really God, and who came to earth to die for the sins of men, but I was told by my professors in college that it was all a fairy tale. But Patsy, no one could ever even *imagine* a fairy tale like that. This Man didn't stay dead, but He came out of his grave alive, and Pastor Anderson told me that He still is alive today. And he says that now He's in Heaven sitting beside God, and praying for each one of His people here on earth. That I thought *really* sounded like a fairy tale, but I know now that it's really *true*! I did what the Pastor told me I should do. I prayed and then found that I believed every word of it. I told this Man, Jesus, that I wanted to belong to Him, and He accepted me, and it's made all the difference in the world in the way I feel. Do you understand what I'm talking about, Patsy?"

Patsy lay quietly, thinking about what Kent had said. Then she slowly nodded, and answered, "Kent, I think I *could* believe it. Right now I'm kind of like you were – I'm lying in this bed, wondering if I'll ever be able to walk again, and having no one to turn to who can really *do* anything for me. Mom and Dad love me, and Penny loves me, and the doctor is doing what he can, but none of them can promise me anything. I kind of feel like I'm in a hole like you described, and that there's no way of getting out of it. Maybe what you've told me makes sense, because from what I remember being taught about God, He is so big that He can do anything. Maybe He would help *me*, do you think so? I guess He kept me from being killed, anyway."

The words spilled out of Kent. "You know what? A fellow a little older than I am sat beside me when I went to their church - I think Mrs. Anderson is his aunt – and he told me that God has a plan for each of our lives. If that's true, maybe we need to ask Him what His plan is for us. Maybe it *is* to help you to walk again. I sure hope so. But I think you have to do what I did: tell Him that you believe in Him – no matter what His plan is for you - and ask Him to come into your heart too! Then we could look for His plan together! What do you think?"

"All right. I certainly can't do anything for myself. I'll do it, Kent, and we'll learn to talk to Him and listen to Him together. There must be a lot in the Bible that we need to learn about and maybe we can learn it together. That *is* exciting, Kent! I'm so glad you told me!" Patsy closed her eyes. "But now I think I need to rest and think about it and maybe try to talk to God myself – and then I'll need to take a nap. I'm really tired!"

Kent sat beside her for a few more minutes, talking to God himself, before he got up and tiptoed out of the room.

Kent was so full of his new experience that he couldn't help talking about it, but not everyone was as receptive as Patsy. His mother was interested, but not excited, and he was a little reticent about talking to his father. Penny was scornful, and blamed God for allowing Patsy to get hurt. When he tried to tell some of his friends, they looked at him like he had two heads, and said, "Man are you *weird!* You must be losing your mind to go religious like this! Don't you know that stuff is just for old people!" Kent was glad that he would not be returning to his college for a while, for he could just imagine what his professors and friends *there* would say!

So he concentrated on learning all he could, and began to attend Redeemer Chapel regularly. He didn't see Josh again but the Pastor and

Julie made it a point to include him in youth meetings at the church and get-togethers at their house. Since there was a Bible study time at each event, he began to feel quite at home with his Bible, and could soon locate verses as Pastor Anderson explained them. Of course he shared all he learned with Patsy, and the time they spent together in studying drew them even closer than they had ever been before.

Chapter 12

*P*enny spent much of her time at the shop with her father. She found herself intrigued by the details of the business, but soon realized that there was much she needed to learn to really be of much use to him.

"Dad, I have something to tell you." It was a slow day for business, and she decided that this was the ideal time to find out how her father would feel about her idea. They sat down where they could see if anyone came into the shop, and John wondered what it was that seemed so important to her.

"Dad, I've been thinking. No, don't laugh," as she anticipated his response. Often he teased her about her wild ideas and about "thinking too much". "I'm serious, Dad. You know you need help here in the office, and I've been learning a lot. But I could be a lot more help if I knew about bookkeeping, and typing, and other things that have to be done. So I was wondering..." she hesitated and John leaned forward in his chair.

"Yes, what have you been wondering, Kitten? I agree that there are a lot of things in running a business efficiently that even I don't know. What do you have to suggest, Honey? I'm listening."

"Well, Dad, you know there's a business school in Charlotte where they teach all these things. I don't want to leave home and go to college, partly because Patsy can't go, and partly because I know you have lots of extra expense with her in the hospital so long. If I could go to business school, I could save you the money you would have to pay to hire some office help, because I could work here during the time when I don't have to attend class. What do you think, Dad? Is it a good idea? I like office work, but I want to know more about it than I do now, and the only way I know how to find out is to take some business courses. Then, too," she added softly, "I would rather work with you than get a job working for someone I don't know – and I do think I should find a job and help take care of Patsy. But I would rather help you, Dad. What do you think?"

John sat quietly for a few minutes, observing his daughter thoughtfully. She seemed to be suddenly growing up, and her concern for him and his family responsibilities evidenced her newfound maturity. He was also impressed at her very sensible suggestion, and could see that she had thought it through carefully before approaching him with it. Satisfied that her plan had great merit (both for the future and the present help she could give him) he finally nodded. Penny had been watching him as closely as he had been observing her, and now she settled back contentedly with a sigh of relief.

"Penny, I think that is an excellent suggestion, and I believe we should get you enrolled immediately. You can continue to work for me during the summer, then you'll be ready to begin classes in the fall session." Then, apparently thinking out loud, he added, "We'll have to see to getting you a car, and I'll teach you to drive during the summer."

Penny could hardly believe her ears. "Dad! Honestly, I hadn't dreamed of that. Guess I didn't think ahead about how I would get there. Wow, that's great!" Impulsively, she jumped up and hugged him. Then sobering, she added, "I don't want to make Patsy feel bad, though. Maybe she'll soon be well enough so that she can ride around with me. Oh, Dad, it's so hard to get used to doing things without Patsy!"

"I know, Honey. We're all going to have to adjust our thinking and our way of doing things to keep her happy. We have great reason to hope, though, because according to the doctor, she may completely recover. We *must* keep hoping, you know, to keep her from being discouraged."

"I know, Dad, and I'm going to *expect* her to get well! Maybe if we keep thinking positively, everything will be all right." Then softly, "I don't think I can stand it if she is crippled because of this horrible accident."

"Well, Honey, positive thinking can't hurt. However, the way I was brought up, I learned that it takes more than that. It takes faith to believe that God will answer prayer, so I'm going to do a lot of asking!"

Penny was startled. "Dad, you sound like Kent. He's always talking about God lately. I didn't know you felt like that! Myself, I don't see that God has anything to do with it, since He didn't even keep her from being hurt!"

John looked at his daughter, his eyes concerned. "I think I must have failed you, Penny, if you didn't know how I feel about God! But believe me, He's always there, keeping guard over us. From now on, I'll do all I can to help you believe in Him, too!"

Penny leaned down, dropped a quick kiss on her father's nose, and almost danced out the door. A new enthusiasm lent excitement to her steps, and she felt new purpose in her spirit. She could hardly wait for the future to begin!

However, as John watched his daughter run lightly out of the room, he leaned back in his chair with a heaviness on his heart. Today he had suddenly seen it for what it was. Penny's words had cut through his conscience and exposed its shameful secret. Her almost incredulous tone of voice echoed in his memory. *"I didn't know you felt like that! I don't see that God had anything to do with it."*

His eyes squeezed shut as he dropped his head into his hands, but he was not able to block out her surprised expression. The realization hit him like a crushing rock. He had let his daughters grow up ignorant of God's Word, of His love and grace. The conviction in his soul was almost more than he could bear.

So it was, that on a cool crisp day in early fall, when the air had just enough bite in it to signal that winter was not far away, Penny parked her new roadster across the street from "Miss Parker's Business College" in Charlotte. With great excitement she gathered her things together to begin this new phase of her life. However, in spite of the fact that she had anticipated this day for many weeks, she felt a little timid, an unusual emotion for her. She suddenly realized that it was because she was alone. There was no Patsy there to give her courage. She lifted her head, squared her shoulders, and marched across the street! After all, this was *for Patsy*, and she wouldn't let her down!

At the same moment she reached the steps leading up to the front porch of the old home which had been remodeled to house the business college, she found herself face to face with a girl, a little older than herself, who was also apparently bound for the same destination. They each stopped politely, then started again, bumping into each other on the steps. Now giggling, they both stopped again, making exaggerated gestures of courtesy. They entered together, then stopped in the hallway to introduce themselves.

"My name is Penny Holt. I guess we'll be classmates! This is my first day here."

"Mine, too. I'm Eleanor Marlowe. I'm glad to meet you, because now I know at least one person here! Are you taking beginning classes?"

"*Very* beginning! I just graduated from High School in June. I've been working in my father's office all summer, and that's been just long enough to discover that I don't know anything about office work! So I think this will do me more good than going to college!"

Eleanor nodded. "I'm enrolled because I want to work with my father, too. I have a brother, but he's a musician and not interested in the business. I've been out of school a couple of years, but have finally decided what I want to do. I'm tired of just going to parties and having a good time. So that's why I'm here – to learn to do something useful!"

Together, the girls approached the desk, and found that they were assigned to the same room for their first class. Arm in arm, they found their classroom, already half filled with eager students. They searched out two chairs together, and sat down to chat. By the time the teacher called the class to order, they were fast friends.

Finding a friend made all the difference in the world to both girls. They looked forward to meeting in the morning, comparing notes, and exchanging little personal items that seemed to seal their friendship. The classes were intriguing, and Penny especially found herself fascinated by the challenges of learning to type and take rapid shorthand notes. The bookkeeping was a little harder for her, but fortunately Eleanor was good at that, and was able to help her. Eleanor's interests were more in business law, as well as bookkeeping, and by helping each other, they both made outstanding progress.

The schooldays passed rapidly, and soon the first term came to a close. As there would be a vacation of two weeks between terms, the two friends got their heads together to make some plans.

"Penny, my cousin Josh (well, he's not really a cousin – more like a brother- and really not any kin to me at all!) but anyway, he's engaged to a real sweet girl from up north, and he's going up to visit her next week. In fact, he's flying up there to spend Thanksgiving with her family. But she's coming down here for Christmas vacation. I'd love for you to meet her, and since my Aunt Julie lives over in Little Rapids, we'll probably have a family get together over there while she's visiting us. Of course we'll have Christmas as always at my Grandma's house here in Charlotte, but during the holidays we'll be over for a party at Aunt Julie's. But what I started to say is that we'll be at Aunt Julie's and Uncle Sig's house for Thanksgiving dinner and maybe we could get together while the family is over there. Aunt Julie and Uncle Sig are lots of fun, even if they do talk a lot of religion, and Josh and Celee are kind of that way, too, but I just listen and let it go in one ear and out the other. I don't put much stock in religion, even though the rest of the family thinks it's real important." She paused for breath. "What do you think, Penny? Would you like to meet my family? I'd really like to meet yours. Aunt Julie and Uncle Sig will be having an open house the day after Thanksgiving and maybe you and your family could come. Do you think they would like to do that?" Eleanor had finally gotten to the point. Penny had tried hard to follow her as she rambled on about family plans.

Penny also pricked up her ears at the names Eleanor was so casually reeling off. Weren't those the names of the people who helped them when Patsy was hurt? Didn't Kent speak about them often?

"Is your uncle a preacher, Eleanor?" she asked.

Eleanor laughed. "Yes, he is, but don't hold that against him. He and Aunt Julie are great fun, and I love them dearly. Why do you ask?"

Penny hesitated before answering. She had not confided in Eleanor about the accident, but had only told her that she had a twin sister. But it seemed that now was the time to tell the whole story.

"I think I met your aunt and uncle. I never told you about my sister's accident, but it was when she was hurt that they stopped their car and helped us. They sure were great, and have been to see Patsy several times, but I didn't know quite what to think of them. They prayed for her like Jesus was right there and they were having a conversation with Him. It was kind of weird, I thought. I never heard anyone do that before, and since I'm not sure there even is a God, it made me feel strange. But I really loved them for the way they helped us. They were so careful to make sure that we were taken care of, and they had never even seen us before."

"That would be Aunt Julie and Uncle Sig. They're like that. I know they'd love to see you again, and Patsy too."

"Well, Patsy is still in a wheelchair, but Dad might be able to get her there, especially with Kent to help. Our friend, Kent, was with us too when that car hit Patsy. He went with your uncle to get help."

"Then we'll invite Kent, too. This sounds great! I'll let you know when the party will be and it will be a chance for you to meet my parents, too. Do you really think your mom and dad would like to come?"

"I'll ask them, Eleanor. But - are you sure your family won't mind having another whole family included in your party? And that your aunt and uncle will be willing for you to expand their guest list like this? I know my parents will want to be sure that we aren't intruding. I know how they feel about things like that."

"Quit worrying, Penny. I know what I'm doing, and I know they will all be tickled to death. My uncle always says, 'The more the merrier' and he means it! I'll call you on the phone when we have the date and the time settled!"

The two girls didn't know it, but this would begin the unraveling of a tale that would involve both families and would reveal a mystery just waiting to be solved!

Chapter 13

*P*atsy spent most of her waking hours thinking about what Kent had told her. He was so excited about what he had learned and was so certain that what his new friends had told him was the truth, that she knew she must very seriously consider her own decision.

"I can't quite understand all that he told me," she thought to herself, *"so I don't know whether I agree with him or not. If it's all real, as he says, I wonder why we haven't heard about it before. We've gone to church and Sunday School all our lives, and it seems like we should have been taught all these things there. Maybe"* a sudden idea popped into her mind. *"Maybe, if these Andersons helped us so much at the time of the accident – maybe they wouldn't mind explaining it to me and answering my questions. That's what I'll do. I'll have Kent ask Mrs. Anderson to pay me a visit so I can talk to her."*

So the next time Kent visited her, she brought up the subject of his new discoveries.

"Kent, you know I've always listened to you, and lots of times you've known the answers to my questions. But this time," she paused and her eyes searched his face as she reached out and took his hand. "This time, Kent, I've thought about what you told me the other day, and there are lots of things about it that I just don't understand. I think I would like to talk to Mrs. Anderson, and see if I could get things straight in my mind. Please don't be hurt that I need to talk to someone else about it. It's just that it's so important to you that I think it should be just as important to me, but unless I have some answers I can't make up my mind. Would you mind asking her to visit me?"

"Oh, Patsy, she would love to come. She asks about you every time I see her. I know she has wanted to come but didn't know if you were able to have company yet. And Honey," he leaned closer to her, "I don't mind a bit that you need to talk to someone else about it. I'm just learning myself, and there's so much I don't know." He squeezed her hand. "I'll let her know right away that you want to see her."

The youth meeting was held every Friday evening, and Kent looked forward to attending the Pastor's Bible study. Kent could hardly wait to get there. He knew Mrs. Anderson would be there too, and he immediately searched her out.

"Hello, Kent. I'm so glad to see you tonight. I hope you're planning to be a regular, and that would be great!" As always, Mrs. Anderson greeted him as though he were someone special. And in truth, he was, for both the Pastor and Mrs. Anderson were deeply interested in the trio of young people that they had helped to rescue.

"Hi, Mrs. Anderson. I was hoping I would see you tonight. I have great news." Julie couldn't help but wonder what it could be that made his face glow with excitement.

"When I went to see Patsy after I talked to the Pastor, I told her all about what I had learned, and what I had decided. Today she told me that she had been thinking a lot about what I had said and wished she could talk to you and ask you some questions. She wondered if you would come and see her. I told her I knew you would and – you would, wouldn't you?" The boy's eager eyes were beseeching. "She really wants to talk to you."

"Why, of course I will, Kent. I'll visit her tomorrow. What would be the best time?"

"Well, you know they keep her pretty busy in the mornings, with the doctor coming in and the nurses getting her ready for the day. But she always thinks the afternoons are long and she gets lonesome when no one comes to see her. Maybe you could go soon after lunch?"

"I'll be there, Kent. You can tell her to expect me." Julie smiled at him and took his arm. "I think we'd better join the group. They're getting ready to begin."

Kent stopped by the hospital on the way home, and reported to Patsy. "I won't come in tomorrow until evening, because I want you to have all the time you need to talk to her. I know she'll be able to answer all your questions."

And Kent was right with only a few exceptions. The question about why she hadn't heard all this before was one question Julie had no answer for. But she countered it by telling Patsy that what was past didn't really matter. It was what she did now that counted.

After making certain that Patsy was familiar with many Bible stories, she asked the question that laid the groundwork for the rest of their discussion. "Patsy, I know you've had some good teaching in Sunday School. But now let me ask you, do you believe that the Bible is true, and that it is the Word of God? Because if you do, everything else I say will make sense to you. If you don't – well, that will be the first thing we discuss. Kent wasn't even sure there is a God, and had been taught in college that the Bible was only a myth. How do you feel about that?"

"Oh, Mrs. Anderson, of course I believe the Bible is true. It's just that I didn't know that those things Kent told me about were in it. You see, my mother and father believe in God, and taught me about Him, but I don't think that even *they* know about these other things!"

"Well, then, we have a good starting point. Just what did Kent tell you, and what else do you want to know?"

"He said that God cares for us so much that He sent His Son, Jesus, to die for us. I had heard that in Sunday School, but I don't know why someone had to die for us. What does that mean?"

Julie took a deep breath. Patsy was ready to hear, and Julie felt that she was also ready to believe. "Patsy, when Adam sinned, he could no longer walk and talk with God, because he had disobeyed Him. He had also given up the right to eternal life, because of his disobedience. And since we are all the children of Adam, we also lost that right. So in some way, if we were ever to be able to be God's children again, someone had to pay for Adam's sin. Since all humans are sinners, there had to be someone who was without sin who could save us. So Jesus, the Son of God, who had no sin, loved us enough to come to earth and by His death on the cross, pay the price for our sin. All that's left for us to do is ask Him to save us and give us a new life, and then believe that He has done what He promised to do. He really does give us a new life, you know, because the Bible tells us that we are 'new creatures in Christ Jesus.' Becoming His child doesn't solve all our problems, but when we trust Him, He helps us get through our hard times, and we know that when we die, we will go to be with Him." Julie paused, and watched as Patsy silently considered what she had said.

"Then came the question that Julie had dreaded. "Does that mean that He may not let me walk again, even if I ask Him to?" Of course that was the most important thing in her life just now.

How Julie wished that she had a different answer for the young girl. "Patsy, He knows all about your accident, and we don't know why He allowed it to happen. And He knows that you're hoping against hope that you'll be able to completely recover. But that's not the important question just now. He wants to know if you'll trust Him, no matter what the future holds. He may heal you. I hope and pray that He does. But if He doesn't, would you still love Him for what He has done for you on the cross, and would you trust Him to go with you through the hard times that you may face? That's a tough question to answer just now. But I won't lie to you and tell you that when you become a child of God, everything is going to be rosy and good. We still have to take what life hands us, but if we belong to Him, we don't have to face our problems alone. He's always with us, helping and encouraging us."

Again Patsy was silent, but her face betrayed the battle she was engaged in. She closed her eyes, as if not wanting anyone to see into her soul, then a tear squeezed out and rolled down her cheek. She really wanted to say yes to God right now, and didn't know that the Holy Spirit was fighting her battle with her. Finally, she opened her eyes, looked straight into Julie's face, and declared, "I guess it wouldn't be fair to try to bargain with God, would it. Especially if Jesus loved me enough to die for me. I guess I could handle being a cripple if He stays by me and helps me. So I am going to believe. Yes, Mrs. Anderson, I am going to do what Kent has done. And I think maybe if I hadn't had that accident, I might never have heard about all of this. Do you suppose that was the reason it happened?"

Julie smiled. "I would say that God has already spoken to you and given you some answers. Honey, let's just thank Him now that you are His child, and we'll keep praying that if it's His will, he will make you walk again."

Julie left the hospital, walking on air. There was nothing else in life comparable to seeing a person, especially a young person, become a new creature in Christ Jesus. Excitement hurried her steps, as she couldn't wait to tell Sig.

Chapter 14

*W*aiting is always so hard! Especially waiting for someone you love who is up in the air and you're waiting for him to land! And if he's a bit late arriving, you can imagine all sorts of things that could have happened!

Celee was in the throes of waiting! Josh should be here any minute, now! She shaded her eyes with her hand and searched the heavens. Was that a speck in the sky? or a small plane? or maybe just a bird? No, it was getting larger and larger, and now she could see that it was Josh's aircraft, sleek and beautiful, like a giant heavenly creature coming down to pay a visit to earthlings!

The playing field had been cleared for the afternoon. All of the classes at Birch Lake Academy had been cancelled so that no one would miss the excitement of seeing the plane land on the Academy campus. As a result, there was a large crowd of cheering students waiting to welcome Josh when the landing wheels of his plane touched the ground.

Of course Bardy was there, surrounded by friends and schoolmates to whom the miracle of flight was still a source of awe and wonder. And Rosi was there, too, almost as anxious as Celee that the beautiful little craft with its precious cargo would have a safe landing.

Plans for this visit from Josh had begun in late summer when Rosi had visited Charlotte and had first met her prospective son-in-law. Thanksgiving had always been a very special time for Dan and Rosi, and unlike most people who preferred to have a huge family get-together, they had their own tradition of spending it, first with each other, then later with their own little family. On the Thanksgiving weekend, they always took the opportunity to spend time with loved ones, but that one day of Thanksgiving was their own. This year Josh, who would soon be a part of their family, would spend it with Rosi, the two girls, and Beth. Then, before he flew back to Charlotte, he would have the opportunity to meet Celee's family and they, of course, would have the chance to determine whether or not he was "good enough" to meet their approval as Celee's chosen life companion. "Not that it really matters," Celee had commented to her mother. "Of course I want them all to like Josh – and I know they will – but I'm the one marrying him and he's *my* choice!" Rosi had smiled and made no comment. She shared Celee's opinion that he would have the unanimous approval of the family, and, with amusement, she recognized herself in Celee's determined avowal of her choice.

It had been decided, during the fall visit to Charlotte, that Rosi, the girls, and Beth would join Josh's family for the longer Christmas vacation. Already that family was planning various visits, events, and elaborate celebrations for Christmas, readily agreeing to excuse Josh for the shorter holiday. It would have been hard to tell whether the Charlotte Marlowes and Wheatons or the Pellston Huebners and Beckmans were more excited over the prospect of entertaining the young couple for their first holidays together.

When Josh's plane was first sighted high in the sky, the crowd of youngsters on the ground shouted and cheered and waved. However, as the aircraft circled and prepared to land, the watchers became silent, hardly breathing as its wheels hovered above the ground and finally made contact with the turf. Then another cheer went up as Josh taxied slowly to a stop. As he climbed out, he waved, then looked around anxiously, and no one doubted that he was looking for Celee, who immediately broke away and ran to give him a hug. Oblivious to the watching students, Josh grabbed her and gave her a long, hungry kiss. In unison, the girls around Bardy gave a long, audible, envious sigh, and the boys grinned at each other, unabashed at this public demonstration by their President's daughter and her fiance. Nor was Rosi embarrassed. She and Dan had never hidden their love for each other, because, as with these two, it had been good and true and unashamed.

After greeting Rosi, Bardy, and Beth, Josh and the family started across the campus to the Wheaton home. Falling in behind them was a parade of some four hundred students, still cheering and whistling and waving. This was better than a ball game any day.

Rosi glanced around and saw that the whole student body was following them. Beckoning to one of the senior boys, she spoke to him briefly, and he took off at a lope toward the gymnasium, entering it only long enough to grab a bullhorn with which he hurried back to her. "Here, Dr. Wheaton, this should do the job." He saluted with a grin, then used the bullhorn to issue a command.

"All right, all you guys – and girls, too, get quiet! Dr. Wheaton has an announcement to make." The group responded except for a knot of boys who were laughing and talking loudly. "Hey, fellows, last call for silence. You're disturbing the peace!" They finally got the message and there was silence.

Rosi took the bullhorn. "Thank you for your welcome to my future son-in-law!"

Again there were cheers and waves. "Now that you have made him feel at home (laughter and more cheers) I have an announcement to make. We will have our school Thanksgiving dinner this evening - just to whet your appetite for the big dinner you will have when you get home tomorrow, (more laughing and clapping) then after dinner we will see you all in the chapel for our Thanksgiving service. At that time you will meet our guest, who has graciously consented to be our speaker." (Cheers and clapping.) "Now if you will excuse us, we will meet you at dinner, and you have free time now to do your packing or use the practice rooms, or do whatever it is that you still need to do before beginning your long week-end." She handed the bullhorn back to the waiting senior, and the students broke into small groups, each going their separate ways. The family made their way slowly to the cottage in the corner of the campus, the same little cottage which had been prepared for them when they first came to Birch Lake. It had been home then, and now, as president of the school, Rosi had declined to move into the larger, more ornate home offered to her, and had instead made that building the location for the ever increasing number of faculty offices. Celee and Bardy had been very happy about her decision, for the cottage had been their home during their growing-up years and they had no desire to leave it.

Celee and Josh had no need for words as they walked together from the playing field. Just being together again was enough for the moment. However, Bardy had no such reservations. It seemed she couldn't stop talking.

"How did you know where to land, Josh? You can't use a road map in the sky, so how do you find your way?" Josh smiled and patiently explained in simple terms how he navigated from place to place in his airplane. His explanations only sparked more questions.

"Do you ever get lost? Can you get directions from airfields on your radio as you go over them? We don't have an airfield here, so you had to find it without help from the ground, didn't you? How long did it take you to learn how to do it?"

Again Josh patiently explained how he filed his flight plan with the authorities before he took off from home, and that if he got lost he would radio to the ground for check points with which to locate his position. Finally Bardy ran out of questions, and her mother quietly suggested that she find something to do until dinner time. Pouting just a bit, she took the hint and disappeared into the house. Rosi pleaded some work awaiting her on her desk, and she and Beth also took their leave. Josh and Celee settled themselves in the porch swing, still not talking much. It felt so natural for Josh's arm to be around Celee's shoulders, and both of them thrilled to the touch and the reality of their closeness..

But soon Josh came down to earth and remembered that he was speaking in chapel later on in the evening. He dug through his briefcase and found his Bible and a notebook.

"Do you mind if I do a little practicing for the service tonight? You know, Sweetheart, you could help me if you would listen to what I've prepared and give me suggestions as to how I might make things clearer – or maybe how I could grab the attention of these kids who are listening to me. You know them better than I do, and since I'm used to working with younger groups, I don't want to talk down to these students. Would you do that for me?"

Celee was thrilled to be asked. "Of course, Josh. I'm not sure how much help I can be, but I'll try."

"Good. Now I thought I would use that passage in Jeremiah where God tells us that He has a plan for every one of our lives. They've had good counsel here with your school chaplain and their Bible teachers, so maybe I won't have to start from scratch like I would with my group at home. However, I want to be sure they know how to be saved, or the rest of the message won't get through to them."

"Yes, they do have a good background in Bible. Our Sunday youth meeting is always a good time for discussion and I think, from listening to them, that most of them have come from Christian homes. They're quite familiar with their Bibles."

Josh sat deep in thought for a few minutes, then, looking at Celee almost sadly, he commented, "Then these kids probably don't know how fortunate they are. I can't help but think of a young fellow in Little Rapids whom I got to know through Aunt Julie and Uncle Sig. After a friend of his was badly hurt in an accident, he was confused and unsure that God even existed. In college he had been taught that the Bible was full of myths and fairy stories and that God was simply an idea that weak people invented because they needed something to give them courage. He had lost what little faith he had because of his godless professors, and was about as hopeless as anyone could be." He paused and then added, "Here at Birch Lake, while it isn't a Bible school, at least God is honored and the Bible is taught as the Word of God. In many colleges and universities, I'm afraid just the opposite is taking place." He repeated, "I hope your classmates recognize how fortunate they are!"

At dinner the guests at the family table included the Student Body President, along with the President of each class. The other students in the dining room looked with envy at President Wheaton's table as its occupants frequently erupted with roars of laughter. Nothing could have better prepared the student body for the evening's speaker.. As a result, the chapel was full a good half hour before the Thanks-giving service was scheduled to begin.

Josh whispered to Celee, "Do you suppose they would like to sing for a while, since they're here so early for the service?"

Celee turned to her mother. "Josh has suggested that perhaps we might have a "sing-along" while we wait for the service to start. Would it be all right? Shall I go down and ask Dr. Goodlet if he would lead it?"

"I think that's a wonderful idea, Celee. But I'll just ask him to come to the platform and I'm sure he'll be glad to do it for us."

So the Thanksgiving service started with an unexpected treat, and the students responded with gusto. The sing-along turned out to be a kind of a pep rally, and by the time Dr. Wheaton arose to introduce their guest, the audience was loudly enthusiastic, and greeted him again with applause and cheers. However, when he stood to speak, they quieted down immediately.

The silence didn't last long, however, for he soon had them roaring and clapping at the funny stories that rolled out one after another, and he had to constantly stop and wait for the cheering to stop. Then, knowing what they were waiting to hear, he told them some of his flying experiences, and gave them an exhilarating account of what it was like to soar above the earth, with a breath-taking view of God's creation. His audience gave him their rapt attention.

Finally, he knew it was the time for a change of pace. His listeners needed another kind of challenge to take home with them on this Thanksgiving holiday. The faces he looked into represented the finest youth of their generation and as he waited for them to give him their full attention, he silently asked God to help him know what to say.

"As you probably know, I serve as a youth director in a small church in southern Michigan," he began. "My kids are not the usual youth group, just out looking for a good time. They *are* interested in having a good time, because they're very normal kids, but they have a larger goal. That goal is to bring into their fellowship kids who are poor, who perhaps run with the bad crowd in town, or who are physically or mentally handicapped in some way. They believe that it is their mission to make a difference in the lives of those who have not been as fortunate as they are. And believe me," he leaned forward and spoke slowly so no one would miss a word, "Believe me, they have not set an easy task for themselves. Occasionally they even find themselves in danger, for believe it or not, not everyone wants to be helped!

"What makes them go out and search for the kids that nobody else seems to care about? Those who may be dirty – both inside and out? Those whom they know will probably rebuff them and perhaps even harm them? I'll tell you why. It's because they know they have something special and they are so thankful for it that they want to share it with others. With others who don't even realize that they are missing out on the most important thing in life and are even hostile about being told.

"What is that 'something' which they possess? It's a gift that anyone may receive by simply accepting it. God provided it when he sent His Son, Jesus, to earth to die for us, and when we believe on Him, the Bible tells us that we immediately have eternal life. Jesus loves each one of us; you, me, and every human being alive, and He longs for us to receive that wonderful gift. My kids want other young people to know that this gift is for them, too, and that God is anxious to give them not only eternal life, but a life that is worth living on this earth.

"I'm telling you this because I believe I'm speaking to the same kind of young people here that I have in my youth group. I understand that most of you grew up in church, and have heard the way of salvation. If you are not one of those, I invite you to talk to me later and let me explain to you what YOU are missing!

" But, tonight, if you are one of those who has accepted God's gift, I'd like to chat with you a few minutes about something else connected with that gift."

He paused for a moment, and looked directly into the faces before him, his eyes darting about from face to face. How he wanted to bring to each of them a new assurance that they were worth everything in God's sight; to help them understand where they came from and why they were so precious to God. He began softly, as every ear strained to hear him.

"I'm not going to talk tonight of why we should be thankful for *things* – because most of us have more things than we need, don't we? (a ripple of self-conscious laughter greeted that question) and usually we just want more! But, you know, the truth is that possessions – that sporty car, the most up to date sports equipment, the newest style in clothes – those are the least important things in our lives.

"And I'm not going to talk about how thankful we should be for our family and friends. I think we all know that they are precious gifts from God.

"Instead, I want to talk to you about who you are, and why you are here. You see, God not only loves you more deeply than you know, but He wants you to have the very best that He can give you. The wonderful truth is that He has a very special plan for each of your lives. And until you understand that His plan is better than anything you could dream up for yourself, you're not getting the best out of life!

"Early in my life a wonderful man told me something that I could hardly believe. He told me that God knew me before I was born, or was even thought of. He told me that God knew what I would look like, what color my hair would be, whether I would have a temper or have great musical ability, or whether I would be a good athlete – or have two left feet! Then he told me that God loved me so much that He gave His Son, Jesus Christ, to die for me so that I could have eternal life. And that piece of information changed my life.

"He made me understand why I am here on this earth. Do you know why are you here? Is it an accident that you and I were born in America? Did our parents just happen to be handy when we needed a mother and father? You may think you made the choice to attend Birch Lake Academy but I have news for you! God picked out this school for you! Believe me, nothing happens to you by accident! You were in the mind of God even before you were born. He *knew* you, and He knew what He wanted to do with your life. He just wants your permission to let Him do it. His plan for you won't fit anyone else in the world except you. Only you. You were special to Him before you were born and you're just as special to Him now!

"You don't believe me? Let me tell you where to find the proof of my statement. God wrote you a love letter, and because we live in America, we each have the privilege of owning a copy of that love letter. Of course you know I'm talking about the Bible." Josh held up his own leather bound copy. "I hope you read His love letter to you every day because on every page He's telling you how much He loves you.

"I'm sure you each have a pen or pencil, or else your friend sitting next to you has one. I want you to write this down, and look it up in your Bible later. Write down Psalm 139," he paused as his listeners busily found pencils and notepads to write on. "Ready? Look up the 139th Psalm, and pay special attention to verses 13 through 16. But right now, I want to put it into everyday conversational language for you, because the King James Version of the Bible is sometimes kind of hard to understand. It says – now listen – it says that before you were born, God knew all about you and wrote your name in His book, and planned every day of your life for you. It says that His eye is on you from your birth until your death and that He loves you so much He gave His most precious possession, His Son, to come to earth to die for your sins. And by giving you this special gift, he made it possible for you to live forever. Forever! That's far beyond the last day of your life here on this earth. It's called eternity. All He needs from you is your willingness to let Him be Lord of your life. I repeat: you are very special to God because you are *you* and He loves you. This is what we should be truly thankful for – not only once a year in November, but every day of our lives.

"This is what makes my kids at home go out and bring in the kids who really aren't nice at all, and who often don't want to be bothered. And that's why my kids know that they must prove to those other kids by their lives that they really have something special – the message of God's love. And that they are willing and eager to share it.

"Now I want you to write down another verse. It's in the Old Testament, too. Write down Jeremiah 29:11. It tells you that God's plan for each of us is good and that it gives us a future that is full of hope. And finally, write down Ephesians 3:20. What He is saying here is that what He has planned for you is unbelievably better than anything you could possibly dream up for your own future!

"Okay, that's it, kids! Now I wish for each of you a wonderful Thanksgiving – made even more wonderful because you know that God has a plan made just for you! Thank you for letting me come and share your Thanksgiving with you."

Josh turned toward his chair, but was stopped by the clapping and cheers from his audience. He turned again and waved at them, but the applause continued until Dr. Wheaton stood and raised her hand for silence. After she had dismissed the group, she turned to Josh.

"I didn't know we were to have a preacher in the family," she smiled.

"Hey, I'm no preacher. I just like to talk to kids," he protested.

"Well, I'm sure these students will remember this Thanksgiving service all their lives. It was a real challenge to them, and I believe it will make a difference in many of their lives." She beckoned to Bardy who came running to join them. "Beth has a snack ready for us at home, so don't be too long, Honey. We have a big day tomorrow, you know!"

Josh thought to himself, *"This is one Thanksgiving I'll never forget. My new family, a chance to talk to a wonderful bunch of kids, and the knowledge that Celee and I are going to live out God's plan for us together! What more could I ask!"*

The Thanksgiving Day *was* one to remember. The dinner was of course as all Thanksgiving Dinners are – delicious – but the best part of the day was the bonding of the little family with their newest member. Beth and Josh found much in common as they shared their experiences, and Rosi felt a deep satisfaction in finding that her future son-in-law was truly all that Celee had said. Bardy was inordinately proud of him, and couldn't wait for her friends to return to school so she could hear their impressions of his visit.

The next day was an exciting one. Early in the morning they piled into the car and made their way to Pellston. There they visited Celia, Rosi's dear friend and mentor, whom they considered a vital part of their family. Then on to Brutus, where Babette and Jesse had gathered the family together for their yearly Thanksgiving party.

For Josh it was not only exciting, but confusing. He had thought the Marlowes were a big family, but here the gathered Huebners and Beckmans presented what could have been a formidable challenge. Instead, as they welcomed him with open arms, and as he was presented to each one, he was made comfortable and immediately felt accepted.

As he sat in the family circle, he mentally revisited each new face, and tried to recall the name and the family connection.

There were, first and foremost, Babette and Jesse Beckman. He sensed how very close Rosi and her girls were to them, and having heard Beth's story, he understood why she was welcomed here in this house as a daughter. Then, after listening to the conversation, he almost felt that he had personally known Vater, Grossmutter, and little Mutter. He marveled at how strong this family was, and what a great heritage they had given his Celee.

Next he met Rosi's brother Karl, whose story he had heard the day before. What a struggle he had had bringing up his motherless children! But what a wonderful job he had done. His eyes searched around and picked out Karl's family. He remembered that Babette's daughter, Margaret, with no children of her own, had "mothered" Karl's children and helped him give them as normal a life as possible. Margaret sat now with her arm protectively around Polly, who in her early twenties was making important decisions for her own life. He wondered why she looked somewhat familiar to him. He finally decided that there must be a family resemblance to Celee, even though Celee was fair with blue eyes, and in contrast Polly had olive skin, a wealth of dark hair and hazel eyes.

He tried hard not to stare at Polly, who looked like the last person in the world who needed protection from anyone, in spite of Aunt Margaret's encircling arm. She had caught his attention from the moment he entered the room. She appeared to be a very self confident woman of the world. Her dark hair was styled in the latest fashion, she wore a chic tailored suit with matching shoes, and her make-up was perfect, not overdone but just right. He wondered how she fit into this family of good, solid people; who were all highly intelligent and capable, but unassuming and somewhat unworldly.

Polly had been introduced to him as Karl's eldest daughter, who worked in Petosky for an art dealer. She had just returned from Europe where she had visited Italy and France on a buying trip. With that introduction he understood her uncommon poise, though he still wondered at the fact that she belonged in this family.

He couldn't wait to ask Celee about her cousin.

She was proud of her cousin, and clearly loved her dearly. "Polly is about three years older than I am, Josh, and I can remember the fun we had together as children. She always kind of looked out for me and Bardy, like she did for all her little brothers and sisters. Mama had been very close to Polly's mother, who was a wonderful artist. We have pictures that Aunt Lisa drew of both of us when we were little. You see, Aunt Lisa's parents never let her go to school, and she was very self-conscious about the fact that she couldn't read and write, though she could do a lot of things other people couldn't. Mama says she had loads of talent, but just had never had the chance to develop it. So Mama taught her to read and write and encouraged her to use her artistic ability in every way she could. You can understand why our families were especially close."

"Yes, I can see that. But what's puzzling me is how she went from the farm to an art shop in Petosky, of all things! The two seem worlds apart."

"Well, Polly, unlike her mother, *did* get to go to school, and while she was in high school, she enrolled in an art class. Of course the teacher immediately recognized her talent, and introduced her to a friend of his, who happened to be a patron of the arts. He kind of took her under his wing, gave her a job that allowed her to leave home and get a place of her own, and he and his wife continued her art education after she finished High School. She now is assistant manager of his art gallery, and is becoming quite well known for her ability to judge art and to make good purchases – as she was doing on the last trip to Europe." Celee's affectionate smile as she glanced at her cousin across the crowded room, spoke volumes as to the pride she took in Polly's success. "She's the only one of the family to have made a name for herself internationally, and Uncle Karl still doesn't know quite what to make of it!"

Josh had listened intently to her recital of Polly's success, but at her last remark he shook his head and commented, "Don't sell the rest of your family short, Darling. Just look at what your mother has accomplished and the good record your cousin Marty made in the war, and what great respect your whole family has in this part of Michigan. I think it's a pretty special family – and I'm proud to be marrying into it!" He added the last with a meaningful look that told Celee that if they had not had such an audience, he would have shown her just how much he thought of this particular family member now standing within the circle of his arm. She blushed as if he had really kissed her, instead of just wanting to, and he was tempted to actually do it! However, reason prevailed as Rosi joined them and the introductions continued.

And that strapping, handsome man at the other end of the porch was Marty, Jesse and Babette's son. He had been through the Great War, and had returned unharmed physically, but with the same lasting inner wounds that he knew Uncle Sig and Aunt Julie carried. He was talking to his uncle Ferdinand, who lived just down the hill from the Beckman farmhouse. Ferdinand had lost a son in the war, and as a parent, would never fully recover from the loss of his only child.

Out in the yard, there was a boisterous knot of young people gathered around a sporty car, which apparently belonged to one of the boys. Josh guessed that these were others of Karl's family, though he couldn't remember all of their names. The happy voices all around him, family members and their friends all enjoying the Thanksgiving party, reminded him that he had been provided a real family when his father, Billy, had been adopted into the Marlowe clan. His thoughts were really a prayer of awed Thanksgiving as he reflected on how good God had been to him.

Chapter 15

On this same day, the Anderson "open house" was taking place in Little Rapids, and members of their church family came and went all day. The Marlowes were all there, and Eleanor waited impatiently for Penny and her family to make their appearance. Of course Sig and Julie had been delighted to invite them, for they had a deep concern for not only the young people, but also for the parents, whom they were sure had been placed in their circle of friends for a purpose.

Finally, in the middle of the afternoon, two cars stopped in front of the house. One was Penny's little roadster, and the other was John Holt's big touring car. Kent and Penny hurried back to the big car, and Kent unfastened the wheel chair from the back bumper. Together John and Kent lifted Patsy out of the front seat as Louise watched anxiously. Finally the little group approached the house where Sig and Julie waited on the porch to welcome them.

The three men gently lifted the wheel chair with its precious load up the stairs to the porch, where Julie had been joined by Eleanor, then escorted into the living room where the Marlowe family awaited them. Introductions all around with hearty handshakes between the men and hugs for each other by the women took but a few minutes, and finally there was a chance for conversation. Julie immediately went over and sat by Patsy, wanting to make sure that she wouldn't feel strange with so many new people around, and Kent promptly fell into conversation with a young man who had been introduced as Eleanor's brother, Robert. Penny eyed Robert curiously, for she had heard a great deal about him from his adoring big sister. She was especially intrigued as he sat down at the piano, ran his fingers experimentally over the keys, and segued into Gershwin's "Rhapsody in Blue". Now she really sat up and took notice. Or all the composers to whom she had been introduced in her music lessons over the years, she was enamored with Gershwin's innovative harmonies and rhythms. Unaware that Robert had noticed her rapt expression as he played, she sat back, closed her eyes and followed the rhythms with a lightly tapping finger, lost in the enjoyment of the music.

The afternoon passed swiftly, and Julie and Sig urged the Holts to share Thanksgiving leftovers with them. Drawn together as they were by the shared experience of the accident, they were soon fast friends. As they drove home in the waning evening light, John glanced into the back seat at his daughter, who was obviously weary from the day's unaccustomed activity. "Are you all right, Kitten?" His voice was anxious.

Patsy opened her eyes and smiled at her mother, who had turned to look back at her with anxiety on her face.

"Mom and Dad, I'm fine. In fact, I've had such a happy day that I'm just having fun remembering every minute of it. I'm so glad we all went to the Andersons, aren't you?" Her voice trailed off and Louise saw that she had fallen asleep.

In a low voice, so as not to wake her weary daughter, Louise confessed to her husband, "John, for the first time I'm feeling hope about the future. Somehow, just being with the Andersons has given me a fresh outlook. Patsy's always been brave about her condition, but I haven't been able to have as much faith as she has. But tonight, I have the feeling that everything is going to be all right."

To her surprise, in response to her words, there was only silence. She waited a few moments, then in the same low voice, this time laced with some anxiety, she asked, "John, is there something wrong?"

This time, there was an answer, but it was slow in coming.

"Are you certain Patsy is asleep?"

Louise turned and carefully studied her daughter. "Yes, she's out like a light. She must be very tired."

"It's been an exciting day for her, getting out and visiting unfamiliar people." He paused and again Louise waited.

"Let's not discuss this now, Honey. We might wake her up. After she's settled down at home and we don't have to worry about awakening her, we'll talk." And Louise had no choice but to wait. However, her mind was troubled, and the waiting was hard.

Louise was greatly disturbed in her mind as she helped Patsy get ready for bed. It was unlike John to be so private and cautious about anything. They had always shared everything, and having secrets between them, even for a very short time, was disquieting.

So it was with some misgivings that she hurried downstairs for the delayed "discussion". He had seemed to thoroughly enjoy the time they had spent with the Andersons, so what could have caused his mood to change so suddenly?

She found him sitting in his favorite easy chair, his chin in his hand, gazing at nothing very intently. When she spoke to him, he turned toward her slowly as if awaking from a dream.

"Now, John, whatever is the matter? Didn't you have a good time at the Anderson's "open house"? I thought you were enjoying the day."

"I did, Louise, I did. I liked the pastor and his wife very much, and it was quite a treat meeting all of the Marlowe family."

"Then what in the world is the matter? I don't understand."

He sighed wearily. He had not anticipated a problem any more than Louise had, for he had become over the years a very sociable individual, always open to new friends and new ideas. The young, ambitious, intense young man had matured into a confident, successful business man, comfortable in his position among his fellow citizens in Little Rapids. However, today the simple mention of a name had shaken him to the core.

"Louise, I don't think we should pursue this friendship. I just don't think it would be wise." As her countenance fell, and a look of disappointment came over her face, he hastened to explain. "You see, we've gone to our own church for more than twenty years, and we have our circle of old friends who are almost like family after all this time." Louise's expression took on even more of a questioning look. He continued somewhat lamely. "I don't think we should have too much to do with these newcomers, because people will think we're going to leave our church and our social group, and feelings would be hurt. People wouldn't understand."

"But, John, think what they did for our girls. We don't want to hurt their feelings either. They haven't pressured you to come to their church, have they?" Louise was totally perplexed at the direction this was going. "Nobody even mentioned church to me today. We were just there to meet the Marlowes, which to me was a real treat. I've heard of them for years, but somehow our paths never crossed before. I think they're lovely people, especially Mrs. Anderson."

"Well, you're right of course that we don't want to hurt their feelings. We owe them a great deal. But we don't have to become intimate friends with them. Being invited to a family "get together" like the one today makes me think that more invitations might be forth coming, and I just don't think we're quite their" he paused to think of the right word. "I don't think we can afford to try to be their social equals."

Louise stared at him in amazement. "John Holt, don't tell me that after all these years, I'm just finding out that you're a snob! At least a snob in reverse! Since when have we ever picked our friends because of their social standing? Is that what you mean?"

"No —no, of course not. Louise, you know it isn't. Just let it go that I'm not really comfortable in pursuing – or even continuing – this friendship. Can't you grant me that? I don't often have this reaction to people, and it bothers even me. But it bothers me even more to think they might become our close friends."

This time it was Louise who answered him with silence. Finally she spoke.

"John, I confess I'm completely in the dark. I don't understand your attitude at all. But, yes, I can grant you that. Personally, I'm very attracted to the family, particularly the Andersons, but you are more important to me than they are. You know that." Then thoughtfully she added, "However, it may cause problems with Patsy and Penny. Penny is great friends with the daughter, Eleanor, and Patsy and Kent have already formed a bond with the pastor and his wife. You'll have to face that, you know."

John nodded but persisted. "That's true, and it's understandable considering what took place the night of the accident. We just don't have to encourage it as a family. Thank you, my dear, for standing with me even though you don't understand why I'm asking this. It's just something that I can't explain even to you. It's hardly something I can explain to myself, but that's the way it must be."

Standing, and holding out his arms to her, he nuzzled her neck and whispered, "I could never get along without you, my dear. I have needed you more than anything in the world ever since we first laid eyes on each other, and I need you now more than ever! I hope you know that."

After a long kiss, she smiled and stroked his face gently. "Look at us after all these years! You are my life, John, and we've always belonged together. Things really do get better as we get older, don't they!"

The next day, Patsy had an unexpected visitor. When Louise answered the doorbell, her eyes hardened as she found herself face to face with the youth who had been the cause of all their heartache.

"Yes?" her voice held no welcome even though the boy standing there looked pathetic enough to evoke pity from the hardest of hearts. "What do you want?"

"I know you would rather never see me again, Mrs. Holt, and I wouldn't blame you, but I really would like to talk to Patsy." Louise shook her head, and his voice trembled as he continued his plea. "Please don't say no. I'm really sorry for all the trouble I've caused her and I'd like to tell her so. Please let me talk to her for just a few minutes."

"Who is it, Mother?" called Patsy.

"Stay here." Louise ordered the unwelcome visitor. "I'll see if she is willing to talk to you." She shut the door in his face and turned to Patsy.

"It's that Jason who ran over you. He says he's sorry and wants to talk to you. But if you say so, I'll send him on his way. You don't have to listen to him, you know. I don't want him upsetting you."

"Oh!" Patsy's shock was evident. "Oh, Mother, we mustn't send him away. I really think we should let him come in. If he's truly sorry then I think we should let him say so."

"Well, all right, if you're sure you're able to handle it. But I'll be right here, and if I see him upsetting you, he'll go right back out the door." Louise's indignation had turned into an almost primal instinct to protect her child.

She opened the door and ushered Jason inside, but took her stance beside the door with arms folded and disapproval upon her face.

Jason looked around him and saw Patsy in her wheelchair. He approached her timidly. "Patsy? How are you?"

She looked at him and almost felt sorry for him. Her voice was gentle. "I'm doing quite well, Jason. I can't walk, as you can see, and I don't know if I'll ever walk again, but I don't have any pain."

He swallowed, tried to speak, and swallowed again. Finally he found his voice. "Patsy, I just want to tell you that I'm real sorry about the accident. I know that probably doesn't make you feel any better, but I can't do any more than apologize. I wish I could. I was driving too fast and after it happened I was so scared that I didn't even stop – and I know I should have. I don't have any right to ask you this, but I wish you could forgive me. I'll always know that I'm responsible for the way you are, and I'll always feel guilty. But if I know you don't hate me, it will make it easier to live with!" Jason had never before, in all his life, been so humble. But now he was afraid he was going to cry. He hadn't known what seeing her in that wheel chair would do to him. He had always been able to talk his way out of things, but this was so final – *this* he was powerless to change, and he *was* guilty! There was no denying it.

Patsy was silent so long that Jason wondered if she was going to talk to him at all. Finally she took a deep breath and nodded her head. When she spoke, her voice also shook.

"A few days ago, I would have given you a different answer. But, yes, Jason, I do forgive you. You were wrong, and I hope you never do this to anyone else, but I can forgive you. You see, I have found out that God loves me and has forgiven me for my sin, and so I must forgive, too. I don't hate you, but" she paused and met his eyes, "I'll never be able to forget what happened, because every day my life is changed. I can't run around or ride my bicycle or dance - or do the other things I've always loved doing. I have to wait for other people to do things *for* me, and that's hard. But I won't think of you with anger." Then slowly she added, "I think I'll be sorry for you, because you'll never forget either, and it will be a hard thing for you to remember all your life that you caused someone to be a cripple."

Standing silently by the door, listening to her daughter's words, Louise marveled. She knew that Patsy had had a long talk with Mrs. Anderson, and if the truth must be told, she had listened in a few times when Kent and Patsy were talking about their newfound faith. To think that now her daughter was able to forgive this good-for-nothing young cur was beyond her understanding, but she figured that it must have something to do with the change that had come over both her beloved young people since the accident.

She decided that perhaps she should talk to Mrs. Anderson herself and find out what this was all about.

Jason listened to Patsy's words with bowed head. "I deserve everything you say, Patsy. And I think you should know that I don't own a car any more. My dad took it away from me after the police found out that I was driving when you were hurt. They took my driver's license away for a year, too. But I had it coming. I'm going to work hard so I can buy another car when I get my license back, but I've learned my lesson. I won't ever be guilty of hurting any one again like I hurt you." He covered her hand with his.

"Thank you, Patsy. I don't think I could have gone on living if I hadn't come to see you. And I'll think about what you said. Maybe what I need is to find God, too."

Chapter 16

The days after Thanksgiving flew by. Christmas always sneaks up on people. With such a few days between celebrations, they suddenly have much too much to do. And it seemed that this year, especially, with everything so different from previous holidays, life took some getting used to. In the first place, Kent made the decision that he must return to college for the semester beginning in January, and Patsy was desolate, though she tried not to show it. She had become more than ever dependent upon her friend, who had been there for her all the time – even to the point of delaying his college education. As for Kent, he had come to the realization that Patsy meant more to him than he had ever guessed, because he had always thought of the twins as his sisters, always in the plural. Now, suddenly, since the accident, he found himself thinking only of Patsy's welfare. Not that he didn't love Penny any more, but now she was the *sister*. Patsy held an entirely different place in his heart, and he knew that she was the one with whom he would spend the rest of his life. He felt he had to declare his feelings to her before he returned to school – and he wanted to do it before Christmas.

So one day early in December, while the trees were bare and there was the smell of snow in the air, he was sitting with Patsy, telling her why he felt that he must return to college. "You know, Honey, even though I've missed a semester, there's still a chance that I will be able to graduate with my class, but I'm going to have to put in some long hours. That will mean that I won't have the chance to come home for Easter, and I may have to go to summer school. So I have something to tell you. I want you to understand why I won't be able to write to you as often as I did before, and I want to be sure that you don't think it's because I've forgotten you. You see, the harder I work, the sooner we can be together again, and I have to get all of this work done because of you." He stopped as he saw by her face that she was totally in the dark about his meaning. She was simply hurting because he was leaving her, and he wanted her to be able to see beyond that. So he started over.

"What I want you to know, Honey, is that I've found out that I can't live without you, and I want to get college behind me while you're still too young to get married. Because I want to marry you, and when I do I have to be ready to take care of you." He stopped again. He was bumbling this and he knew it. He took a deep breath.

"What I'm saying is that I can't formally propose to you until you're at least eighteen. I know both of our mothers would say that. But I can let you know that I love you and that I plan to propose as soon as you're old enough. But by then I want to be free to make definite plans for our marriage – if you'll have me – (she was staring at him with unbelieving eyes) and I want you to have time to think about it and be absolutely sure what your answer will be. That means I have a big job ahead of me, and if I'm not here for you as much as I have been, you'll know it's because I'm working my head off so that we can always be together." Finally having said it to his satisfaction, he waited anxiously for her response.

It was slow to come, as she studied him with solemn eyes. Then softly she spoke.

"Kent, I love you, too. I think you know that. But just think what you'd be taking on for life – a cripple who might never walk again. I have to face that fact, you know. It wouldn't be fair to you. I would be a burden to you all of our lives. Could your love for me endure that?"

"What I couldn't endure would be life without you." He reached for her hand. "I believe that true love can endure anything. And besides," he added, " now we have help that we wouldn't have had before your accident – we both know the Lord, and He'll help us. I'm confident of that. The real question is, would you wait for me and would you keep loving me. Knowing that you would – well, I think that would give me the strength and encouragement to do what I have to do."

A sudden thought struck him. "But – am I asking too much, Patsy? Am I? Maybe you will meet someone else to love. Maybe it wouldn't be fair of me to ask you to make a promise that you might not be able to keep." His face fell. "All I want is for you to be happy and cared for, and selfishly, I want to be the one to do it."

Tears filled Patsy's eyes. "Kent, there never has been anyone else, and there never will be. I think I've always loved you, first like a brother, and then, in the last few months, in a very different way. I would keep my promise because I couldn't help it." She brushed away a tear or two. "Yes, Kent, I can give you my promise, as long as you understand that all I want is for you to be happy too. I can let you go back to school, and I can keep busy getting ready to marry you. I need to learn a lot of things, too. After all, I'm not helpless, and there are a lot of things I can do. I just have to figure out ways to do them!"

Then, unable to help himself, Kent took her in his arms in anything but a brotherly way. He kissed her tenderly, then pulled away. Looking deep into her eyes, he gently told her, "Now that will have to do for a long, long time. It's probably a good thing that I won't be able to come home too often, because I have to keep my mind on my studies. And if I'm here, my mind is always on you!" He smiled and stood up. "Let's keep this to ourselves, okay? It will be our secret, and we can pull it out and think about it whenever we get discouraged, and it will give us the courage to go ahead. Would you do that?"

Patsy returned his smile, and he tucked that smile away securely in his memory. "Yes, Kent. It will be *our* secret!"

In the process of getting his life in order, Kent felt the necessity of having a long talk with his father. He had something to make right with him. It had nothing to do with his and Patsy's secret, but it was something that had been preying on his mind ever since his talk with

Pastor Anderson. As he was growing up, he had always made fair grades, and had been a quite model son in most ways, but he had never been the outstanding student he could have been. He knew his father was somewhat disappointed that his son was never at the top of the class, and had not been totally approving when he had decided to delay his college education for a semester. So Kent had some fence-mending to do before his conscience was comfortably at rest.

With the conviction that this was the time to face up to it, he appeared at the door of his father's office the next day. Gordon looked up in surprise, then his face broke into a welcoming smile. "Well, this is a surprise! Come in, Son. Give me just a few minutes and then we'll sit down for a good chat. We haven't had much opportunity for that with everything that's been taking place, have we?"

"No, Dad. And I've missed it. You go ahead with what you're doing. I don't mind waiting."

Gordon turned to his secretary, and finished dictating the letters that Kent's arrival had interrupted. Then he dismissed her, turned to his son, and inquired, "What's on your mind, Kent? You look very solemn and serious this morning."

"Well, Dad, I have something to tell you. It's something that I should have said – and done – long ago."

His father eyed him with alarm. Was this something so serious that Kent had hidden it from him and Mary Ann? "Go on, Son. Let's have it."

"It's not anything bad, Dad, it's just something that you should know. You see, I know I haven't been the student I could have been, either in High School or in College. You've spent a lot of hard earned money on me, and I haven't given you a very good return on it. I'm really sorry, Dad. I was having too much fun, I guess, to really get serious about my grades. I was just satisfied to make it. But things are different now."

"How so, Kent? You've never failed or gotten into trouble. I haven't complained, have I?"

"No, Dad, but I know you were disappointed many times. And now I wish I had tried harder. But what I want to say is that when I go back to college in January, things are going to be different. I'm going to really work and make you proud, but I have another reason, too. You know that I've had a lot of conversations with Pastor Anderson, and I've learned that God is real (which I had come to seriously doubt) and that I want to do my best for Him because He has done so much for me. I'm really different, Dad, because now God is a very important part of my life. And I know that He expects my best from me, just as you have always done. So now I have the incentive to do what I should have done years ago. Dad, I'm going to graduate at the top of my class. You see if I don't. I'll make up for all those years I fooled around."

Gordon was stunned. He *had* often been disappointed that his son did not show more ambition and seemed content to just coast along. Kent had always been enthusiastic about his sports, and was one of the most popular fellows in his circle of friends. With that, Gordon had been pleased. But he certainly had shown a lack of interest in what Gordon thought *should* have mattered the most to him – his future. He had sincerely hoped that the boy would shape up as he matured – but suddenly he was shocked to find that that his son's maturity had sneaked up on him when he wasn't looking! He responded with relief and enthusiasm.

"Son, if you do that, there will be a place waiting for you here in the bank when you graduate. I've hoped you would step into my shoes, but I admit I've had my doubts as to whether you would be able to take hold of things as you would be required to do. Thank you, Son, you have really put my mind at rest."

Kent was shaken as he detected the emotion in his father's voice, and he stared at his father in surprise. "I never knew you wanted that! I never really thought of coming into the bank with you – but I guess that's because I just didn't have any ambition." He smiled and added, "I guess that solves a problem for me, too. That will give me something else to work for, because jobs aren't that plentiful." He and his father stood up at almost the same instant. Gordon put out his hand. Kent grabbed it, then the two men parted with a father-son bear hug, both of them marveling at the change a few minutes of heart-to-heart talk could bring in each of their lives.

But Gordon had something else to think about, too. Like Louise, he wondered at the change that had come over Kent, and determined that he must have a talk with Pastor Anderson. There was something here that he didn't understand, and he wanted it cleared up.

As Kent strode home in the crisp, cold December air, he marveled at the way the events of the last few days had worked out. It almost seemed that Someone was going beside him and putting into his mind things he must do. Was this the way the Plan worked? Pastor Anderson and Josh had both talked about it. But Pastor Anderson had also warned in one of the Bible classes that everything would not always be smooth. That it would take faith and courage to keep on when things went wrong. Well, it was good to be warned, but at the moment all Kent could think about was being thankful that just now everything looked good. If only Patsy could walk again, things would be perfect!

John Holt was struggling with his decision to separate his family from the Marlowe influence. Following up on his declaration to Louise, he set out to find a way to satisfy his family and still accomplish his purpose. He knew there would be questions and objections and he must move carefully.

First he wanted to separate Penny and that Marlowe girl. Providentially, it seemed, he learned that a small business school was being organized right in Little Rapids. It was presently advertising for students, and, after investigating the credentials of the educational staff, and finding them satisfactory, he set out to sell Penny on the idea of enrolling here, instead of continuing at Miss Parker's.

"Kitten," he approached Penny during a lull in their schedule one morning. "I need to talk to you about something."

"Yes, Dad. Just give me a few minutes to finish this pile of invoices, then we'll sit down and have a cup of coffee together." She smiled at him. "I'm having so much fun learning how to manage the office here, that I'm even considering suggesting some procedural changes. Is that presumptuous of your newest office clerk?"

John chuckled. "Well, I won't fire you for making suggestions." Mischievously he added, "But I might fire you if they don't work!"

"Oh, Dad! I know you won't do that!" Then grinning, she shot back at him, "But if you do fire me, I have had experience now and could get a better job than this! What do you think about that?"

Both laughing, they settled down to enjoy their coffee, and John felt that he had found just the right opening to make his suggestion.

"Honey, did you know that there is a new business school opening right here in Little Rapids? They're enrolling new students right now and they have an excellent faculty. There would be small classes and a lot more individual help for the students, and I think it might be a good idea for us to patronize it. It would save you a lot of traveling time and would therefore give you more time to put in here, and you and I both know that the work is beginning to get ahead of us here in the office. What do you think?"

Penny was stunned. She had come to feel very comfortable at Miss Parker's, and had made excellent progress. She also enjoyed her close friendship with Eleanor, and her first thought was a total rejection of the idea.

"But, Dad, I'm doing so well over there. And I haven't nearly learned everything I need to know. I don't mind the travel, you know, and I really love the school and the teachers! It's not boring like so much of high school used to be, because I'm learning things that I really need to know to do my work here in the office. Changing schools would be kind of like starting all over again!" Her face betrayed her dismay.

"Listen to yourself, Kitten." His voice was gentle as he realized how much his suggestion had upset her, but he persisted. "You'd be studying the same subjects, your typing would continue to improve, and maybe you would learn even more up-to-date methods here than you have learned in Charlotte. I've investigated the teaching staff and find that they are well qualified, and much younger than the average staff member at Miss Porter's. I think you would fit in perfectly, and in addition, you would be on the ground floor of a new institution. That's always exciting." As he noted the storm cloud still hovering over her brow, he added, "Besides, remember that you do really need more time here in the office. I hope – and believe - that within a year or so you'll be able to completely take over the office and organize it as efficiently as you wish. When I hire more office staff, I want to be able to put you in charge and then you can install those new procedures that you were mentioning a few minutes ago."

Penny was silent as she thought about the changes that would take place in her life if she agreed to this plan. They would be upsetting but not necessarily painful – except for the fact that she would no longer be seeing Eleanor several times a week. But she had to face the fact that the changes would affect only *her* feelings, and that she would be selfish not to think about the advantages – both to the business and ultimately to the family.

"Dad, can I think it over a couple of days? I can see your point, and I'm beginning to see the wisdom of your suggestion, but I need to get used to the idea." She toyed with her coffee cup, then looked up straight into his eyes. "Dad, I want to do what's best for the company, because you and I are in this together, and to me it's more than just a job. It's our family business, which Grandpa started, and that you've built up, and I'm proud of it. Can I have a couple of days to think about it?"

"Of course, Kitten. As you say, we're in this together and we have to make decisions together. But I'd appreciate it if you would very seriously consider what I've said."

"I will, Dad, I will. I promise. After all, the work here is much more important than where I go to school. I wouldn't be quitting, I'd just be moving on."

John smiled as she jumped up and hugged him and exclaimed, "Now I have to get back to work."

As he finished his coffee and returned to the shop, he thought to himself, "Well, step one seems to be successfully accomplished. I don't think that was too hard for her to accept!" Then he added to himself, *"It really is best for the business, and besides, it had to be done!"*

Louise, still puzzling over their strange conversation of a few nights ago, approved heartily of the changes her daughter and husband were contemplating, for having her daughter on the road back and forth to Charlotte so much of the time had worried her. She realized what John was doing, and while she still couldn't understand his attitude about the matter, she accepted the fact that this was important to him. She tried over and over to think what might have upset him that Thanksgiving afternoon, but found herself at a complete loss. However, she wasn't sorry to see this opportunity to loosen the tie between Eleanor and Penny. While Eleanor was a refined and lovely girl, there was something about her attitude that bothered Louise. In contrast to the rest of her family, Eleanor seemed to be cynical of the solid standards and beliefs for which they stood, and even appeared to mock them by her tone of voice and her comments. She didn't want Penny adopting such ideas and attitudes, and was relieved to know that in the future the girls would not be spending so much time together. She wondered where in the world Eleanor had gotten such ideas, and how the rest of her family felt about her differences. She was sure it must bother especially her grandmother, whom Louise had observed regarding Eleanor several times that afternoon with a quizzical, mildly puzzled expression.

John's intention was to try next some gentle suggestion with his other daughter. However, he found himself delaying approaching her for she had become calm and even seemed happy in the last few months since her accident. Having observed her apparent acceptance of her disabilities, he was reluctant to say anything at all that might upset her. In addition, she and Kent seemed to be all wrapped up in each other and in the new ideas introduced to them by the Andersons, which he thought might have something to do with her newly acquired peace of mind. He wasn't at all concerned about the very obvious attraction between the two young people. Kent was like part of their family, and somehow John had known intuitively for a long time that at some point their brother/sister relationship would blossom into something deeper. Not only was he not disturbed by it, but he watched it develop with great satisfaction. He was also aware that the two young people believed that it was their secret alone, and he smiled to himself. No matter, he trusted Kent implicitly. The only thing bothering him was the attraction that they both seemed to have for the Andersons. In his present frame of mind, he found himself uneasy and was at a loss how to go about minimizing it. However, he told himself sternly that it *must* be done.

As it turned out, Kent solved the dilemma for him by announcing that he was returning to school in January. This, he was sure, would put an end to opportunities for the Andersons to influence his family. Not that he had anything against the Andersons. They were without doubt lovely people and his gratitude to them was deep. But Mrs. Anderson was a Marlowe. And it had become an obsession with him that any connection between the Marlowes and his family must end. Someway it must be worked out.

Chapter 17

The interval between the Thanksgiving holiday and the beginning of the festive Christmas celebrations was soon over. John had said nothing about his concerns to Patsy, for when Kent left, he felt there would be little enticement for Patsy to continue the relationship she had developed with Mrs. Anderson. Besides, Kent had been the connection, and he would no longer be attending youth meetings at Redeemer Chapel.

The Holts and their close friends and neighbors, Mary Ann and Gordon Walters, had, through the years, developed seasonal traditions that were now an automatic part of their lives as the time for Christmas activities rolled around. The excitement of decorating their homes and their adjoining lawns occupied almost all of their spare time. Secrets and whispered plans for surprising each other were pursued with just as much glee as when the twins and Kent had been children.

One special project that the two families always looked forward to was decorating the tree that stood almost on the dividing line between the Holt and the Walters properties. Immediately after Thanksgiving, the outdoor decorations were hauled out, and the three children always loved the excitement of running up and down the ladders, stretching precariously to place each treasured item at a critical point on the lovely tall cedar tree. John and Louise watched anxiously as Patsy sat in her wheel chair, now able only to observe as Penny and Kent decorated the tree. With relief they saw that if she was disturbed, she didn't show it. She seemed to enjoy bossing the other two, becoming quite dictatorial in insisting that they follow her orders – which they did with good grace, including her in the fun.

Over the years their outdoor tree had become a very popular place for the townspeople to visit during the days between Thanksgiving and Christmas, for when it was completed, the display was spectacular. At the base of the tree, John and Gordon always set up a spot-light, trained aloft, and placed carved wooden life-sized figures of not only Santa Claus and his sleigh and reindeer with the little elves gathered around, but also the creche of the Holy Family. The two fathers had created these figures when the twins were little more than babies, and setting them up each year was an activity that was very important to the two families. They were always happy to share their efforts with all their friends in Little Rapids and the street past the Holt and Gordon homes was continually busy between the two holidays.

Parties and church events as usual crowded the calendar. But one day Penny realized that she had only a few days left, and she regretfully told Eleanor of her new plans. To her dismay Eleanor burst into tears.

Fortunately, the two girls were sitting in relative privacy at the picnic table on the school lawn, which had been placed there specifically for the use of the students at lunch time. However, it was much too cold now for that use, but the two girls had bundled up and gone outdoors for a short walk before classes resumed for the afternoon. At Penny's suggestion, they stopped at the picnic table to be by themselves for a few moments, and she chose this time to break her news.

"Eleanor, I hate to tell you this, but things are going to be different after Christmas. I've decided to transfer to a new business school in Little Rapids to be closer home. I won't be spending so much time on the road, and will be able to put in more time at the office. My dad is planning to turn the management of the office over to me when I've had enough experience and training, and this change will help me to be ready sooner. I – why, what's the matter, Eleanor? We don't need to stop being friends, we just won't see each other so often." Penny got up, went around the table, and put her arm around her sobbing friend. "I hate it too, because you're the best girl friend I've had since I finished High School, and I've missed doing things with Patsy so much that I don't know what I would have done without you. Don't cry, Eleanor. I've felt bad ever since I decided to make the change, but I know it's the best thing for the business and for my family. You see that, don't you?"

Eleanor nodded, and wiped at her eyes. "Yes, of course, Penny. I understand. It was just a shock. But in the same circumstances, I'm sure I would do the very same thing." She sat quietly now, and then made what seemed to Penny a very strange comment.

"You see, Penny, I've come to kind of a crossroads, too. I've been working very closely with my father for the last few months, and am finding that I never knew him very well, and that I really didn't understand the business at all. I'm not sure that I can ever be the person he wants me to be. That is, I don't know if I can ever measure up to his standards." She sighed. "It doesn't matter to him, Penny, that I'm a girl instead of the son he had always hoped would take over the business some day. But it seems that he has some very strange ideas – at least they are strange to me - about how his successor must continue to run things, and I don't understand how those ideas make sense in running a successful business. They certainly aren't in agreement with what I've been taught that businesses must do to stay solvent. But somehow he's managed to do things his own way (which was the way that his father and Grandpa Underhill did things) and their efforts have built the largest corporation in the state of Michigan." Again she paused thoughtfully. "You see Penny, I find myself at the point where I have to convince myself that I can either accept his ideas and measure up to what he expects of me, or tell him that it's no use and he will have to look for someone else. That I'm just not ever going to be good enough to satisfy him. And he's going to be devastated. I love my father very much and - do you see my dilemma, Penny? At present it's all up to me, and I'm not sure what to do."

Penny was speechless. Eleanor had just told her more than she ever would have guessed about her family relationships and she had had no idea of the crisis that her friend was facing. What in the world could she say – if anything? This was almost beyond the bounds of friendship: - this was Eleanor baring her soul and Penny was almost embarrassed.

"Eleanor, I don't know what to say. But I can imagine how you must feel. Have you talked to any of your family about it? Maybe your grandmother or Mrs. Anderson?"

"No. I've just been struggling with it in my own mind. I guess I'm not very good at making decisions. I had so hoped that working with Dad would work out for both of us, and I just hate to give up the idea."

"Well, I can't give you any advice, but if it were my family, I think I would talk to my grandmother about it. Old people lots of times understand our problems better than we do. I remember when I was a little girl, my grandmother was always the one who seemed to have the answers to things that puzzled me. Grandmothers sure know a lot more than we do. They've had a lot more years to learn all the answers. Now come on, Eleanor, dry your eyes. We have to get to class!"

In the few days they had left together, the subject was never mentioned again, and Penny had no idea how – or even whether - Eleanor was able to solve her problem.

However, being able to talk to someone about it had seemed to clear the older girl's mind, and she suddenly realized that Penny had given her some excellent advice. Why *not* go to Grandmother Christy, and just lay it all out before her? Why hadn't she thought of that before? A quick rush of hope arose in Eleanor's heart, and she wondered how she would be able to wait to hear what Grandma had to say. Well, she knew she would *have* to wait, because she had tests to pass and assignments to complete within the next few days, and it would be at least a week before she could pay that beloved lady a visit. Not realizing that her own sense of determination and self- confidence had been inherited from Grandma herself, she gritted her teeth and set out to do what she had to do to complete the school term successfully. After that was over, next week for sure, she would pay Grandma a visit. Maybe *then* she would be able to come to a decision. She had no idea what an important visit that would turn out to be!

The days passed rapidly, filled with long hours of study and then with examinations which both girls passed with ease. The sense of purpose that spurred each of them put them both at the top of their class. After the final assembly was over and the term was officially ended, Penny and Eleanor reluctantly each went her own way. But not without promises to keep in touch.

"Penny, you'll be hearing from me. Mom and Grandma and I are planning a luncheon for Celee, Josh's fiance, and you're invited. You know their wedding is planned for early fall, and there's going to be lots of excitement in the family between now and then. Celee and her family will spend Christmas with her grandparents, then will come back in February to stay for a couple of weeks. That's when we're planning our luncheon. It won't be anything formal, just a get together for us all to get better acquainted. Please tell me that you'll come."

Penny thought of her father's insistence that there be no more interaction between the families, and she hesitated. Then, feeling a surge of resentful independence, she made her decision.

"Thank you, Eleanor. Of course I'll come if you want me to. And we'll write to each other often between now and February. Our friendship means a lot to me, too, and I don't want to lose touch with you. After all, Charlotte and Little Rapids aren't that far apart, and I think perhaps we can get together quite often."

That moment was Penny's "declaration of independence". She had never before intentionally disregarded her parents' wishes, but she believed that they didn't realize how much Eleanor's friendship had meant to her. Thus, though her decision made her slightly uncomfortable, she told herself that now she was old enough to decide for herself who her friends would be. She had no idea how important that sudden assertion of maturity would be to her – and to her whole family.

Now Penny turned her full attention to getting ready for Christmas, but Eleanor found her mind filled with unfinished business. Somehow, some way, she must find a way to work out her problem - hopefully before the New Year rolled around.

Eleanor found her grandmother busily baking, and mouth-watering scents filled the house. She was immediately transported in imagination back to her childhood when her favorite thing at Christmas was to "help" Grandma Christy make cookies. Her job was to carefully cut the rolled dough, using cookie cutters that were bent into all the imaginative shapes that meant Christmas to children. Grandma always said that she couldn't have completed her Christmas baking without her only granddaughter's assistance. Eleanor now knew, of course, from the lofty view of an adult, that she had probably always been more of a hindrance than a help, but Grandma never let on. She was forever patient, loving, and encouraging, and those fun times had knit the two together with a solid bond of affection. And, for Eleanor, they had built up a feeling of dependence upon her grandmother, greater even than she felt for her mother. She loved her mother with all her heart, but somehow, Grandma Christy had always been easier to talk to.

So today, her first day of freedom from classes, she had again sought out her grandmother, with questions and problems that she seemed unable to solve by herself.

"Eleanor, my dear, how did you know I needed you?" called Christy from the kitchen. "You know I could never make cookies without your help!"

Eleanor laughed, delighted at her Grandmother's greeting. "Oh, Grandma, you know that I was always in the way. I had great fun, and you always told me I was helping, but I know better. Sometimes I wish I were that size again, and didn't know the truth!"

"Well, if that's what you think, you still don't have a handle on the truth! Because the truth is that your help was *exactly* what I needed, and I need it now. Get a plate, will you, and unload this pan of cookies while I get another ready to go in the oven! Time's running short, and I'm behind!" Christy thrust a spatula into Eleanor's hand, and ordered, "Now get to work! You know where the plates are, and those cookies each need one of those candies pressed onto their tops while they're still hot."

Eleanor grinned at her grandmother, grasped the spatula in one hand, and with a holder in the other took the pan of cookies from the oven. Her questions could wait, for this was a treat she hadn't counted on. *This*, now, was really Christmas!

When the two finally sat down, having a massive batch of cookies cooling, and a satisfied feeling of accomplishment, Grandma Christy turned to her granddaughter and came right to the point. "Now, Eleanor, I know you must have something on your mind. I appreciated the help with the cookies, but since you didn't even know I was baking until you came in the door, I know there was another reason for this very welcome visit. Are your classes over for the year?"

"Yes, Grandma, and much as I enjoy business school, I'm glad to have some time off. Classes don't begin again until the middle of January, so I'll have more time to spend with you and the family."

"When will Robert be home?" Christy wondered.

"Not for another week, I think. He was lucky to be able to get home for Thanksgiving, with Christmas so soon after. But he won't have to go back until February, so this will give him a good vacation. But Grandma, I have a question to ask you," she paused and thought for a moment, then added, "or maybe it will turn out to be two or three questions! Do you have something else you have to do, or can we talk?"

"I've done all I intend to do for today, my dear. At my age, one big project a day is enough! Sometimes more than enough!" Christy chuckled as she spoke, privately thinking to herself with a hint of sadness, that not that many years ago, baking cookies would have been just one incidental chore among many others. *"Growing old gets more and more frustrating!"* she thought, as her chuckle turned into a silent sigh.

"All right, Grandma, I'm going to put you on the spot, and I hope you can tell me what to do. You see, I love working with Daddy in the office, and I'm learning lots about the business. I really think, you know, that business law is going to be what I specialize in. But in the meantime, I'm trying to learn all I can about Underhill Associates. And what I'm learning puzzles me. In business school I'm taught that certain things are essential if a business is to make money, and that only if those principles are followed will a company stay solvent. It sounds good, and on paper it all makes sense."

"So what puzzles you, my dear? Your father's business is certainly solvent, or so I've been led to believe."

"It's not only solvent, but we're making money while other businesses are failing around us right and left. The depression hasn't seemed to affect Underhill at all."

'Then what's the problem, Eleanor? I don't understand."

"Well, Grandma, what Daddy is doing and what Grandpa Underhill and Grandpa Marlowe did, is all opposite to what the current business philosophy is. He's doing everything backwards, but it seems to work. His reasons for operating the way he does just don't make sense to me, and I don't know that I agree with all the reasons he gives me when I ask why. I'm very confused."

"Then suppose you tell me more specifically what you disagree with, and maybe I can begin to understand what's bothering you. Though I think it would be more to the point to talk to your father about it.""

"I've tried, Grandma, but he just gives me a puzzled look, and there's a question in his voice as if he doesn't understand what I'm talking about. It's kind of like I'm talking Greek instead of English. That's why I came to you. Maybe you can help me figure out a few things so that he and I can communicate. What I'm really wondering is why he gives back so much capital to the associated stores and factories. He could be making so much more money, and it just seems silly to me that he should be treating them as if he were working for them instead of them working for him. They wouldn't be able to stay open in this present negative business environment if it weren't for him, and yet he isn't taking advantage of the situation. Why not? Wouldn't it be better business practice for him to put the extra money into some kind of safe investment so it would be there when he needs it?"

"Well, Honey, as I understand it, you've just answered your own question. He is making the safest investment possible – putting the money back into the businesses that are a part of the association. You just told me that they wouldn't be able to stay open if he didn't do that; so if they had to close, what advantage would that be to him? Mr. Underhill started the business on the premise that his associates would be his partners, and that everything the company did would be for their mutual advantage. And your grandfather continued that policy, as has your father. And when your father has to pass it on to someone else, he wants these very successful methods to be continued. And as you say, it has worked, hasn't it?"

Eleanor was silent, looking at her grandmother with amazement. She certainly was able to boil things down and make them sound reasonable. Who was the businessman here, she wondered?

"But, Grandmother, they actually *give* stock to their employees! And bonuses that are unbelievably big, considering the present state of the economy. Are they trying to make the factory employees and the store clerks rich? It doesn't make sense."

"Look at it this way, Eleanor. None of the employees of the associate firms have been in a soup line or has lost his home. None of the firms have gone bankrupt. Now would it be better for your father to be rolling in money at the expense of his associates, while those same associates would be paying starvation wages and maybe would – or maybe wouldn't - be able to hardly hang on, barely meeting expenses? Besides, what I've noticed about a great number of formerly successful businesses, is that they have gone bankrupt, the millionaires have become paupers, and their employees have gone hungry. Now which method makes the best sense?"

Now totally speechless, Eleanor sat and stared at her grandmother. She knew that Christy still had more to say, but she herself was speechless. Her mind was reeling with the unbelievable words she was hearing, and with wondering how those few words could have so completely overturned what she had thought were rational ideas.

Then her grandmother continued, "But, Eleanor, that wasn't the most important consideration in both Mr. Underhill's and Matthew's minds. The impelling factor was the justice and the fairness of the plan. Neither of them could have lived with themselves if they had gone into business just to make themselves rich or to take advantage of other people. In his youth, your grandfather read and reread the teachings of Jesus in the Gospels, and on those principles he built his business. He knew he could never carry on a business successfully unless he could do it in a way which served humanity – he always had to treat his fellow man as he himself would want to be treated, and that meant total honesty to himself and to God. And God was very real to both him and Mr. Underhill. They both believed that they must answer to God some day for the way they lived their lives here on this earth." Then she added softly, "And I believe they both heard God say, 'Well done, good and faithful servant'."

Now Eleanor *was* in over her head. "You mean this has something to do with religion and not just business? And that Daddy is carrying on that idea?"

"No, dear, it has nothing to do with religion. It has to do with a personal relationship with God, which I'm happy to say, directed the actions of all three men. That's why your father is so determined that whoever takes over from him has the same philosophy of business and knowledge of God's will that he has."

"Well, I guess that lets me out." Eleanor stood, picked up her purse, and started for the door, not even remembering to kiss her grandmother good-bye. Her whole world seemed turned upside down. She had to think. She didn't *want* to believe that she had no chance, but she knew for certain now that she didn't measure up. But what to do? This was just too confusing!

Her grandmother watched from the window as she marched down the sidewalk, banged her car door, and roared off down the street. And as she watched, she prayed. This was something she could not help Eleanor with. Her decision must be her own, and Christy was well aware that her granddaughter knew what she must do. She had been exposed to that knowledge all of her life. She only hoped and prayed that she would do it.

But Eleanor had another shock in store for her.

Chapter 18

At breakfast the next morning her father announced, "Eleanor, I have to go to Lansing today to check out two or three of the associates located there. Instead of going to the office, I'd like you to go with me. All you have had a chance to do, so far, is to work on the Underhill books. I'd like to have you meet some of the people with whom we deal. The associates are what the business is all about, and until you actually get into the field, and see what goes on in the real world of business, you won't have a true picture of what our company does."

"But, Dad, I'm not finished with that posting job you gave me last night. You said it had a deadline on it."

"Well, the deadline isn't so imminent that you can't let the job wait for one day. Anyway, I need you to go with me, so please be ready in about half an hour." With that, Dan excused himself, and left the room.

In spite of her objections, Eleanor found herself excitedly looking forward to the trip. She hurried to her room, changed into a chic business suit and picked up a fur coat as she started downstairs. She was actually waiting for her father when he appeared, car keys in hand.

"Good. You look very professional, my dear! And it's a good thing you're taking a coat. That gray sky looks like there may be some heavy weather coming. So let's be on our way!"

Both of them were relaxed and enjoyed the outing. However, as they drove into the outskirts of the city, Eleanor grew quiet. This would be exciting, she was sure, but she really wondered what to expect. Some business conferences, probably, and maybe a tour of one or two of the associate firms.

And her guess was right on the money for the first stop. The manager of the store welcomed them into his office, and willingly answered questions that Dan put to him. Eleanor was impressed with her father's intimate knowledge of the firm's organization, and with the thorough attention he gave to the financial records he was given to inspect. She also proudly observed the obvious respect given to him by the manager, and also by the owner who joined the conference a few minutes after their arrival.

The assistant manager was summoned to join them also, as they began a tour of the store. And again she was amazed, for many of the workers greeted Dan with open friendliness, and he in turn called many of them by name. Not only did he call them by name but he often asked about their families, and showed concern for problems they might be having in their private lives. How did he know them all so well? She also noticed that some of the older employees mentioned her grandfather's name and would recall incidents in which he had done something for them which had changed their lives. She found herself wondering if this was standard business practice. Somehow she had never realized that there was a truly human side to running a successful operation such as this seemed to be. The business philosophy that had so engrossed her in her business school classes began to seem rather distant and irrelevant.

The next associate was a factory, located in a part of the city new to Eleanor. She had never had reason to go into this section, which was across the railroad tracks in a very seedy area.

Dan turned down a side street where the houses were small and poorly maintained.

"This doesn't look like an area where one would find a thriving business of any kind, Dad. Look at that ramshackle building." She pointed to a very small, run-down shanty which boasted a sign advertising groceries for sale. "Can you imagine going shopping for food there? It's a wonder the building hasn't been condemned – much less being allowed to handle food!" Her voice had the hint of a sneer in it.

"My dear, that grocery store – years ago when it looked just as bad as it looks now – was run by one of the most caring, generous, good men that I ever met," her father responded. "I was just a small boy when my father brought us, your Uncle Billy and me, that is, over to see him. He fed much of the neighborhood with what little he had, and Father used to bring him money to buy more food for hungry people."

"How in the world did Grandpa ever get to know such a man, Dad? He certainly didn't have much interest in a community such as this, did he?"

"Yes, Honey, your grandfather had a great interest in this community. You see, this was where your Uncle Billy lived when his mother died, and Father had this man to thank for taking care of Billy until he could do something for him himself." He pointed to a tiny house close to the road. "That was where Billy and his mother lived. After she was taken to the hospital, the owner locked Billy out, and he had nowhere to go except to this kind man in the grocery store. When Father found him, he arranged to have Mrs. O'Conner buried in Maple Hill Cemetery and Uncle Joseph and Aunt Ruthie adopted Billy. You know the rest of the story, because you've heard it all your life."

"But Uncle Billy lived in a place like this? I can't imagine such a thing! I knew he was poor, but here!" The aristocratic Nell was almost holding her nose. "How can people live like this!" and as she spoke she pointed to three little barefooted boys squatting down in the dirt flipping pennies. "Dirty little urchins!"

"Eleanor." Dan's voice was hard. "These are people, just like us, but very unfortunate. You've had the best of everything all your life, and I'm sorry to see that it has made you unfeeling and snobbish. Billy's mother was a lovely Christian lady, from all I know of her, but her husband died, she had no money, and this was the best home she could find for her and her son. Billy was just a youngster trying to do a man's work to support his mother when my father found him. Do you know any better person than your Uncle Billy?"

"No, Dad." It was only a whisper from a very humbled Nell. She just hadn't known. It hadn't sounded so bad when Uncle Billy told the story, but to *see* it! It was beginning to occur to her that rather than being so full of pride, she needed forgiveness from somewhere – or from someone – for her haughty attitude. If she had been confused before, she was now mired in self-reproach and actual disgust for the person she was finding herself to be. And even worse, she had a feeling there was more to come.

Dan drove on through the unfamiliar streets and pulled up in front of a four story factory building. "This is our next stop, my dear. And I suggest that you watch yourself, that your attitudes do not show. At least, if they are like the ones you just displayed when you saw Uncle Billy's neighborhood. The people who work here also live in this area, and though their houses may not be pretty, they are good, hardworking people who are trying to keep their families fed and clothed. And," he added with a stern look at his daughter, "these are the people with whom we partner, in an effort to make their lives better in any way we can. Now, let's get out and go into the office."

They made their way up the uneven stone steps into a cold hallway, and entered a tiny office barely warmed by a small coal heater. Again Dan was greeted with great warmth and deep respect, and Eleanor had the feeling that there was genuine friendship between her father and his associates.

After a similar conference to the first one she had witnessed, Dan turned to the owner and requested, "Jim, I wonder if you would give my daughter a tour of the factory. She's working in the business with me now, and I feel she needs to see the operations of the various associate firms."

"I'd be happy to, Mr. Marlowe. But I must warn you that it's pretty cold in the factory today. We ran out of coal yesterday and the furnaces got cold during the night. However, since she has a good warm coat, it may be all right."

Dan gave the man a searching look. "I noticed in your books that money is running pretty tight. Do you have enough to keep the place sufficiently warm? Your production is going to plummet if your people have to work in a cold building."

Jim squirmed and looked down at his feet. "Mr. Marlowe, I've been making it, but it's been tight, as you say. If we have a real cold winter, I'm going to have problems. However, my workers don't complain. They know they have it so much better than the other factories round about, that they're willing to endure some hardships."

"Well, I don't like it that they have to suffer. You cut my percentage down by half for the present, and use that extra money to heat the building. I don't need it just now, and you can make it up to me later. Now let's take that tour."

Eleanor now felt that her "educational" tour was becoming almost more than she could handle. New sights, sounds, ideas, emotional shocks bombarded her from every side. She wondered if her father had any idea what this trip was doing to her. Had her grandmother had anything to do with it? Their conversation of yesterday kept hammering at her consciousness, as she related what Christy had told her to what she was seeing and experiencing today.

As they walked the aisles in the factory, she noted that the workers were bundled up against the bitter cold, and that for some it was difficult and even dangerous for them to be trying to work in such heavy wraps. Again she couldn't help but notice that her father called many of them by name and asked about their families. And he was greeted with genuine delight by the workers. Occasionally there was a new face, and with dignity they were introduced to Dan and were acknowledged with the same innate respect and obvious pleasure that he would have displayed to any of the social class in which he moved daily. And as before, she was introduced and acknowledged as a friend by people who, in her daily experience, she would have scarcely noticed – much less spoken to.

As the car headed back to Charlotte, the gray clouds finally began to release their snowflakes on the earth below, and Dan slowed down and drove carefully. There had been mostly silence between Dan and Eleanor during the drive home from Lansing, but suddenly Eleanor let out a long sigh, which turned almost into a sob. "Dad, I truly didn't understand until today what our business is all about. And now that I know – and have seen what it means to so many people - I see how wisely it was set up and why it has survived the depression when so many other corporations have folded. What would have happened to all those people who work for the associates if Grandpa Underhill and Grandpa Marlowe hadn't had the foresight to protect them?"

"Who knows, Honey. All we can do is look around us and see the current state of the economy and presume that these people who are now earning a living wage would have instead been in the bread lines. God had a purpose in the founding of such a business as ours, and it's our privilege to keep it going and to watch it helping so many people. I wish my father and Grandpa Underhill could have lived to see it."

"You really think God had something to do with it, Dad? Do you think God really has an interest in such things as business and factories and the economy?" Nell's voice revealed a deeply rooted skepticism.

"No. I don't just *think* He is interested, I *know* He is. He has a concern about *everything* that goes on with people. He's interested in *people,* Nell, all kinds of people. Even dirty little urchins flipping coins in the dirt. *Especially* in those little urchins, because He loves little children in a very special way. Maybe you need to get out your Bible and start reading it, my dear. You'll find answers to a lot of your questions in that Book."

Eleanor realized with a pang in her heart that she didn't even know where to find her Bible – the one she had received when she joined the church as an early teen. With a sudden determination, she vowed to herself that she would find it, and try to fit together some of the things she had just learned from the conversations with her father and Grandma Christy, and from the things she had witnessed today.

"Dad, when did you last talk to Grandma Christy?" she wondered aloud.

"Oh, it's been several days. I plan to pay her a visit tonight. I've been so busy that I'm afraid I've neglected her lately, and I need to make it up to her."

"Then he hasn't talked to her since I went to see her yesterday. I thought maybe she suggested this trip today! Maybe God Himself is showing me the answers to my questions! Could it be?" Eleanor felt a sense of awe at the thought that God would even bother with her after the way she had treated Him for most of her life. For the first time she really had an urge to pray. *"Dear God, please help me to find my way. Help me to understand what you want me to do. I don't want to disappoint Dad and Grandma Christy, but somehow most of all, I don't want to disappoint YOU!"*

Chapter 19

Christmas that year was all that could be expected of it. Between the Wheaton home festivities with Grandma and Grandpa Wheaton, and the many events planned by the Marlowes, the holiday passed quickly and by the time it was over, the two families were fast friends. Even Eleanor and Celee found each other good company, and Grandmother Christy observed the friendship with great relief. She assured herself that evidently Eleanor was finally growing up, and felt hope in her heart that her granddaughter would soon find her place in the world and know peace in her heart.

Billy, along with Rosi and other adults in the family, watched Josh and Celee together and thought that they had never seen two young people who seemed so right for each other. All in all, Christmas was a huge success and everyone looked forward to the happy events that were planned in the year that followed.

In Little Rapids, Christmas was also memorable, but with a sadness between Kent and Patsy, who both dreaded the year to come when they would be separated for so many months. However, to them both, Christmas had a new meaning. Their newfound life in Christ had changed them both, and the Holts and the Walters, though mystified by the change, observed their children with satisfaction. They had never believed that what was such a terrible catastrophe to them could be endured with such courage and peace as Kent and Patsy displayed.

Penny watched them with dismay, and felt that she was the only one who was really suffering as a result of the accident. How could Patsy be so uncomplaining and sweet about her condition, and didn't Kent really care at all? Penny was not only puzzled, but for the first time in her life, she felt that she didn't understand her twin, and that something had been taken away from them. They loved each other as always, but the sense of being "one", the sense of connection, was just not there. She was comforted by the thought of her friendship with Eleanor.

However, there was one event that for a time brought them all together again in the old way.

Just before Christmas, Barney had paid John a visit.

"You know, John, I've had a great idea, and with your permission I'd like to work it out for Patsy. I know how much she loved to ride, and I've been trying to figure out a way to make it possible for her to mount a horse. I think she could ride all right if she could just get on from the wheelchair."

John was listening with great interest. "I agree. And what do you have in mind, Barney?"

"I believe I could build a ramp up to a mounting platform so that we could get her wheelchair up. The horse could wait beside the platform and we could help her from the wheelchair onto the horse's back. Once she could get her feet in the stirrups I think she could ride like she used to. What do you think?"

"Barney, I can't think of a better Christmas present for her. Just let me talk to her doctor and make sure she is able to do it. I'll talk to him tomorrow."

"Great. In the meantime I'll experiment with building the ramp and the platform, so we can show him if he wants to inspect it. Then you and I together can make sure it's safe and solid. You know something? That horse of hers will be just as happy about this as Patsy will. Sweet Girl sure misses her!"

The next day John, with great excitement, reported to Barney that the doctor was pleased with the plan. "He was very enthusiastic, Barney. His only caution was that we strictly supervise every move she makes, and be sure that the horse is very dependable. He thought that would be excellent therapy for our girl!"

Barney slapped his knee in glee. "We both know that Sweet Girl is as gentle as they come, so there'll be no problem with that." And the two men proceeded to work together secretly, finally satisfied that the mounting platform was built to their satisfaction. As excited as two boys, they managed with difficulty to save their big surprise until Christmas Day.

After all the presents had been opened, Christmas dinner had been eaten and pronounced the best ever, everyone was ready for a nap. However, John could wait no longer to spring his surprise.

"I'll give all of you just one hour to digest that huge dinner, then we're going for a ride. I have one more present to give my girls, and I want all of you to go along to see it."

"Dad, what in the world could you give us that we don't already have? Just look around you! We have more presents than we had toys when we were little girls! What else could we want?" Patsy truly felt that her parents and friends were spoiling her, she supposed because of the accident, and it embarrassed her.

"Well, Honey, think of something that you haven't been able to do since the accident — something you always loved to do. One of your friends suggested a way to help you do it again, and he wants it to be a surprise. So that's all I'm going to tell you. Now remember, everybody, the old family bus leaves in one hour, sharp!"

The "old family bus" took off on schedule, with the Walters car following close behind. As they wound their way through the woods, Penny exclaimed, "Dad, this is the road to Barney's Stables! Are we going there?"

"Just wait and see, Kitten. Don't spoil my surprise," John smiled. He could hardly wait himself to see Patsy's face.

And he was not disappointed. At first she was puzzled when she saw the mounting platform, then slowly it dawned on her. "Dad! Did you and Barney fix that so I could go riding again?" Her face glowed. "What a wonderful idea! Oh, Penny, think of that! We can ride together again! I wonder if my own Sweet Girl will remember me?"

"Well, you'll soon see. There comes Barney leading Sweet Girl now. Here, I brought an apple for you to give her. That will help you get reacquainted again!"

However, the apple was welcome but unnecessary. Sweet Girl nuzzled Patsy affectionately, and seeming to know how important this reunion was, held very still as Barney and John helped her into the saddle.

Kent and Penny were on their favorite mounts, waiting for Patsy to get settled and secure. It was truly the best Christmas present of all. John pumped Barney's hand in appreciation.

"You don't have any idea how much this means to Patsy – and to all of us." There were actually tears in John's eyes. "We still don't know if she will ever walk again, but this will give her the gift of freedom, and that's one of the things that she has missed so much! Thank you, my friend, for such a wonderful idea."

"You know, John, I haven't had so much pleasure out of anything in years. Just to see her excitement when Sweet Girl stepped off and she felt herself riding again! It was worth everything in the world to see how happy it made her. That was *my* best Christmas gift, and I hope to see her out here often to enjoy it!"

Of course, the New Year brought changes, as New Years always do. Again Josh and Celee had to endure separation, but only for a time. There was much to do to get ready for a wedding, so for Celee the time would be full of activity and preparation. For Josh, too, there were plans to make, a business to run, and frequent hops in his Cessna to see Celee.

On a cold February day, Josh straightened up, pulled out his handkerchief, and wiped the sweat from his forehead. It was warm here in the hanger, even though it had started to snow outside. He fingered the little part he had just removed from his beloved aircraft, and looked at it thoughtfully. It just needed a slight adaptation to fit properly and do its job adequately, but it was beyond his power to do the job. He would need to look up an ironmonger and describe what he wanted done, and hope that the man could do the work.

He slipped the part into his pocket and walked toward the office, racking his brain with the effort to think of someone to whom he could take his problem. He was sure that he had heard of some metal works nearby, but he was positive it wasn't in Charlotte. He needed the job done – and done quickly – as he had an appointment the end of the week to fly a client to Petosky.

His father was sitting at his desk in the front office. "Son, you're looking mighty solemn. What's your problem?"

Josh pulled the part from his pocket and explained what he needed to have done. "You know, Dad, I'm sure there's an iron works somewhere nearby, but for the life of me I can't think where it is. Do you happen to know? I really need to get this done in a hurry."

Billy knit his brow in deep thought. "You know, I think you told me one day that your Aunt Julie mentioned one over in Little Rapids. You didn't tell me the name, though, so I guess that's all the help I can give you."

"That's it, Dad! That's it! Do you remember when Aunt Julie and Uncle Sig helped the young people who had the car accident? The father of the girl who was hit has a metal works over there. That's the one!" Josh was jubilant. "I'll run over there tomorrow and see if he can help me. I know Aunt Julie said he does some exquisite ironwork, so maybe he's my man. Thanks, Dad!" Josh started to the door. "You about ready to go home for the day? Shall we lock up and go see what Aunt Ruthie has for supper? I'm ready to eat!"

Smiling, Billy stood, locked his desk, and proceeded to close the office. Josh checked the hangar, and made sure it was properly closed and locked. The two boys who worked for them had left an hour before, so he double checked to make sure that they had left everything in order.

Fortunately, the snow fall had been light, and there was only a white dusting on the roads in the morning. The night before, Josh had made a drawing of the part he wanted, so with the part and the drawing, he set out early for Little Rapids. He would swing by Aunt Julie's and get directions from her.

Her directions were precise and he quickly located the Holt-Waggoner Metal Works. He brought his roadster to a stop in front of the "Office" sign, and, grabbing his briefcase containing the part and the drawing, he headed for the entrance. Then he saw the small display window and came to a sudden halt. Those little old fashioned iron toys and penny banks, the same display that had captured John Holt's eye many years ago, had caught his attention. In spite of his haste, he found himself mesmerized by the small figures. They were constructed with superb skill and great artistic imagination. 'An *almost loving touch*' he thought to himself. What a talent their creator had! He stood in wonder and in admiration of such beauty to be found in such a mundane place as an ironworks factory!

He was greeted by a young girl, who rose from behind her desk as he entered the room. "Good morning." Her smile lit up the room. "Can I help you?"

"Yes, thank you. I would like to see Mr. Holt. I have a small but very important job to be done, and I need some expert help. Mr. Holt comes highly recommended."

"Of course you may see him. If you'll wait just a few moments, I'll get him. Have a seat, please," and she motioned to one of two comfortable chairs, the only furniture besides her desk in the room.

As she left the room, Josh's attention again turned to the display window. He longed to pick up the toys and examine them more closely, but decided instead to ask about them first, and learn who made them.

He had waited only a very few moments when the shop door opened and John Holt entered. He smiled as he saw the interest with which Josh was regarding the display.

"My father-in-law, Albert Waggoner, was the artist who created those toys. He had a great talent and loved making toys more than anything in the world. You don't see many iron toys any more, do you? I treasure those – and others that he made – a great deal."

"I was admiring the intricate detail with which they are constructed. A man would have to love his craft to produce such pieces. Even the expressions on the faces and the movement captured in the animals are perfect. He was quite an artist, wasn't he?" Josh could hardly bear to bring his attention back to business, however, he knew he had little time to get his own job done.

He stuck out his hand, and the two men introduced themselves. "What can I do for you, Mr. O'Conner?" asked John.

"Just call me Josh, if you don't mind. Now do you have a table where I could lay out a drawing and explain what I need?" asked Josh. "I brought a small part from my Cessna that needs some adapting and I've made a drawing to show you just what I have in mind."

As John and Josh pored over the drawing and Josh explained what he needed, John nodded his head with quick comprehension. "I can do that, Josh. I believe I see what has to be done. This part is small, but if it is a matter of safety, it needs to have a strong lock on it, which could be done this way." John grabbed a pencil and made a quick sketch.

"That's it!" Josh exclaimed in delight. "That's exactly what it needs. Can you do the job?"

"I certainly can. When do you need it?" John liked this young man and the feeling seemed to be mutual.

"As soon as you can do it. I am in a bit of a rush."

John nodded. "How about tomorrow morning? I can work on it this afternoon, and it shouldn't take but a couple of hours to do the job."

"Great. I'll pick it up sometime before noon tomorrow." Josh was turning to go when the girl reappeared in the office door.

"Dad, there's a call for you. Shall I have them call back, or can you come to the phone?"

"I'll be there in a minute, Penny. Josh, this is my daughter, Penny, who is learning about the business, and is about to make my office into the most modern, up-to-date, efficient operation in Little Rapids!" John grinned as she blushed with pleasure at his evident pride in her. "I didn't mean to embarrass you, Honey, but I don't know how I managed before you grew up enough to take over!"

Josh acknowledged the introduction, and suddenly remembered that this was the family that had suffered the tragedy his aunt and uncle had witnessed. He wondered about the injured girl, but felt it would not be right to even inquire about her, since they were not aware of his family connections with the Andersons. However, this had been an interesting trip, and as he headed for home, he reflected that this contact might be a very useful one in the future. It often took more time than he liked to get parts that he needed, and to have such a resource close by would be very convenient.

With the accelerator to the floor, Josh headed back to Charlotte. He was anxious to do his pre-flight inspection, because he would have to take off almost immediately after he picked up the part and got it installed. The flight up to Petosky would take only a short time, but he never flew any distance without going over the Cessna thoroughly. He had an excellent safety record and he intended to keep it that way.

Unbidden, that beautiful smile on Holt's daughter's face flashed through his mind. She was certainly an attractive girl, and he wondered if her twin was as pretty as she. He prayed that she wouldn't be a cripple the rest of her life, and his thoughts drifted to the young man who had been so terribly upset by his friend's accident. He sensed that there was something more than friendship there, and he smiled to himself. When one was in love, it seemed that everyone else should be enjoying the same wonderful feelings! And he couldn't help but wonder if that young fellow had had his questions answered. He would have to ask Uncle Sig. It was important that he have those answers, especially if he was going back to the same college where he had lost his faith.

Deep in his thoughts, he found himself turning into the shop driveway almost before he knew it. As he breezed through the front office, Billy called to him, "Josh, Mr. Wenzel called to verify your appointment to fly him up to Petosky. Wants you to call him back. I guess that trip is pretty important to him."

"Thanks, Dad, I'll do it right now."

He dialed his client's number, and with a very short conversation, assured the man that the flight would be on schedule, the only variable being the weather. "You know that, though, without my telling you. However, the outlook for tomorrow is clear, so we should have no problems."

John Holt had the part ready for him on schedule, and Mr. Wenzel was awaiting him when he returned from picking it up. It took only a very few minutes to snap the new piece into place and it fit perfectly. Soon the two men were on their way, and, finding each other to be good conversationalists, were quickly getting acquainted.

"Have you been up in this part of the state much, Josh?" asked his talkative passenger.

Josh smiled and nodded. "Yes, sir. As a matter of fact, I'm engaged to a girl whose family lives just a ways north of Petosky, in a little place called Pellston, so I've been up here once or twice."

"Ah, yes, Pellston. That brings back memories. When I was a boy, we lived in Pellston for several years. Nice folks there. Mostly German, especially in the little town just south of Pellston, called Brutus. Don't suppose you ever heard of Brutus. It's just a little stop on the railroad track."

Josh laughed. "It's a small world, sir. I spent Thanksgiving with my fiance's family, some of whom live in Brutus. There was quite a family gathering there, at a big farmhouse on a hill, where her aunt and uncle live."

"Would that be the Beckman farm, by any chance? My parents and the Beckmans were good friends."

Josh turned to his passenger in amazement. "Well, as I said, it *is* a small world! Yes, Beckman is their name. My future mother in law is Mrs. Beckman's younger sister!"

"Well, my friend, you are marrying into a fine family. Jesse Beckman is probably one of the most respected men in this north country. As a matter of fact, his wife's family, the Huebners, are good people too. They all came over from Germany about the turn of the century, and are hard-working, honest people. I went to school for a year or two with one of the boys, Karl, but he had to drop out of school to help his father in the mill, I think it was. I kind of lost track of the family, but

I did hear the sad news that Karl lost his wife, and was left with several children to raise without their mother."

"Yes, I met some of Karl's children when I was up here. I think he had four, if I remember right. He seems to have done a good job raising them. They seemed like nice kids."

"I think he had a lot of help from his family."

The two men chatted on for a while about one thing and another, finding several subjects of mutual interest. Suddenly Mr. Wenzel returned to the subject of Karl Huebner's children. "You know, I just remembered. Karl had two more children, but I don't know where they are. I don't know if anyone knows. It seems that Karl's wife died when they were born – they were twins, you know – and even with all his family around, Karl couldn't take care of them. He had to adopt them out to someone, and that was sad. It must be hard to have to give away some of your children."

The subject was dropped there, because Josh had to give all his attention to landing the Cessna safely. Mr. Wenzel took care of his business in short order, and the conversation on the way back to Charlotte took another direction. But Josh couldn't shake off the sad feeling that had come over him when he heard about Celee's Uncle Karl having to give away his newborn twins. No wonder he had seemed so sad and quiet, even in the midst of a family reunion. Josh wondered if one could ever get over having to give his children away. His heart ached mightily even thinking about it, and he felt great sadness for Karl.

Chapter 20

(Kent to Patsy, January 12)

"Dear Patsy. No, I'll try that again. My darling Patsy. Yes, that's better! Honey, it feels good just to write the words, but I do so terribly wish that I could not only say them to you, but could hold you close while I tell you how much I love you! However, I'm not complaining. I know you're waiting for me, and I know also that I have to keep my mind on my work, so that I can be ready when our time comes to start a home together! Just thinking about you helps me get through the day, though. You give me a reason for working at my studies, even when they get boring and tiresome!

"And believe me, some of them almost make me want to curl up my toes and die before my time! (Not seriously, Honey, because I intend to stick around until we're back together again!) The business courses are fine; they are about things I really need to know. But I am required to take a course in Philosophy, which to me is a waste of time. It's all about what *men* think, and a lot of it isn't at all what Pastor Anderson has taught me and which I now know to be the truth. The main thing I've learned is that it doesn't really make any difference what men think, because what they think isn't necessarily the truth, and the truth is really the only thing that matters. However, I have to listen, because I have to pass the tests! I manage to stay awake, but you would laugh at how many of the students catch up on their sleep in that class!

"I have a good roommate this semester. He's a lot of fun, but not like Tim – my last roommate - was. Tim was crazy all the time and never cared about studying. My new roommate is someone I can talk to, and we exchange a lot of ideas. But when we study, we study! His name is Roger, by the way. You remember I told you that when I was here last year I had to go to the library to find a quiet place to study. There's a large percentage of my classmates who seem to just come to college to have a good time – and they think that's what everybody else is here for, too! So having spent a year with Tim, I really appreciate Roger!

"I did see Tim and some of his crowd a day or two after I got back, and we got into a discussion about the class in "Bible As Literature". I told the guys that I had come to believe that the Bible was true, and I sure got laughed at! Tim started to call me 'Preacher' and the other boys took it up, so now that's my nickname. You know, they mean to humiliate and tease me by calling me that, but I really don't mind at all. I remember that they called Jesus names that were a lot worse than Preacher, so I guess I can stand being laughed at a little bit!

"Strangely enough, my favorite subject this semester is American Literature, and since you know that I'm not a great reader or scholar, I'm sure you'll be surprised at that! But I've been amazed to learn that the "Fathers of our country" and those who wrote the important documents that we study both in Lit and History say the same things that Pastor Anderson does about what they believed. And they sure made it pretty clear that they gave God the credit for bringing them to a new land where they could find freedom. Once I realized that, I knew that I was in pretty good company!

"Gotta run, Honey. I have some big assignments and I better get started on them! Don't forget for a minute that I love you! Your picture is setting on the desk right in front of me, so I can imagine I'm talking to you as I write these words! Without your picture, the whole room would be dark and terribly dreary! I'm yours forever, Kent."

*

(Patsy to Kent, January 16)

"Darling, I live for your letters! You know how much I love my family and how hard they try to keep my mind off my problems, but somehow Little Rapids is empty without you! Penny is very busy at Dad's office, and when they talk about business I'm pretty much in the dark. But I'm glad Penny is happy and I know it saves Dad a lot of money to have her working with him. And he declares that the improvements she has made in office procedures have been worth a fortune to him!

"My best times are when Penny and I can go out to Barney's and ride. Sweet Girl is always so glad to see me, and it almost seems like she knows she should be extra careful when I'm riding her. The mounting platform that Dad and Barney made is wonderful. Even though they have to help me mount and dismount, I don't feel like a cripple when I'm riding.

"Last week when we were out at Barney's we saw Pastor and Mrs. Anderson there. They asked about you, and said they wished they had seen you before you left to go back to college. We only had a few minutes to talk, because they came just as we were getting ready to go home, and Dad seemed to be in a great hurry. I had the feeling that he didn't want them to be talking to us. I know that's silly, because they are such good friends and there's no reason why we shouldn't see them from time to time, but maybe he really was in a hurry. He did work late that night – I guess because he had taken time out to go with us to Barney's stables.

"I know you've only been gone two weeks, but, Kent, it seems like two months to me! I love to read about what you're doing, and I can picture you going about campus and attending classes. But I wish you would describe your roommate in more detail, and tell me more about what he's like. And tell me how your room looks. How have you decorated it? What do you have on the walls? I know this sounds silly to you, but I want to have a picture in my mind of where you spend your time and how you live. It just would make me feel closer to you, and Honey, I miss you so much I need every little detail I can get!

"Do you sometimes wonder about the times when we were growing up and were just like brother and sister? It's so different with us now, and sometimes I wonder how it happened that suddenly we were in love! Do you suppose that God had this in store for us all the time, and just gave us our childhood together so we could get acquainted with each other? My love always, Darling. Your Patsy."

*

(Kent to Patsy, February 12)

"Sweetheart, I miss you so much. I can't even tell you how much. But your letters keep me going. Please keep them coming. The days I don't hear from you aren't worth counting!

"You asked about my roommate, Roger. His last name is Dawson – Roger Dawson. Well, he's a good looking fellow and a good athlete. He's about as tall as I am and is really into basketball. But like I told you, he's a good student too, and takes his studying seriously. He has red hair, but without the disposition that most people associate with red haired people. I guess he could lose his temper if he were pushed hard enough, but mostly he's easygoing and everybody seems to like him. I know I do, and I think I'm really lucky to have him for a roommate.

"I want to tell you about what happened yesterday. I knew it had to happen sometime, but I wasn't expecting it so soon. It was an interesting encounter, but I'm glad it's over! I was on my way to the dining hall when my former science professor, Dr. Hopper, fell in step with me. He asked me about the semester I was out of school, and told me how sorry he was to hear about your accident. He's a pretty decent fellow until he gets started on the subject of evolution.

"And it didn't take long for him to get started! He had heard some of Tim's crowd make wisecracks about some student they called "Preacher", and he finally found out that it was me they were laughing at. He seemed shocked and disappointed to hear that I had told them that I didn't believe that evolution was even scientific, and that I had come to believe the Bible account of creation. He was aghast to think that I would admit it even if I do believe such a 'ridiculous' thing (as he described it)! I told him that I had given it a lot of thought, and found it much easier to believe the book of Genesis than to believe in evolution. When I told him that to me the Bible made a lot more sense than the theory of evolution, I thought he would explode! It was like I had committed some great, unthinkable crime or that somehow I was being blasphemous! He told me that I was being very foolish and that if I wanted to be respected in either the business world or the scientific world, I should never let anyone know how I felt. I replied that I didn't care who knew what I believed, and that, furthermore, I believe the Bible in more ways than just the creation story. I think he really is convinced that I have lost my mind!

"You know, Patsy, somehow I'm relieved that he came to me and that we got the subject out in the open. I know he thinks I'm a fool, but I don't care one bit. I'm just as entitled to my opinion as he is to his, even if he is a professor! And this year, he can't fail me for not agreeing with him, because I've already passed his course with honors! Last year I put down what I knew he wanted to hear when I took his exams, and I always aced them! But now, I don't think I could do that. As a matter of fact, now that I know the truth I'm pretty sure I would do it differently. Maybe I would answer the way he wants, then add that I really don't believe any of it, and tell him why! Of course then I was being honest, but if I had it do over again, my honesty would demand that I tell him how I really feel about what he taught me. Well, I guess it's a good thing that his classes are behind me!

"Need I say again how much I look forward to your letters? I know I'm asking a lot of you, but if there's not a letter from you in my mailbox my day is spoiled! So I don't mind it even when they're short. Just seeing your handwriting gives me a 'shot in the arm' and keeps me going!

"And I haven't forgotten that Valentines' day is nearly here! There's a package in the mail and I hope it gets to you on time.

"So, as always, darling, I love you and I promise you that I always will! Kent."

*

(Kent to Patsy, April 1)

"Have I told you lately how much I love you, my precious Patsy! I just don't want you to forget it!

"I stay so busy that time is really flying by. I hope it's passing quickly for you too. Something so exciting has happened, that I can't help but be glad I came back to school, even if it meant leaving you for a time! Just listen to this!!

"First, as I told you, my roommate and I frequently exchange ideas, and sometimes we get into quite heated discussions. (It's good practice for us, because we're both in the debating club.) We never get uptight, but just argue things for the sake of arguing, and try to apply logic properly – and mainly, of course try to offer indisputable proof that our side is the correct one!

"We have so much fun with it, that other fellows have begun slipping into our room to listen in, and occasionally they get into the discussion. One of our favorite subjects is Evolution vs. the Bible, and I guess we get onto that subject more often than anything else, even though politics, ethics, war, and other things have their turn. Anyway, I'm always at an advantage because I've learned so much from Pastor Anderson.

"The exciting thing is that the group has grown so much that we've had to move down to the lobby to have more space, and our discussions have turned into kind of a club, with the members all serious about searching for the truth. I told the fellows that it was when I really began believing the Bible to be true, that I also began to understand the things it taught me. I also told them that I had accepted Jesus Christ as being not only the ultimate Truth, but my personal Savior. Instead of laughing as I expected some of them to do, they became very quiet and thoughtful, and yesterday Roger told me that he had accepted Christ, too! Wow, that was great, and even greater, I think some of the others will soon admit to believing, too.

"And were we ever shocked when, one evening, Professor Hopper slipped quietly in and sat down to listen. He didn't say anything (which surprised us) but just listened, then slipped out as quietly as he came in. I am hoping, (though I can hardly believe it to be true), that he's seeing that evolution just doesn't make sense. Apparently, he doesn't intend to make trouble for us, (at least we haven't been told to stop our meetings yet), and just maybe he's starting to think about what he heard there. Wouldn't that be a miracle if he should change his mind? According to Pastor Anderson, "with God anything is possible!"

"Keep those letters coming, Sweetheart! They're like food and drink to me and just as necessary!

"All my love, Kent."

Patsy always devoured Kent's letters, for to her they were now the only link she had to her new life. She would share with Penny and her parents bits of news concerning his school life, but, of course, his letters were her own. She knew Penny felt left out, but she had promised Kent to guard their secret, and she intended to keep it close to her heart. She also knew that no one else in either family would really be interested in what was so exciting to him – and to her. They would politely listen when she tried to explain what she and Kent had come to know through the Andersons, but there was no real interest. Penny would just look at her, shake her head, and change the subject.

Often she would have liked to talk to Mrs. Anderson after receiving one of Kent's letters, but it had been a long time since she had seen the Pastor and his wife. She wistfully remembered the few times that she had really been able to share her feelings with someone who understood and could give her answers. It was terribly lonesome without Kent, not just because they were in love, but because she felt isolated. However, she wrote him nearly every day, and this always helped her feel better.

She was painfully conscious of the widening gulf between herself and Penny. There was no way that she could discuss with her twin anything that she had learned from the Andersons. Penny still went to church with the family regularly, but never had a comment on anything she heard there. Patsy was convinced, however, that both her mother and father felt that church attendance was very important, and that Penny would not have risked hurting them by refusing to attend church. That left Patsy saddened because, for the first time in their lives, she and her sister seemed unable to communicate about something that really mattered.

However, there was something that she *could* share with Penny; something that she had not even been able to tell Kent yet. It wasn't that she was keeping secrets from him. It was just that she couldn't tell him until she was sure that it would not cause him to worry. He couldn't afford to be distracted from his studies at this crucial point in their lives. Her family and Kent's family were as excited as she, but had promised not to say anything to him just yet. If it was true that a miracle was possible, and that she might really walk again, she would tell him, but until then she wouldn't raise his hopes.

Easter vacation had come and gone, and Kent had not come home. He had felt that he must use the extra time to do some research and write a paper that would count for one complete course, thus increasing the possibility that he could graduate with his class, in spite of losing one semester. Both of them had been disappointed, but agreed that it was the wise thing for him to do.

But now she was elated that she could give him something to raise his spirits, and she couldn't wait to tell him the news. No longer was it a secret, but it was a real possibility. It was a ray of hope that perhaps their lives could become normal again. They had both accepted the fact that she might never walk again, so this news filled her with almost unbearable anticipation. Of course she had to keep reminding herself that it was just a hope – not a reality – but for now that was enough.

(Patsy to Kent, June 6)

"My Darling Kent, I have some exciting news for you and I can hardly wait to get it down on paper! I've been waiting to tell you until I could give you the whole story, and not have to make you wait and worry for the next 'installment!'

"The doctor has been hinting around for a month or two that he might have some good news for me, but wouldn't tell me more than that. I was almost afraid to believe that I could hope to walk again, and he didn't say that, but seemed unusually pleased with my progress.

"On my last visit, he made an extremely detailed and careful examination of my injured leg and hip, then made an appointment for me to go to the hospital for some additional x-rays. I wondered what this was all about, because I had been doing fine and felt that he was pleased with my progress. He seemed to be very satisfied with what his examination revealed and that made me even more curious. After the x-rays were over, he took me into the consulting room and called Mom and Dad in, too. He acted as if he didn't have another thing to do that day, and just sat down with us to talk. I supposed he would tell us about the x-rays, but he didn't even mention them.

"'I have something that I want to discuss very seriously with you,' he began, and my heart fell. I thought it must be something bad. Instead, he said, 'Patsy, you've made great progress – better than I ever expected. To be honest, I never – until now - had any real hope that you would ever walk again, and I've tried not to give you any false encouragement. However, just recently I heard of a new procedure that holds out some real possibilities. I want you to know that I've done a lot of research on it before I even dared to mention it to you, but I'm convinced that it is something that we should look at. It can be performed in our hospital here in Little Rapids, but I would have to have a specialist come and do the operation. It's not something that I would dare to do myself and, to be totally honest, it's not without risks to you. That I want you to understand.' By this time I was so excited I was hardly listening to him! But his next words caught my attention again.

'If you are satisfied with the status quo (and Darling, you know I'm *not*) and since you are getting around very well with your wheel chair and adjusting to life as you are living it now – then you may not want to even consider what I have to suggest. However, all reports that I have read on this new procedure indicate that – though there *are* risks involved – they indicate that we might be able to return you to a nearly normal life. You might always have some stiffness in your leg, but if the operation is successful, you would be able to walk unassisted and function normally in every way. Now – mind you' he lifted his hand for silence as Dad started to speak. 'I can't guarantee anything, and I want both you and Patsy to think this over very carefully. If the operation is *not* successful, she might not be as well off as she is now. (My heart sank at that!) So this is not to be decided in haste. I have some detailed information available if you care to see it, and I also have accounts of some cases in which the outcome was very successful. But I don't want to influence you. I just want you to know what has become available in the last year, and you must make your own decision.'

"It was very quiet for a few minutes. I was bursting with excitement, but couldn't seem to get the right words out. Then Dad asked his question. He really put in words what I was thinking. After all, if this were really a possibility, but so very new that it was still risky, he wondered if it wouldn't be wise to wait a bit until the procedure had been tested and refined. 'Doctor, could we wait for more information and perhaps more proof that the operation will be successful and not so full of risk before we make a decision? You know, this is Patsy's future that's at stake. Since she's doing so well now, it wouldn't hurt her to wait, would it?'

"The doctor smiled and nodded. 'That's exactly what I would recommend, John. Since she is steadily improving in her general health, and has learned to live with her disability, it would not be a problem to wait a year, or even two years. By that time we will know more about this procedure, and the odds of success should be greatly increased. But I felt that now I could safely hold out hope for the future to your girl, and that in itself will help her to regain her strength and peace of mind.'

"We left the doctor's office, and I still couldn't believe what I had heard. You know we've prayed for my deliverance from the wheelchair that seems still to anchor me to the earth. My first reaction was to try anything – *anything* – that would give me my freedom again. But the risk just seemed too great. Now I see that God has given us hope and I don't mind waiting – because somehow now I know that one day I *will* walk again. Now I can share that hope with you, and it will help both of us to go on doing what we have to do! We can pray together about this, and maybe God is really going to let us have a normal marriage after all! How I would love to be able to *walk* down the aisle on Dad's arm! But, Kent, whatever God does is all right, because I know He will give us what's best for us. But, Honey, isn't it wonderful to have *hope!*

"I would love to talk to Mrs. Anderson about all of this, but for some reason Dad doesn't want us to have much to do with the Andersons. He seems to feel that they would take us away from our old friends and the church we've always attended. I know they wouldn't, and maybe someday he'll realize that. But for now, I don't see them at all.

"Somehow, Sweetheart, the future looks so much brighter, and life is really exciting again since that visit to the doctor. I hope this letter makes you feel that way, too!

All my love, Darling,
Your Patsy"

*

(By return mail)

"Darling, did you hear me whooping and hollering way over in Little Rapids? What wonderful news! Isn't the Lord good to us!!!! With a prospect like that, the next six months should be a breeze! Add to that great news the fact that it's now certain that I can graduate with my class. And when I get home, we can start making real plans for the future! (I just noticed that almost all of my sentences ended with one or more exclamation points! That's just the way I feel right now – like one BIG exclamation point of praise!) I love you, Patsy, more than I can ever tell you. It will take the rest of my life and eternity for me to show you how much you mean to me! (There go some more exclamation points! This letter could never be written without them!) As always, my love, Kent."

Chapter 21

*P*lans and preparations for a wedding seemed endless. Especially to a prospective bridegroom who would like to just visit the preacher with his bride and with no fanfare say "I do, with all my heart!" Josh was excited and impatient, but understanding, all at the same time. He knew that he and Celee would have this wedding to remember all their lives, and he was content. As for her mother, his grandmother, Aunt Julie, Grandmother Christy, and everyone else in the family, they would be heartbroken if they couldn't put on this wedding exactly as it should be done. So he tried very hard to listen with patience and interest to all the plans. They were seemingly endless! Details of fabrics, colors, dinners, wedding parties, showers, and numerous other items that he could never even have imagined, seemed to dominate everyone's thoughts and conversation. He assented to everything and smiled, happy to see the pleasure and excitement the preparations gave to those he loved.

However, one important development made everything fall in place and gave him great joy. It came about one evening, as the Wheaton family was gathered in the comfortable family room, now the focal point of all the planning. It was also where the lives and memories of the elderly couple hung on every wall and were scattered on the mantle and every small table where there was space. There were pictures of Celee's father Dan, his brother Frank, and his sister, Fran (better known as Sis) in their growing up days. The lovely, old-fashioned wedding picture of Grandma and Grandpa Wheaton was to Josh the centerpiece of the room! A rosy glow from Grandma Wheaton's prized Tiffany lamp lent a coziness to the room, and highlighted the sheen on the beautiful rosewood grand piano in the corner.

Together, Josh and Celee had inspected every picture in the room and Josh felt that he had been given a special introduction to each person shown there. Comfortable in the knowledge that this would be *his* family, too, very soon, he tried to remember the story about each picture. Tonight he had let his eyes travel from picture to picture, reviewing the names and events pictured, as he had done in Babette's home, and silently lifted his heart in thanksgiving. *"You've been so good, Lord, in giving me such a wonderful family. How blessed I have been to be Billy's son, and to have not only the Marlowes, but now also the Huebners and Wheatons as loved ones, and to know that they all love me as if I were their own. But most of all, Lord, thank you for Celee and the privilege you are giving us to start our own home together. Help us to always keep You at the center of our lives. Your faithfulness to us is amazing, Lord! Thank you again."*

"Josh, how do you feel about Grandpa's idea? Would it be good for you?" He was suddenly aware that he had not heard the discussion, so involved had he been in his own thoughts.

"I'm sorry, Honey. Forgive me, Mr. Wheaton. I was wool-gathering. No, to be truthful, I was pondering on how good the Lord has been to us, and I didn't hear a word."

"That's all right, Son. You have a right to be preoccupied, but I think you'd better listen up now. I have a suggestion, and if it's all right with you and Celee, and is agreeable with Celee's mother, I will be more than pleased. However, if it's not to the liking of everyone concerned, that's fine, too. This is your wedding and you must have it just as you want it."

"Thanks, Mr. Wheaton. What was your suggestion?"

"First of all, I'm Grandpa to you. After all, you are marrying my granddaughter, so let's have no more of this 'Mr. Wheaton' stuff." Josh smiled and nodded his head. "So here's my suggestion, and if you'll humor an old man, it will give me great joy. Since my son Dan can only be with us in spirit, I would like to stand in his place as a father to Celee and give her the wedding as he would do if he were here. Rosi, you know how much Dan meant to us, and how important you and our granddaughters are to us. So, if it would be agreeable to you, I would like to suggest that we have it in our little church here where Dan grew up." He turned directly to Rosi and added, "I hope it wouldn't make it too difficult for your family to attend, my dear, and I'll take care of any expense to see that they get here." Settling back in his chair, he continued, "Then we could have the reception right here in our house, which would please *my* sweetheart no end!"

Grandma Wheaton interrupted breathlessly, "Oh, please let us do this for you. It would bring such joy to us to have such a special wedding here, and we wouldn't interfere in any of the planning – but we would love to pay for it." Then with a touch of sadness she added, "Since we didn't go to Dan and Rosi's wedding – a sad fact that we have always regretted – and since Sis doesn't show any signs of ever wanting to get married – well, you can see how much it would mean to us!"

Rosi left her chair, went across the room and kissed each of the old couple's soft, wrinkled faces. "Of course, Father Wheaton. I would be grateful to have your help, and if it's agreeable with Josh and Celee, I think it would be perfect. And I know it would have made Dan very happy."

Josh looked at Celee with a question in his eyes, and was satisfied with what he saw. His heart had leaped at the suggestion, because this was what he had wanted (prayed for and hoped for) that they could be married in the little church just outside the city of Charlotte, that was so dear to his heart. It had been the scene of so many of the meaningful events and decisions of his life, and it was his spiritual home. However, he had known it was up to the mother of the bride to provide for the wedding, so the financial aspect, while a wonderful gift, hadn't really entered into the picture as far as he was concerned. But he knew how much easier this plan would make it for Rosi. She would have all the responsibility of planning for a new school year, plus the details of a wedding if it were held up north. This way she could enjoy the preparations for her eldest daughter's wedding, without the exhaustion that so often went with such a large event, as this was sure to be. So he looked at Grandpa Wheaton with a smile and gave him the answer he wanted to hear.

"Grandpa Wheaton, I think that would be perfect. It would be a dream come true for me to be able to be married in my own little church home. And it would certainly make *my* family happy too! Thank you!"

At his reply, Grandma and Grandpa Wheaton visibly relaxed. They had so hoped that their offer would be accepted, but they had been very hesitant about 'butting in' as Grandpa put it. Now they couldn't wait to begin planning the details. So now that the location was established, the family conference proceeded full speed ahead!

Suddenly, in complete innocence, Celee asked a question that placed a pall over the group. Her grandparents were so shaken that she was immediately sorry she had opened her mouth. But the damage was done.

"Have you heard from Aunt Sis lately, Grandma? I was wondering if she would come and play the organ for our wedding? I've only seen her a few times in my life, but I know she's a wonderful musician."

There was a heavy silence for a moment, then Grandma Wheaton answered quietly, but with a quiver in her voice.

"My dear, that's a lovely thought, but I must sadly admit that she hasn't been home in several years, and we actually haven't heard from her at all for the last six months. I'm afraid she doesn't consider this her home anymore. Of course we'll always love her, but I'm not sure she has much love for us." And Grandma wiped a tear from her wrinkled cheek.

Grandpa put his arm around her and pulled her close to him. "We seem to have no daughter anymore, but Rosi, you have done everything to fill the void. You're our daughter now, and you've given us our two beautiful granddaughters. You've brought us more joy than we can tell."

He smiled at Rosi and Grandma nodded her head as she continued to wipe her eyes. "We're happy that our son Frank keeps in close contact with us and hopefully he and his family can come for the wedding, but I'm afraid you can't count on Sis for anything." He shook his head sadly. "She seems to have inherited all the unpleasant characteristics from both sides of the family – as well as a tremendous musical talent. I guess that talent has maybe gone to her head, because her success has been phenomenal. She just doesn't need us any more. So, my dear," turning to Celee, "we'll have to make other plans for the music."

Josh had just the right answer. "I know my cousin Robert would be happy to play. I could ask him, if you like. He'll be home from the conservatory just in time for the wedding, and he's like a brother to me, so would you let me take care of that detail?" Josh's heart ached at the pain he saw in the eyes of the old couple, but he was thrilled to be able to ask Robert to be a part of this most important event in his life.

His suggestion lightened the atmosphere again, and from there on the family conference was like a party with everyone talking at once. Celee was busily taking notes, and Grandma Wheaton hurried to the kitchen for munchies which she always kept on hand. By the time the evening was over, the plans were well under way.

"Josh, do you suppose Eleanor would be one of my attendants? Of course I want Bardie to be my maid of honor, but I'd love to have Eleanor stand up with me, too. I want the two of them, and Polly, if she will." Celee had clearly already put a lot of thought into plans of her own.

Josh was delighted. "Honey, I think that's a wonderful idea. You know, Eleanor and Robert are the only 'siblings' I have, and to have them both in the wedding would be perfect. I've thought about my attendants, too, and my choices may surprise you. I want my dad and Uncle Dan to stand up with me, and my third one would be the youth director who works with me at the church. Jimmy's a good friend, but I want my dad to be my best man!"

Grandpa looked at Josh in surprise. This would be a highly original move, but as he thought about it, he understood the boy's choice. "You know, Son, I believe that both of them will be tickled to death, and the fact that you're asking them shows how close your family is. I know not everyone knows your story, but even not knowing your reasons, your choice would be an admirable one."

His announcement also delighted Rosi. She was continually learning new things about her prospective son in law, and so far they had all been good! She reflected that Celee had made her choice wisely, and the young man whom she had chosen would clearly command love and respect from all the family. "I think that's a wonderful idea, Josh. I agree with Grandpa that it will probably mean more than you know, to both your father and your uncle."

Josh spoke softly, but with great tenderness in his voice. "You know, if the Marlowes hadn't rescued my dad and given him a home, I wouldn't be here now. Who knows who I would be or where I would be. God has been very good to me, and when I try to confront the 'what if's' in my life, it becomes incomprehensible to me that God cared enough about my dad and about me to work out such a wonderful plan for our lives." He paused a moment, then added, "And the plan is still being developed, now with Celee in the picture." He grinned. "And you can see it's getting better every minute!"

Celee blushed under his unabashedly adoring gaze, and she quickly turned the discussion back to details of the wedding. Time passed quickly as ideas were exchanged and details were developed, until suddenly Grandma's rocker came to a halt, and she rose from the chair.

"Children, I am weary, so I will leave you and make my way to bed. And I think you all had better do the same thing. It's almost midnight, and tomorrow's another day. Come, Father, let's lead the way. If anyone wants anything more to eat, you know what's in the icebox and you're welcome to any or all of it. Goodnight, my dears." And she took Grandpa's arm, pulled him up from his comfortable Morris chair, and headed for the stairway.

Rosi quickly followed them, leaving Josh and Celee to say goodnight to each other. For a long moment, Josh held Celee close, breathing in the sweet scent of her. As she yielded to his embrace, she gave a little sigh and whispered. "It won't be long, now, Sweetheart. And isn't it wonderful how things are working out. I think our wedding is going to be even more beautiful than I dreamed it would be!"

Josh was slow in answering, too involved in savoring her nearness and the yearning that he felt. Finally, as he smoothed her fragrant hair, also exulting in the fact that their waiting was nearly over, he murmured, "The Lord's working it all out for us, Celee. He's just as interested in our wedding as we are. And since it's in His plan, it is going to be perfect! You'll see!" And after a lingering kiss, Josh headed for the door.

"Be sure you lock up after me, Sweetheart. Sleep good and dream of me!"

"I'll be sure to dream of you, Darling, because you'll be the leading man in my wedding dreams!" Celee turned her face up for another quick kiss. "Be careful going home, Josh. You know I love you!" she called after him. As she shut the door and turned the key in the lock, she leaned back against it and closed her eyes. Then she pinched herself to prove that this was real and not a dream. She grinned at herself for being so silly, and ran up the stairs to bed.

Chapter 22

There was a good bit of travel back and forth between Birch Lake Academy and Charlotte during the next couple of months. Josh set up a schedule of counseling appointments with the pastor of the little Covenant Church, which meant that Celee made the trip to Charlotte frequently. Rosi came as often as she could get away, and Bardy always teased for permission to miss school in order to come to Charlotte with her mother. Sometimes Josh flew up to get them, and other times they drove down in Rosi's big touring car, and when they drove down, Beth would come with them.

Grandma Christy, Eleanor, and Josie had been busy planning for the luncheon which would honor Celee, and would also give the families another chance to bond. It was to be quite an event, even larger than at first intended, as the guest list continued to grow. Aunt Julie would be there, and of course Grandma Wheaton and Rosi. Since Rosi had driven down from Birch Lake this time, both Beth and Bardy would also be there, along with Celee's cousin Polly. Then Eleanor added Penny to the list, and wished aloud that Patsy could come also. She remembered well the sweet girl in the wheelchair at Aunt Julie's open house, but was unable to figure out a way to entertain her, without a man to handle the wheelchair. She decided that there would have to be another event, in which she could have both the twins as well as that good looking young man that had been so attentive to Patsy. This one would have to be strictly a "hen party".

Grandma Christy was especially excited as it was to be held at the old brick house on Lawrence Avenue. It had been home to Christy for many years and had been the scene of momentous and 'historic' Marlowe events. Today would be a delight for she would see gathered together many of the people she loved best in all the world. And she was not at all averse to including some newcomers, whom she intended to add to that group! She figured that her old heart was still big enough to embrace them!

Penny arrived in time to have a few minutes with Eleanor and Eleanor's mother and grandmother. Christy remembered Penny from Julie and Sig's open house, and knowing of the two girls' close friendship, now observed her very closely. She noted with relief that Eleanor's friend seemed to be good for her. She wasn't one of those painted and sassy girls that Eleanor used to run around with, thank God! Penny's skirts were a decent length, she wasn't chewing gum, and she appeared to be a polite, intelligent girl. Christy approved.

By the time the Wheaton car arrived, Penny felt at ease with the Marlowes and was ready to meet some new people. She had been nervous when Eleanor told her who would be attending the luncheon. Then Eleanor had added, "It's going to be nice, Penny, but nothing fancy. Celee and her family are really lovely people, and you'll like them all. You've met Aunt Julie, and she thinks the Wheatons are great. So just come and have a good time."

Eleanor ran out to meet them as they got out of the car, and Penny watched from the big bay window in Christy's living room. She tried to guess who was who, but had no clue to the identity of the poised, fashionably attired lady with the gorgeous dark brown hair, beautifully styled, with just a hint of auburn in it. In contrast, her skin was milky white, and while she was not beautiful, she was a compelling figure, sure to attract attention in whatever room she entered. She was introduced as Celee's cousin, Polly, an art dealer in Petosky, and when she turned to acknowledge the introduction, Penny looked into snapping brown eyes, and thought that she had never seen anyone lovelier. Then Polly flashed her lovely smile and Penny's heart was immediately captured. She had never met anyone like Polly before, and was immediately drawn to her.

But then she heard her name called, and turned to meet the rest of the family. She was in awe of Dr. Rosi Wheaton, but Dr. Wheaton's two girls looked like great fun. The lady named Beth seemed to be a favorite of all of them. And Grandma Wheaton reminded Penny of her own Grandmother Katherine, who had passed away many years ago when the twins were still in grammar school. Penny decided that this was the most beautiful group of women she had ever seen gathered in one room. Only Aunt Julie was still missing, but Penny knew she belonged. She would fit perfectly into this gathering. Penny wished that her mother and Patsy could have been here with her. She knew that they would have fit, too!

Then Aunt Julie arrived, and the group was complete. Eleanor, Josie and Grandma Christy had outdone themselves preparing the festive lunch which was as beautiful as it was delicious, and by the time she started home, Penny felt like she had been visiting another planet. This was like a dream world. She had often attended lovely affairs in Little Rapids, but somehow this one, in an entirely unfamiliar and obviously wealthy setting, had taken her out of herself. She knew she would never forget it.

Of course, most of the talk had been about the coming wedding, and Celee had invited her to attend. She had thanked Celee, but really doubted that she would be able to come. In her heart, she was sure that her father would disapprove, even as he had questioned her acceptance of the invitation to lunch. She had come in spite of his objections, but loved her parents too much to cause them any more concern. Better to leave well enough alone, for a while at least. But how she would love to be able to accept the invitation!

At home, her mother and Patsy wanted to hear all about it, and Penny enjoyed reliving it for them. She described each person in great detail, and when she finished Patsy leaned back in her chair with a sigh, and whispered, "Some day maybe I'll be able to go out and enjoy such things again. At least, now I have hope!" and Penny rushed over and hugged her sister.

"You will, Patsy. You will. I know you will. I was wishing you were with me today. It would have been much more fun if you had been there, too." And for the first time in many weeks, the twins recaptured some of their familiar closeness. Louise watched them and smiled contentedly. Even if Penny's determination to have her own way had upset John, it was worth it to see her girls happy together again, even if just for a few minutes.

A few weeks later, when Rosi was again in town, Josh found it necessary to make a trip to Little Rapids to visit the iron works. He always made it a point to look in on Uncle Sig and Aunt Julie on such trips, and this time he took Rosi and Celee along, with the intent of giving them another opportunity to be together before the wedding. Today, he would swing by the metalworks first, then they would share lunch with his aunt and uncle, who had been delighted at the prospect of the visit.

On the way, he related his conversation with the client whom he had flown to Petosky, and asked Rosi if she recognized the man's name. She hadn't known him, but verified the story he told. "Yes, Josh, that was an unbelievably difficult time for my brother. It broke his heart that he could not see the twins grow up, but my older brother, who adopted the girls, was adamant that they must never find out they were adopted. I'm sure that was hardly realistic on his part, because I think that someday someone in the family will find them and tell them. But ever since he and his wife took them home to wherever they lived, we have had no contact with them. It's like they disappeared from the face of the earth. We often wonder what the girls look like - if there's any family resemblance, but I guess we'll never know unless God brings us together in some way."

Celee had been listening silently but suddenly she burst out. "You know, I don't think it was fair to the twins *or* to their brothers and sisters, to be separated like that. I know Uncle Kuno wanted them to believe that he is their real father, but just think how much they're missing not to know any of the others in their family! I know I just *love* to be with my cousins, and I can't imagine life without having a big family close by. I wonder if they're lonesome?"

"Honey, they might have brothers and sisters of their own by now. We just don't know! It's the absence of any contact at all with our family that leaves an empty place in our lives. But maybe we're just feeling sorry for ourselves. We may be wasting sympathy on them. We can sympathize with their real father and brothers and sisters, but probably they themselves are very happy. I hope so, anyway." Rosi smiled at her daughter. "So, my dear, since there's nothing we can do about it, I suggest that we just try to forget it and enjoy our day with Josh."

Celee nodded and grinned teasingly at Josh. " I don't think that will be too hard, Mom. Somehow I kind of like the guy. At least he's a good tour guide, and knows a lot of fun places. I think I'll keep him."

Josh reached over and playfully punched her arm. "I think you'd have a hard time getting rid of him, young lady! He's already addicted to you and addictions are hard to shake, you know! Besides, this addiction is a very serious one, which is going to last a lifetime, so you might as well get used to it!" They were all laughing as he drew up beside the Holt-Waggoner Iron Works and pulled into a parking space.

As he held the door open for Rosi and Celee, Josh saw that Penny was at her desk in the front office, and was again struck with her resemblance to someone he knew – but he still couldn't think *who*. Penny smiled a welcome as she hurried forward to greet them.

"It's so nice to see you both again. Josh, I met Dr. Wheaton and Celee at Eleanor's luncheon in Charlotte." She turned to Celee and Rosi, "We had a wonderful time, didn't we?"

Then the shop door opened and John Holt strode forward with his hand out. Josh proudly drew his guests forward.

"John Holt, I want you to meet my fiancée and her mother. Celee and Rosi, this is my very special friend, one who has the genius of being able to listen to me, read my drawings and make for me any part that I need to keep my Cessna in working order. I don't know what I would do without him," and Josh laid an arm across his shoulder in heartfelt friendship. "And this is Penny, his beautiful daughter and office manager." Josh beckoned her into the circle. "When I found John so near by, and learned what an expert he is, it was one of the luckiest days of my life!"

Suddenly Josh was aware that neither John nor Rosi was listening to a word he said. John reached out to take her hand, then seemed to pull back as their eyes met. Rosi's face went white, and Josh reached out to her, wondering if she suddenly felt sick. She shook her head at him and completed the handshake, but the expression on her face was as though a mask had dropped over it. He had never before seen such a look on his future mother in law's face, and he was at a total loss to understand what had happened.

John also seemed to be in shock. However, he pulled himself together, shook both Rosi's and Celee's hand, then turned to Penny. "Honey, I need the papers on that big order that came in by truck yesterday from Detroit. Would you get them together for me right away?" His hand guided her away from the visitors and back toward the filing cabinets behind her desk.

Turning back to Josh he asked, "Now, my friend, what can I do for you today?" Josh laid his briefcase on Penny's desk and pulled out his order.

"Nothing unusual today, John. Just some supplies for the store and a couple of standard parts for the Cessna. If you'll get them together for me, I'll pick them up this afternoon before we start back to Charlotte."

"I'll have them ready for you. How's the ferrying business going? I've sent a couple of my customers over your way, hoping they would bring you some business. You have a good reputation around here, Josh. Your safety record is unblemished, and I'm proud to be able to help you keep it that way!"

Josh noticed that Rosi appeared to have taken a great interest in Penny's movements, and was also watching John as though she expected something more from him. But he politely ushered them out to their car, with hardly another glance at her. Josh found himself extremely puzzled at the little drama he had just witnessed. However, he was destined to keep on wondering. The only comment that Rosi made was in answer to Celee's wondering observation.

"Mom, does that girl Penny remind you of anybody we know?"

Rosi's answer was slow in coming, and didn't give her daughter much satisfaction.

"Maybe. But many times people I meet remind me of someone else I know. I really didn't notice any unusual resemblance – either today or at your party."

And as they made their way to the Anderson home, the conversation turned to other things. They admired the town of Little Rapids, and nothing more was said about their visit to the metalworks.

Josh soon forgot about it as Aunt Julie and Uncle Sig welcomed them with open arms. The lunch was perfect, as always, and the afternoon was a delight. They enjoyed each others' company and the time flew by.

As soon as John had assembled Josh's order and had it ready for pick-up, he told Penny that he had an errand to do and would be back in the office within an hour or two. However, his "errand" took him straight home. When he walked in the door, Louise looked up in alarm. It wasn't that he didn't often come home during the day; it was that he looked tired and worried, and suddenly old.

"John, what in the world is the matter with you? Are you sick?" She hurried over to him and he allowed her to lead him to a chair. He leaned back as if no longer able to hold his head up, and audibly sighed as if in great sorrow. Louise's alarm increased.

"John, what is it? Tell me this minute. If you're sick we need to call the doctor."

"No. No, Honey. I've just had kind of a shock. I'll be all right in a few minutes. I just had to come home and try to get my head together."

"What kind of a shock? Is there something wrong with Penny? Has something happened at work? Tell me, John, or I'll go into shock myself!" She picked up a pillow from the couch and put it under his head. "How does that feel, Dear? Does that help your headache?"

He reached up, grabbed her hand, and pulled her down onto his lap. "Louise, something is bothering me – and is about to drive me crazy! I can't imagine why, after all these years, that I'm questioning the wisdom of our decision to never tell the girls that they were adopted, but lately I've had a feeling of – almost guilt - as if we're living a lie." Then thoughtfully he muttered "and I don't know what else to call it but a lie! What do you think, Louise? Have we done the right thing to separate our girls from the rest of their family? Have we been fair to them? Was it fair to their real father to take them completely away from him?" He shook his head, brushed his hand across his eyes, then covered his eyes with his hand. "It's been nagging at me for the last year, and I didn't want to bother you with my doubts, but I just can't keep them to myself any longer. What are we going to do, Louise? What *should* we do?"

Now Louise was as disturbed as John was. She understood at last what had caused his strange obsession to keep the girls away from any new friends who were not part of their tight circle. She still didn't know what had triggered in her husband this attack of – conscience? If it *was* conscience, it must have been lying dormant for all the years since the girls had come to live with them, for it hadn't seemed to have bothered him until recent months.

Her mind turned wistfully to memories of how happy they had been to bring the twins home, and how carefully they had kept their secret from everyone except her mother. Perhaps, like John, she too had realized deep in her soul, that someday their decision would come back to haunt them. As John pointed out, they truly *had* been living a lie before all their friends for many years.

Even her best friends, Kent's parents, had no idea that the girls were not their own. She had found ways to keep the truth from them; had spun a complicated web of deceit to keep Mary Ann and Gordon from suspecting anything. When she had her last miscarriage, she had not wanted to go out among her friends whom she knew would pity her, and she just couldn't take any more pity. So she and John had said nothing to anyone outside the family about the loss of the baby. Instead, they had let it be known that she would have to stay in bed and be very careful for the remainder of her pregnancy. They had stuck to their story, not knowing how they would ever explain it when the time came, and had even let their friendship with Mary Ann and Gordon cool so they could keep up the subterfuge. Katherine Waggoner had been extremely disapproving and very outspoken about it, but had agreed to lend credence to the lie by supporting their daughter and her husband, whom they knew wanted children more than anything else in the world. The opportunity to get the twins had providentially come just at the right time, or so they believed. As Louise had been out of circulation for several months, their story was believed without question.

Now, the two adoptive parents sat quietly, thinking back over the deception that they had nurtured almost their entire married life. Suddenly the thing that had been so unbelievably wonderful, took on a tawdry, dishonest aura, and their guilt confronted them. How could their good life change so suddenly, not by any earth shaking event, but by their own accusing consciences?

"But, John, we did it to help their father out. He couldn't have looked after those two babies at all. He would have had to give them up to someone he didn't even know. That would have been worse than what we did, wouldn't it? We've given them the best home they could possibly have, all the love and care that any children could want or need, and they've been happy. Very happy. You and I both know that. Could it really have been wrong?"

John groaned. "No, Honey, that part wasn't wrong. It was very right. I think the problem was the way we did it. We caused their father great pain by our insistence that the twins never know the truth, and I, at least, confess that I was selfish in wanting people to believe that Penny and Patsy belonged to us. I've been very proud of them, and you know how much I love them. But all the time I've had that guilty feeling, way down in my heart, that I was living a lie, and – God help me – enjoying it!"

"Well, there's not much we can do about it now, is there?" Louise stood up and straightened her dress and hair. "After all this time, we can't just come right out and say to our daughters 'you really aren't ours at all. You were born to someone else'. John, it would be such a shock to them that they might never get over it. We may have been wrong, but I can't think of any way to put it right after all these years."

John sat for a few minutes without answering, holding his head in his hands. To her consternation, she saw tears trickling from between his fingers. She knelt beside his chair, her arm across his shoulders.

"John, there's something more bothering you. Can't you tell me what it is?"

Lifting his head from his hands and looking at his frantic wife with tortured, red-rimmed eyes, he replied in a husky, quavering whisper, "It's not just the girls, Louise, and it's not just Karl. It's God! I think He's looking at me with disgust and condemnation for living a lie all these years." He sniffed and brushed the tears on his face with unsteady fingers. "And He's been really hammering me, Louise, ever since Patsy's accident."

Again he paused and shook his head. "You see, my mother and my grandmother knew God very well, and they taught me – especially Grossmutter – that when we sin wilfully, some day God will allow us to suffer the consequences of that sin. And – I think maybe Patsy's accident was the result of our lying to everyone and being so selfish." A hiccup that sounded more like a sob escaped him. "Louise – honey- what are we going to do?"

Now Louise felt the burden of guilt descend on her shoulders. "I – I don't really know, John. I don't know who could even help us find out."

"I guess we could talk to Dr. Phelps, but his sermons never have much to do with the Bible, and Louise, I think our problem is with God."

"Yes, you're right. I wouldn't be comfortable confessing to him anyway."

Suddenly she remembered that there was something else she needed to know. "John, what happened today that gave you such a shock? When you walked into that door, you looked like you had seen a ghost!"

"Maybe I did. I'm not sure just now what I did see. But I think I saw someone out of my past, and just the sight of her frightened me. I'm still not sure if she was who I think she was, because we didn't speak. We just looked at each other. But it brought the past back to me – as if it had been yesterday – and I couldn't let down in front of Penny and the strangers who were confronting me at the office. I had to come home to you – because only you and I share that past, and only you and I understand what we did in that past." He knew how badly she wanted to know whom he thought he had seen, but he couldn't bring himself to tell her. "Honey, I think perhaps this person only reminded me of someone. I'm not sure I really recognized her at all. And that's all I can tell you. I may never see her again, but it sure brought all those guilt feelings out in the open – in my mind at least."

Now Louise was the one who was distraught. Sometimes in her dreams she would find herself reliving those days, and would wake up in a cold sweat of fear that their secret would be discovered. But by morning she always succeeded in burying her memories, and only the sensation left by a bad dream remained with her. Now it was no longer a bad dream. It was a reality that had reared its ugly head and must be confronted. She was nauseated with dread.

"John, we must talk to someone who can help us. We can't live with this hanging over us any longer!"

For a long time, John didn't answer. Then he sat up with new determination. "You are right, my dear. We must soon make things right. But now I must get back to the office. A customer will be picking up an order this afternoon, and I should be there. But we will see them soon. That's a promise!"

Chapter 23

*P*lans for the wedding were coming together. As the early fall date approached, everyone was nervous except Josh. There were endless details to be attended to, and Grandpa and Grandma Wheaton kept thinking of things which they wanted to do. It was their intention that this would be a *perfect* wedding, and their excitement in having a part in it was endearing to watch. The phone lines were kept buzzing between Charlotte and Birch Lake, and the Cessna was frequently in the air.

On one occasion, Eleanor flew up to Birch Lake with Josh. The bridesmaids' dresses were ready for final fittings, and excitement was at a high pitch. Josh had watched with delight the friendship developing between Eleanor and Celee, and was relieved at evidences of Eleanor's late-blown maturity. Of course Celee's decision to ask her to be one of her attendants had done much to cement their friendship, which at one time had seemed impossible.

Eleanor settled herself into the co-pilot's seat, strapped herself in securely, and reveled in the excitement of the take-off. As Josh leveled the plane for the flight, he looked at his cousin and grinned.

"You really enjoy flying, don't you, Nell? Aren't you a bit afraid?"

"Afraid! Of course not. I love being way up here, able to look down on earth but not having to worry about anything that's happening down there. It's just us and the clouds, and I think it's the most peaceful place I know."

"You're right. I never get tired of it. It's nice to be able to make a living at something I really enjoy."

Eleanor nodded her head. "You know, Josh, I'm beginning to finally understand the truth of that statement. Working with Dad is fascinating, and the business is growing on me in a way I never expected."

Josh nodded. "Yeah, I've noticed that you've gotten pretty involved in it. I'm pleased as punch, but I must admit it has surprised me. I thought for a while you would never get serious about anything." He turned a teasing but affectionate smile on her. "When Uncle Dan took you on to help him in Underhill Associates, I wondered what he was thinking. I really thought that maybe he was losing his mind! You know, it's a far cry from Arnold and the Roarin' Roadhouse!"

An uncomfortable, telltale blush crept up Eleanor's neck and suffused her face. Looking down to avoid Josh's eyes, her words tumbled out in a mixture of embarrassment and anger.

"You don't have to bring that up, Josh! That's way in the past. I never did like Arnold anyway, and I liked the Roarin' Roadhouse even less! But I was bored, and I didn't know what else to do. I didn't want to be going to church all the time, and that seemed to be all you and Robert could think of! Now will you please forget it?"

"Sure, Honey." Josh was now all seriousness. "I didn't mean to make you mad. I was just teasing. As a matter of fact, I can't tell you how proud I am of you. The way you've taken hold of things at Uncle Dan's office has given him a new lease on life. He has come to depend on you tremendously. He really needed someone in the family to take an interest in the business, and he seems to be tickled pink at the arrangement."

"But, Josh, I'm worried. He may be depending on me too much. I'm not sure I can measure up to what Dad expects of me. I love what I'm learning about the business, (which, by the way is truly unique) but I'm afraid he expects something additional of me that I can't give. I suppose you know that religion had something to do with the founding of the business, and Dad expects me to believe the way he does if I carry it on. I'm willing to do things according to the principles by which it was founded and still operates, but you know I don't go in much for this religion thing. That's no secret to you, of all people."

"I'm not quite sure what you mean, Nell. What is it that you can't accept about it? You've seen how well the Corporation is doing, and how much it's helping the people who work in the associate companies. You just told me that you wouldn't change anything, so what's bothering you?"

Eleanor sat quietly, trying to figure out how to answer Josh. The problem was that it wasn't clear even in her own mind. She just knew that she lacked something important that the rest of the family seemed to possess. They were all so – religious. And in spite of all the days she had spent in Sunday School and church, she still didn't know what was so important about it. She continued to insist that she didn't want to get involved with anything – *religious*!

She was quiet for so long that finally it was Josh who spoke.

"Correct me if I'm wrong, Nell, but I think you're fighting the obvious. You're fighting anything that you think smacks of religion, but you're wrong. It isn't religion that's bothering you, it's the fact that you're not willing to give up trying to run your own life. You think you know better than anyone what's good for you, but ('scuse me for being blunt) so far you haven't made really great choices, you know! You see, Honey, it's not religion you're fighting. It's a Person. The Lord Jesus Christ wants you to give Him a chance. He wants you to admit that life is too much for you to handle all by yourself. If you let him, He'll take over for you, and give you direction- and the peace that goes with it!. You know, Nell, He has a plan for your life, tailored especially for *you,* and all that you have to do is ask Him. Ask Him to forgive you for being so ungrateful, and let Him come into your heart. He'll give you a new life and make you a new person." He looked at her with a sympathetic grin, and added, "Then you'll know what the rest of the family knows!"

"Are you are talking about what we learned in Sunday School, Josh? About God giving His Son to die on the cross for us? Is that really true? I always thought it was just a story."

"It's a wonderful story, Nell, and a true one. If you remember the rest of the story, He not only died, but He came back to life, and He lives today. That's why He can change your life and help you to understand why Grandpa Marlowe and Mr. Underhill set up the business the way they did." He paused thoughtfully. "And you know what else? Robert and I were able to get you out of that nightclub before you were disgraced, but it was God who helped us do it. He loves you very much, and is just waiting for you to trust Him. You could do that right now, Nell, and your whole life would be changed immediately."

Again there was a long silence. Finally a small voice said, "Okay, Josh. God wins. I'm tired of chasing around, always looking for something I can't find. I'll let Him show me."

Josh reached over and squeezed her hand. "That's great, Nell. Let's thank the Lord Jesus for saving you." And still holding her hand, he prayed, "Dear God, thank You for answering our prayers for Nell. Thank You that she's now part of your family. Help her to immediately feel the joy of your presence as she commits her life to you. Amen!"

Eleanor suddenly felt tears of relief in her eyes and a lightness in her soul. She hadn't realized before how heavy a load she had been carrying. She had only felt the effects of her anger and discontent.

"Josh, is this what makes Celee such a lovely person? You know, when she asked me to be one of her attendants, I felt guilty because I really didn't like her at first. I-I guess because you were going to marry her. You know, I always thought you belonged to me, and I was just plain jealous. I couldn't understand why she would want me to be in her wedding."

"You're right, Nell. She's a wonderful Christian, and she's been praying for you – like my dad and I have, and Grandma Christy has, and your dad and mom, and Robert, and a lot of the people at church. Now you can tell them the good news that their prayers have been answered. You have no idea how happy they'll be!"

The conversation had taken up much of the flight time, and now Josh had to turn his attention to landing the Cessna safely. The athletic field soon came into view, and as the wheels set down, a crowd of boys came running to greet them. The students were now accustomed to seeing the small plane land at their school, and Josh was a favorite of theirs.

As soon as they could get away from their admiring fans, Josh and Eleanor hurried toward the President's little home. Celee came on flying feet, followed closely by Bardy, and together they all trooped in to hug Rosi. Josh didn't have to say a thing, because Eleanor burst out with her joyful news.

"I have something to tell you all! On the trip up here, I accepted the Lord Jesus as my Savior, and now I'm a member of God's family just like you! And oh, does it ever feel good!" And this time the hugs were more than just family hugs. They were welcoming a new member of the family of God.

The fittings over, and the dresses duly admired, Josh and Nell made their way back to Charlotte. Josh was delighted with the change in his cousin, and the eagerness with which she shared her good news with the family there. She made it a point to quickly visit Grandma Christy first, then she had a memorable conference with her mother and father.

"Dad, I want you to know that I understand now about the business, and I'm so thankful for Grandpa Matt and Grandpa Underhill, and their vision in starting it. There's something more important than money, and now I know what it is."

"Honey, I couldn't be happier to hear you say that. But ever since you came to work with me, somehow I've been confident that God would work it all out for us. He's always had His hand on the business in a very special way, and this is just one more evidence of it." And he held his daughter close. "Welcome home, Honey."

Josh, to his friends and close family, resembled the cat that swallowed the canary. His anticipation was infectious, and while he paid careful attention to every detail of the planning, it was clear that the only thing he was really interested in was the moment when he and Celee would finally exchange their vows. When it came time for the rehearsal, his cousin Robert challenged him.

"Josh, I've always heard that both brides and grooms invariably get cold feet about getting married. Is that true? I haven't seen any sign that you've gone through that stage yet. What about Celee? Do you think she will actually marry *you*?" He grinned mischievously. "Are you sure she knows what she's getting into, or should I give her all the gory details and warn her about the risk she's taking?" Josh regarded his cousin with a look that suggested he must have three heads. "I don't know where you heard that, Rob, but I can tell you it isn't true and we don't need your help, thank you! Neither of us has any doubts about what we want, and as far as I'm concerned, I can hardly wait! If I were you I wouldn't waste my time worrying about either one of us." Then he grinned at Robert. "I know you're just kidding, but let me set you straight! It's right for both of us, God intends for us to be together, and it *will* happen. On schedule!" As an afterthought, he added, "And you might remember that for future use! I've seen the way you look at Bardy, and I'm guessing that you just might need that advice – sometime in the not too distant future!"

Now it was Robert's turn to feel his ears burn. "Aw, Josh, Bardy's too young. I would have to wait for her to grow up!"

Josh grinned, aware that his dart had hit the bulls-eye!

This wedding was one that the church family remembered for a long, long time. And it did, as Josh predicted, go off on schedule. Grandpa Wheaton spared nothing to ensure that it would be perfect for his beloved granddaughter. The local florist hadn't had such an order for years, and the decorations were the biggest and best money could buy. The bridesmaids were as beautiful as the flowers in their lovely pastel dresses, and Celee's 'one of a kind' bridal gown was complete with Grandma Christy's own treasured lace veil. This in turn was set off by a tiara of delicately scented orange blossoms , flown in from Florida on a special order.

Josh and his three groomsmen were resplendent in their tuxedos, and the ushers were proud members of Josh's youth group, also dressed in their best for the occasion. They solemnly escorted the ladies to their seats, and watching parents wondered at their sons who seemed to have suddenly grown up – right before their eyes! As the church filled, it was obvious that the entire congregation had accepted Josh and Celee's invitation to be their guests.

Robert held the guests captive with his professional performance at the organ, and Rosi took note of his talent. She was always looking for prospective faculty members for the music department at Birch Lake. The mothers and grandmothers were joyfully tearful, joined in their emotion by Beth and Babette. The groom was eager, and could hardly refrain from urging the pastor to hurry things up. However, with Billy and Dan and the youth pastor as steadying influences, and with Uncle Sig smiling benevolently on them from his position beside the pastor, everything went as planned. Finally Josh and Celee made their public vows, and Josh kissed the bride with unhurried possessiveness. Uncle Sig gave them the final blessing.

"May the peace of God, which passes all understanding, rest upon Josh and Celee as they begin their life together. Dear God, we thank you for their lives and for their consecration to you. May the years ahead be ones of blessed service, of loving dedication to each other, and of joy in their union. We pray in the name of our Savior and Lord. Amen."

And all the people echoed a heartfelt, "Amen".

The reception at the home of the Wheaton grandparents was also the product of Grandma's determination that her beloved granddaughter and her husband would have only the best to remember from their wedding day. The house was full of laughter and good wishes as most of the church family had also accepted this invitation. Grandpa had enlisted the services of the only caterer in Charlotte, and Grandma had baked and baked some more, and had hired two women to clean the already spotless house from top to bottom. No one except Celee and Josh had more fun than Grandpa and Grandma Wheaton. This celebration was not only for their granddaughter, but also for Rosi and her beloved Dan, whose wedding the old couple had not even attended.

They were celebrating both unions today, and hoped by their efforts to atone for that mistake made so many years ago.

Finally alone, having been given a sendoff in a hail of rice, Josh and Celee set off on their honeymoon; a trip to Florida in a new Buick coupe, Uncle Dan's wedding gift to them. Josh drove to one of their favorite spots, a nearby lakeside park just outside Charlotte. He stopped the car under a spreading tree, and took Celee into his arms. "Now, Mrs. O'Conner, you have taken on this very imperfect human being, and promised to keep him forever. Please give him a hint of how you feel about him – well, he would rather have you *show* him how you feel about him, if you don't mind!"

"And Mrs. O'Conner would *love* to show her very own 'imperfect human being' how she feels about him. She is so happy that the marriage ceremony included the words 'for as long as we both shall live'. And for us, that means eternity, Sweetheart, and I couldn't be happier!"

Josh folded his wife in eager arms, and finished the kiss that he had begun at the close of the ceremony. Then he had wanted it to last forever, and now there was no one to cut it short. The two lovers repeated their vows now in the privacy of their new car, beside the placid lake, with the smile of God enveloping them. Their new life together had begun.

Chapter 24

*I*n the meantime, there had been a joyful reunion in Little Rapids. Kent had two free weeks, and had come home to spend his vacation. He had brought along his red headed roommate, Roger Dawson, and soon realized that there would be no problem in entertaining him. Roger and Penny seemed drawn to each other like the opposite ends of two magnets.

Kent and Patsy observed this attraction with amusement. The two were so enamored with each other that they hardly knew anyone else was around. Roger haunted the metalworks during the day, and John had to find things to keep him busy so Penny could do her work. Surprisingly, Roger showed a sincere interest in the works, and John began to enjoy teaching him as Albert had taught him. In the evening, the two were frequently at the piano, Roger singing in a pleasant baritone and Penny brushing up on her playing. For the last year, Penny had seldom filled the house with music as had been her habit in their growing up days. Life had become too serious and uncertain, and Penny had been too involved in taking on the responsibilities with which she eased her conscience. But now music again gladdened the household!

"Maybe Roger can talk to Penny better than any of us have been able to," Kent confided to Patsy. "I have the feeling that she has been a little resentful of us, and she's plainly resentful of our involvement with the Andersons. I'm glad Roger knows the Lord now. I think he might be the one to help Penny."

"Oh, I hope so, Kent. I feel so sorry for Penny. She's really unhappy, I think. She won't admit it, but I know she is. We used to be able to share everything with each other, but now she feels shut out, and I don't know how to open the door. I do so hope you're right."

All of John's former determination to keep the Holts and the Andersons apart would have been of no avail as soon as Kent was at home again. He attended everything he could at Redeemer Chapel while he was home, and John surprised Patsy by seeming glad for her to go with him. And because Roger wanted to go, Penny went along. She told herself that she would just go for the fun of it and wouldn't listen to anything the pastor said, but in spite of herself she found herself intrigued.

In the course of his regular Bible Study meetings, Pastor Anderson had been teaching Revelation. He had reached Chapter 4, verse one, where John was called to "Come up" to Heaven, and this was where he started teaching on the night that Kent and Patsy, along with Roger and Penny, attended his class.

"We know that John represents the church, and we observe that from here on, we don't find the church mentioned again until the very last chapters of Revelation where it returns with Jesus at the Glorious Appearing." Pastor Anderson began. "So where do we find all the believers who make up the church, which is called the Bride of Christ? They certainly aren't on earth, because Jesus promised that His church would not go through the terrible tribulation described in Revelation.

"Class, we know that the church must be in Heaven, for the simple reason that they come back to earth with Jesus when He returns. We find that promise in Revelation 19 where we're told that He will come back riding on a white horse, and that the saints (that's us) will return with him, clad in white and also on white horses! So how did we, who are believers - the true church - how did we *get* to Heaven?"

"The early church had the answer, but for almost two thousand years, many teachers and church leaders ignored it. But during the nineteenth century the teaching was revived again, and in the twentieth century it began to be widely taught. The answer was a great event, which we call the Rapture, even though the Bible doesn't use that word. In I Thessalonians 4:16 and 17, we are told that '...the Lord himself shall descend from heaven with a shout, with the voice of the archangel, and with the trump of God: and the dead in Christ shall rise first. Then we which are alive and remain shall be caught up together with them in the clouds, to meet the Lord in the air; and so shall we ever be with the Lord.' The word 'rapture' means 'caught up" (a phrase we see in verse 17), so we understand that the Lord is going to call his children home before the great tribulation. I remind you that John represents the church, and when he was called to 'come up' to heaven, it was a picture of what would happen for all believers. And notice that it happens *before* the description of the great tribulation is given. Jesus promises that His bride (us) will not go through the tribulation!

"These verses tell us that the Lord Himself will come with the sound of a great trumpet, and those of our loved ones who were believers and who have already passed away and been buried, will rise and be 'caught up' together with us into Heaven! At the same time, we will receive new bodies that will be perfect, even like that of the Lord Jesus Himself!

"I know what you're thinking! You think it sounds like a fairy tale and is too good to be true. But I remind you that this promise is in God's own letter to us, the Bible. And God always keeps His promises.

"I would also remind you of a promise in a passage of Scripture that is very familiar and very precious to us. In the Gospel of John, chapter 14, verses 2 and 3, we read, 'In my Father's house are many mansions; if it were not so, I would have told you. I go to prepare a place for you, and if I go and prepare a place for you, I will come again, and receive you unto myself; that where I am, there you may be also.'

"The sad thing is that there are going to be people who have heard the gospel but have not believed, and they will miss that wonderful trip to Heaven. They will be left behind to endure the tribulation, unless they accept God's gift of salvation.

"For this reason, we are told to spread the Word to our families, our friends, actually to the whole world, because God doesn't want anyone to be lost. He gives us this commission in Matthew 28:19-20, and it's up to us to be his voice until He comes and calls us up to Heaven to be with Him."

At home the four friends were gathered in the Holt parlor, in animated discussion about what they had just heard. "Man, I sure learned a lot tonight. That pastor is some teacher!" Roger was more excited than Kent had ever seen him, even at fast played basketball games. "Of course I knew about the life of Jesus in the Gospels, and I knew that He arose from the dead. But I never heard before about His coming back to earth someday! As a matter of fact, I don't remember ever even hearing a sermon on the book of Revelation before. Wow, if what we heard tonight is true, Christians sure have something great to look forward to!"

"You can count on it being true! Pastor Anderson is a real Bible scholar. You know He attended that Bible School in Chicago – I think it's called Moody Bible Institute. I'd like to go there myself some day, but I don't plan to be a preacher – even though I seem to have been conferred that title at college." Kent laughed as he remembered Tim's efforts to make fun of him. "However, if we go to his church when I get home from college to stay – well, I guess I won't need to go off to Chicago. I can just listen to Pastor Anderson."

Patsy had been quietly reviewing in her mind what she had heard. After she had been wheeled into the house, and they were all four settled comfortably in the living room, she spoke quite shyly about what had impressed her. Penny pricked up her ears, because Patsy seldom referred to her condition.

"You know what caught my attention? Pastor said that when Christians are taken up into heaven, that they will all have new bodies – bodies that will never be lame, and that we'll be like Jesus. That means each of you – and *me!* Isn't that wonderful? It's going to be hard waiting for my new body!"

Penny could be still no longer. "I've been listening to all of you, and I can't believe I'm hearing you say that you really believe all those far-out things Pastor Anderson said! Listen. We're all sensible people, and we know he couldn't have meant that all that stuff is really going to happen! Can you tell me honestly that you swallow that tale about some day all Christians just disappearing from the earth? And that someday Jesus is coming back riding on a white horse and that all Christians will come back with Him on horseback? Of course I'd like to believe that (about the horses, I mean) but I never heard anything about horses being in the Bible at all – unless Noah took them into the ark!"

Roger was quick to answer. "And do you believe that Noah really built the ark and took all the animals in? If you believe that, Penny, why couldn't you believe the Rapture (I think that's what the pastor called it) could really happen?"

To that Penny was just as quick to answer. "Well, we were taught about Noah in Sunday School, but I never heard anything about the Rapture there. And I always thought the story of Noah and the Ark was probably a fairy tale, too, when I grew old enough to really think about it at all!"

Kent cut in rather sadly. "Penny, if I didn't know better, I would think you had been attending our college. You sound just like those professors and students who don't believe in God or the Bible at all." There was an almost stern note in his voice as he added. "I can tell you, Penny, you're wrong. God is real, and the Bible is true. No, I don't understand everything I heard tonight, but I know it's true, because it's in the Bible and I know the Bible is God's Word."

Dismayed by Penny's revelation of doubt, Patsy leaned forward, wishing she could get up and go to Penny. "Oh, Penny, no wonder we can't talk things over like we used to. Oh, please tell me that you'll accept Jesus so that we can all go up to meet Him together in the Rapture. I know Mom and Dad are believers, and I do so want you to be one too!" Patsy was almost in tears.

Sheepishly, Penny got out of her chair and went over to kneel beside Patsy. "Oh, come on, Pat. It isn't all that serious. Now let's talk about something else. The boys won't be here much longer, and we have to make our time count."

An uncomfortable silence greeted her suggestion. Finally Roger spoke in very serious tones. "Penny, there's nothing we can do more important than to pray for you. And whether you want me to or not, I'm going to be doing just that, here and after we get back to school. You see, there's nothing I want more than to see you become a believer." The look he gave her was full of tenderness and meaning, and Penny blushed. "You see, I want to spend eternity with my family and - best friends. So I want to be sure you're there!"

The evening ended on that note. The boys made their farewells for the night, and promised to be back right after breakfast the next morning. Penny helped Patsy to get ready for bed, and as Patsy hugged her goodnight, she whispered, "Penny, do you remember how people always said we were like two peas in a pod – until recently. I've been lonesome for you, and now I know why. I'm going to pray for you, too, along with Kent and Roger. I want our family to always be together – in heaven like we are on earth!"

Kent, Roger and Patsy had made their point. Sleep was not peaceful for Penny that night. There was too much to think about. She tossed and turned, slept fitfully, and dreamed that she woke up and everyone she loved had suddenly disappeared from the earth. In alarm, she reared straight up in bed, her heart beating a rapid tattoo in her breast. Then, realizing that it had only been a dream, she sank back upon her pillow, but found that she was afraid to let herself go to sleep again. She threw the covers back, leaped out of bed, and began hunting for her Bible. She tried to remember just where to look for those passages Pastor Anderson had read, and found that her search involved a lot of reading. Before long, dawn began to creep through her windowpane, and she finally fell asleep.

John was sorry to see the boys return to school for he was very fond of Kent and he highly approved of Roger. But the bond with the Andersons had been renewed, news of the Wheaton-O'Conner wedding had filtered through via the Andersons, and John was constantly nagged by the knowledge that he must get his problem with God solved.

However, soon all was quiet again, and life resumed its usual pattern. He continued to go about his daily duties, though constantly lurking in the back of his mind was the nagging awareness that something must be done —and soon - if he were to ever be at peace again.

One evening, after Patsy was in bed, and Penny had gone out for the evening, Louise felt she could keep still no longer.

"John, you're as nervous as a cat. Are you still worrying about the twins? I thought we were going to visit a counselor and see what he would advise us to do."

"Yes, Louise, I think the time has come." He got up from his easy chair and began to pace. "We've always known that sometime it would come to this. We just never wanted to admit it."

Again one of those long silences filled the room, so heavy that Louise found it hard to breathe. But she knew the truth of her husband's statement, and she also knew that it could be put off no longer. She finally took a deep, quivering breath and broke out in a sob. "But now that you feel so strongly about it – I'm afraid we can't ignore it any more. Now we *have* to admit to ourselves that what we've done is wrong and try to find a way to make it right. I still have no idea what we can do about it, but somehow we have to try."

John was silent, but sat down, this time facing her. She took his hands in hers and her voice was steady even as the tears rolled down her cheeks. "We know that's what we must do, don't we, John? We have to start working through our memories, and try to find a way to make things right. But can we do it without letting the girls see that something has changed – that something is wrong? Because, above all, we must keep our struggle to ourselves. I'm not sure I can, John, but I'm afraid of what this will do to our family if we're not able to control our feelings."

John nodded, but still sat silently. He pulled away and put his head in his hands. Louise arose, paced back and forth for a few minutes, then sat down in the other easy chair, leaving the question hanging in the air, her hands nervously wringing the bit of lace handkerchief with which she had dabbed her eyes a few moments before. Their guilt lay between them, almost palpable in the silent room, as each searched for some answer to their self-inflicted dilemma.

Finally John gave another heavy sigh, as if he had reached a painful conclusion. "I think, Louise, that there's no way we can handle this ourselves. I think we both need help – from someone outside our family. From someone who can give us counsel from a purely objective point of view." Then he shook his head with a hopeless expression on his face. "But I have no idea who that might be. I don't think I know of anyone to whom we would want to go for advice."

Louise suddenly had an idea, but was almost afraid to voice it. "John?"

"Yes, Honey. What are you thinking?"

"Have you noticed the tremendous change in both Kent and Patsy? Do you remember what I told you about Patsy's meeting with that young Jason who was driving the car that hit her? Somehow Mrs. Anderson, that preacher's wife, helped them to find the strength to accept what happened, and to be happy in spite of it. Do you suppose…"

"Are you suggesting that we should talk to the very people that I have been trying to keep out of our lives? Louise, you know how I feel. That is exactly what I've been trying to avoid."

"I know that, John, but maybe we're wrong about them. Maybe they could help us like they've helped Kent and Patsy. Couldn't we try, John? Or at least think about it? I don't believe I could talk to our own pastor about something like this, but I have a feeling that only God is going to help us find our way out of this mess without hurting our girls. Couldn't we just think about it, John?"

The distraught husband finally, with great hesitancy, nodded his head. "All right, Louise, we'll think about it. But let's still give ourselves a few days to – well, maybe even to pray about it. I agree that it's too much for us, and we do need God's help. But let's try for a few more days to just keep things normal around here. It's going to be hard, but I'll do my best if you will."

Louise met his eyes, and they were suddenly locked in each other's arms. Her head on his shoulder, her tears flowed freely and his tears mingled with hers. How had such a wonderful event in their lives – the coming of their precious twins – turned into this sorrowful burden which weighted them down today? They had finally faced the question, but now they had to find a solution to the problem they had created for themselves so many years ago. Their very lives and future happiness depended upon it.

Within two days, John knew he must act. This feeling of guilt was killing him and he knew that Louise was caught in the same web of confusion. So he picked up the telephone and did the inevitable. He dialed the number of Redeemer Church, hoping to find Pastor Anderson in his study. He was rewarded by a hearty "Good Morning", and suddenly found himself tongue-tied.

"Hello, hello! Can I help you? This is Pastor Anderson speaking."

John finally found his voice. "Pastor, this is John Holt. Perhaps you remember me. You and your wife helped my girls when Patsy was hit by a car…"

"Of course I remember you, John. How is your beautiful daughter doing? My wife and I often think of her and wonder if she's making any progress in learning to walk again."

"As a matter of fact, there is progress, thank you. The doctor is holding out hope that, with a new surgical procedure that is being developed, she may actually walk again. We're almost afraid to believe it, but he thinks that perhaps within a year, it will be safe to try it." John had taken a couple of deep breaths, and had found his voice. "But that's not what I was calling you about, Pastor. My wife and I have a serious problem that we need some advice on, and we wondered if we might have an hour of your time." He added quickly, "Just whenever it's convenient with you. It's not an emergency, but we would appreciate having an opportunity to talk it over with you, and thought perhaps you could help us." He knew he was almost stammering, trying to find the right words, but the pastor didn't seem to notice.

"Why, of course, John. Would you be able to come in late this afternoon, perhaps after you close your shop? I'd be happy to listen, and certainly help you if I can. I'm glad you felt that you could call me." Truthfully, he was very puzzled. The Holts, if anything, had been cordial but very reserved the afternoon after Thanksgiving when they were at the Anderson house. He had had the feeling that they were a very private family, perhaps the last people he would expect to ask for counseling.

"Thank you, Pastor. We'll see you about four-thirty then, if that's all right with you."

John immediately called Louise, and hoped that the prospect of confession relieved her burden as it did his.

Sig greeted them warmly, and ushered them into his comfortable study. He pulled three chairs into a casual, conversational circle, and they immediately felt at ease. John surveyed with interest the book lined walls, and noted that there were also little plaques hung about in conspicuous places, on which were printed either Bible verses or pithy little sayings, some of which he had heard before. One of them read, "With God all things are possible" and he found himself thinking, *"if that's really true, maybe there is an answer to the mess we've made of things."* Then suddenly he found himself praying, *"Dear God, we need your help. We've never really asked for your help all these years, but You were always good to us. Even Patsy's accident could have been worse. She could have been killed! Please help us now."* And a peace seemed to descend upon him as though God wanted him to know that He had heard his prayer.

As their story unfolded, Pastor Anderson sat forward in his chair, listening intently, interrupting only to ask a brief question now and then. Having finally completed the account of how the girls came to them, John suddenly dropped his head and, with an air of desperation, exclaimed, "Pastor, we know it was right that we take the girls. They needed a home. But the way I did it was inexcusable, and after all these years, I'm finally admitting it. My wife is not to blame – I was the one who insisted that the twins never find out that they were not born to us. I was selfish enough to want to keep them all to ourselves. I didn't want them to ever know that they had another family. Now I know what pain it must have cost their father to agree to it, but then I didn't care. All I could think of was that now we would have the family we had so badly wanted – and had been denied."

Louise interrupted him. "John, you can't take all the blame. I agreed to it, and it was together that we made up the lie and acted it out. We are equally guilty. But, Pastor, now we are concerned about the twins. How can we make things right without hurting them? We're the only parents they've known, and how can we tell them that it has all been a lie?"

Sig let the question hang in the air for a few minutes as he silently prayed for wisdom to give the right counsel. He realized that for the two distraught people sitting before him, this confession was a catharsis for them. Louise was again sobbing, and it crossed Sig's mind that the look on John's face was what a criminal might look like when caught red-handed. But now it was time for the advice and comfort for which they had asked, and which they so badly needed.

"Dear friends, I think you have done penance long enough. Your intent in adopting the girls was loving and compassionate and your love for them was never a lie. You've given them a wonderful life – possibly far better than they would have had otherwise." He paused, noting that Louise had stopped sobbing and was listening intently, and John had raised his eyes to meet his own.

"Then you made a mistake, and I think it *did* cause needless pain to the children's father. And perhaps it deprived the girls of certain family ties. But you provided a secure and loving family for them, so perhaps that evened out. As I see it, now the need to make things right is probably more important for you than it is for anyone else, after all these years. It would seem that you have repudiated your own siblings, John, in order to live this lie, and in so doing have denied yourself – and your wife and children – the joy of having an extended family. Such an experience is one of God's gifts to us. I know that having the Marlowe family close by is one of our greatest blessings, for each one of them enriches our life in a very special way, and in turn we have the privilege of reaching out to them and sharing their lives. There is nothing to equal the feeling of belonging to an extended family.

"So now what to do about it? I think I know what God wants you to do, and I think you know, too. I think it's as simple as picking up the telephone and making a call that will set things right. And I do not think you need to be afraid to do it. I believe the joy of reuniting with loved ones will far override any feeling of blame that the twins' father or any other member of the family would have."

"But how will the girls feel? Will they hate us for lying to them about who they are? I don't think I could endure that?" Louise's voice shook.

"I believe you will always be their beloved mother and father. Without you, Louise, they would never have had a mother, and they will never love anyone else as a father except you, John. Yes, it will be a shock to them, but young people are resilient. It will soon be a memory, but it will be a memory that brings the joy of new relationships, so it will not be bitter. My friends," he stood, placed a hand on each of their shoulders, and spoke with deep compassion, "the initial step will be the hardest, but God will work it out for you because you are doing the right thing."

He reached down, took them by their hands and raised them to their feet. "Let's ask Him right now to give you the help you need."

John and Louise bowed their heads as Sig talked to the Lord. "Father, you know the hearts of these dear people, and how heartily they repent of the mistake they made so many years ago. Thank you for their love and care for the dear twins, and now give them the courage and the wisdom to make things right with their family. Father, comfort their hearts, let them feel Your love, and bless them as they begin a new life, one no longer based on deception but on full restitution of the wrong they've done. And we ask that you will work in the lives of the ones who were wronged that there be nothing but forgiveness and gratitude for the loving care the twins have had in this precious family. Thank you for hearing and answering our prayer." And John and Louise joined him in a sincere "Amen".

Sig had one more question to ask his visitors. He couldn't let them go without making sure that they themselves were truly children of God.

"My friends, before you go, I must ask you. Do you know the Lord Jesus Christ as your Lord and Savior? Have you made a commitment to Him of yourselves and your home? Because if you haven't, you can't really ask God for a miracle, you know. He's good to us even when we don't deserve it, but if we really want His blessing on our lives, we have to put our total trust in Him."

He had been almost certain of their answer, but to his surprise John lowered his eyes. Louise was nodding her head that she was certain of her relationship with God, but she turned to John in alarm.

Pastor Anderson spoke quietly. "Do you have another problem, John?"

John was obviously deeply troubled as he met the Pastor's eyes. Then he looked at Louise as he searched for the right words.

"Pastor, for many years I have carried hate in my heart for an old man – my father – who is dead now, but who in a drunken rage almost killed my little sister. And somehow it was easy to hate again when that reckless kid crippled my daughter. I'm – I'm tired of hating, but I'm not sure God will forgive me."

Sig gently placed his hand on John's shoulder. "Friend, all you have to do is ask Him. If you are truly sorry, God won't hesitate to forgive."

John looked up, doubt still dulling his eyes. "Are you sure, Pastor? Somewhere in the Bible I remember it says that hate is like murder. Will God forgive a murderer?"

Sig smiled. "My friend, He would have even forgiven Judas if he had repented. You have no cause to worry. God will welcome you with open arms."

John nodded, relief now flooding his eyes. "I can do it now, Pastor. Will you pray for me?"

With joy in his heart, Sig led in prayer for this troubled couple before Him. Then John, in a faltering voice, asked God to accept his confession and give him peace.

John and Louise looked at each other and smiled. The thing they had dreaded no longer held any fear for them. John spoke. "You know, Pastor, God has blessed us abundantly and has never let us down, in spite of our neglect of Him."

Louise added, "We've realized recently that we haven't lived as we should, because we've watched our children, Patsy and Kent, and have seen their lives changed since they came in contact with you and your wife. And we do thank you for what you did for them. It made us see how far away from the Lord we had gotten."

Pastor Sig smiled broadly. "Yes, I've had some fascinating letters from Kent since he went back to school. He's having a great impact on his fellow students – and even on the very professor who led him astray. I'm proud of that boy."

Now John couldn't wait. His first act was to call the Wheaton home and ask for a telephone number. Then he dialed long distance.

Chapter 25

Bardy answered the phone. "Mr. Holt? Yes, of course I remember you. How are you?"

"Fine, thank you." John's voice shook, but this time it was with excitement and anticipation. "Miss Wheaton, could I please speak with your mother?"

"Of course, Mr. Holt. Please wait a moment until I can call her to the phone." Bardy couldn't imagine what the purpose of this call might be, but she could tell from John's voice that it was very important. She hurried to her mother's study where Rosi was deep into plans for the new school year.

"Mom, you're wanted on the phone. It's Mr. Holt, from the metalworks in Little Rapids. I can't imagine what he wants, can you?"

With a look of wonderment on her face, Rosi looked up at her daughter. "Maybe I can, my dear. We'll soon see if I'm right." And she hurried to answer the call.

A questioning, wary voice greeted her. "Rosi?"

"Yes, Kuno. This is Rosi."

"I – I wasn't really sure if that was you with young Josh O'Conner the other day. But it was you, wasn't it?"

"Yes. I recognized you, but was quite sure that you wouldn't want me giving away your secret. Your daughter was right there, and we had promised not to tell. I wanted to keep my promise."

"You were right, Rosi. That day I *didn't* want Penny to know who you were. But, Rosi, when I saw you standing there I realized all of a sudden how much I have missed my family all these years. And there's something else, too..." his voice faded out for a long moment.

"What else, Kuno? You know, there's been an empty place in our family, too. We had no idea where you lived, and we always wished we could know the twins, but we never stopped loving you, and we understood your silence."

"But, Rosi – there's something else I must tell you...the reason for this call. And this is very hard to say, but both Louise and I want to make things right. We know now that we should never have isolated the twins from their real father and the rest of the family. It wasn't fair to Karl, and it wasn't fair to them. We – I – was selfish in wanting them all to ourselves, and we didn't even consider the pain we would be causing Karl. This has really been bothering me, especially for the last year, and when I saw you so suddenly that day, I knew that we had to make contact with the family and try to make up – as much as possible - for what we had done. But, Rosi..."

"Yes, Kuno – or John. To me I guess you'll always be Kuno."

"Rosi, to you I'm still Kuno. But, Rosi, what frightens us is that maybe Karl and the family won't forgive us. Do you think he will? I called you because I didn't have any way of getting in touch with him, and I knew the Wheatons could give me your number. I wouldn't blame him if he hates me, and I still don't know how the girls will react to learning that they are adopted. But we have to go through with this. Will you get in touch with him for me, and ask him to call me?"

"Kuno, you and Louise don't have to worry. He will be ecstatic, and so will Polly, their oldest sister. You know how much she wanted to keep them and care for them. I think probably he will not only call you, but I expect that you will see him at your door as soon as he can get there. Kuno, your decision will bring joy to all the family. You and Louise can be sure of that."

Rosi heard a huge sigh of relief at the other end of the line, and a voice calling out, "Louise, it's all right. It's all right! We can thank the Lord it's all right!" Then he returned to his sister.

"Thank you, Rosi. Thank you! You don't know how much this means to us. And tell Karl that we want to see him – the sooner the better!"

As Rosi hung up the telephone, she put her head down on her arm. Immediately Bardy was hovering over her.

"Mom, what did Mr. Holt want?" Then in alarm, "Mom, are you all right? You're awfully pale. Wait, I'll get you a glass of water!"

Rosi reached up and caught her daughter's arm. "Bardy, I'm fine. I was just thanking the Lord for a great miracle, one I have hoped for but wasn't sure I would ever see. Honey, call Beth, then the two of you sit down here with me, and let me tell you about it. Then we'll plan to get over to Pellston as soon as possible to see your Uncle Karl!"

The three laughed and cried and talked, hardly able to believe what had just happened. Then Rosi thoughtfully observed, almost to herself, "Kuno mentioned thanking the Lord. I wonder about that. I don't remember that he had any concern about God before. Of course he knew that Grossmutter trusted God for everything, but it seemed that he always kind of scoffed at her beliefs – not openly, though. He would never have dared to do that. But his attitude always was that he could get along very well without God. Oh, I hope he *has* changed, and that your cousins have been brought up in a Christian home." Then she stood up, and, as was her habit, automatically straightened the things on the telephone table before she pushed her chair into its place. Her tone was businesslike as she spoke.

"Bardy, I want you to call your Uncle Karl and tell him we plan to drive over to Pellston this afternoon, and that we have something to discuss with him. Don't tell him anything else. I don't want to deliver this news over the phone! And tell him if he can have Polly there, I would appreciate it. Now I have to finish the plans I was working on when Kuno called, and you help Beth make lunch."

****

The touring car that pulled into the parking lot of Holt – Waggoner Metalworks was loaded. Rosi was at the wheel, with Karl beside her in the front seat, and Bardy between them.. Babette, Beth and Polly occupied the back seat. Everyone was in a mood of high anticipation, and Karl was almost beside himself. Polly seemed in kind of a daze, hardly able to believe that she was going to see those babies that she had fought so hard to keep. She could hardly comprehend that they were no longer babies, but grown up – almost eighteen years old! Young ladies! She wondered if they would look at all familiar.

Karl suddenly realized that his tightly clasped hands were white-knuckled, and he tried to relax. He laughed self-consciously, and commented, "Rosi, it's a good thing you're driving and not me. I'm not sure I would have been safe. I think I would have tried to make this car fly instead of keeping to the road!"

Rosi had been aware of the tension in her brother. "I think you can be excused for that! If I were about to see my children for the first time in nearly eighteen years, I'd be worse off than you are! But the waiting is about over. I told Kuno we would meet him here, and he'll lead the way to their home. I'll go in and tell him we're here." She opened the car door and had stepped to the ground when suddenly the office door burst open and her brother came hurrying out.

Now Karl was out of the car, running to meet him. The two men embraced, then stood apart with hands clasped, looking at each other. Finally John spoke.

"Brother, will you forgive me for keeping you from your children all these years?" There was pleading in his voice.

"Forgive you? Forgive you for giving my girls a good home and caring for them as though they were your own? Kuno, there's nothing to forgive. I'm in great debt to you." And the men embraced again.

Now Babette was beside them. John reached out to hug her, then he turned to Rosi. "Thank you, little sister, for not giving me away when you first saw me. I don't think I could have handled things that day, with Penny there. But now we have told the girls about their family. I still don't know how they really feel about it all, because they haven't expressed themselves too much. They've been very quiet and thoughtful ever since we talked to them. However, they seem to still love their mother and me and for that we're happy – and very relieved! We'll see them in a few minutes. I'll just close up the office and we'll be ready to go. Penny stayed home today so she could greet you there. But first, introduce me to these three lovely young ladies."

Rosi smiled and reached out to Polly. "This is the twins' oldest sister, Polly, and my younger daughter, Bardy. I'm sure you remember meeting my daughter Celee when we were here. She's now married to your friend, Josh O'Conner. We must tell them what's taken place as soon as we can, but they are at present on their wedding trip. Josh was very aware that something happened that day between you and me, but of course I couldn't tell him that I had recognized you. But now not only Josh but his aunt and uncle will be glad to know. He was telling us that they helped the girls when Patsy was hurt."

"They know, Rosi. It was Pastor Anderson who helped Louise and me decide that we must call our family and make things right. They're pretty wonderful people."

Babette stepped back and put her arm around Beth. "And this lovely young lady, John, is my adopted daughter, Beth. Her mother was the best friend I ever had, and when she died, Beth came to live with us."

John warmly acknowledged each of them, then unhooking a bunch of keys from his belt, he turned away, and with a lingering look at his visitors told them, "I'll close up and get my car. The house is just around the corner, so we'll be there in two minutes."

The reunion was something they would never forget. In spite of Karl's exuberance, he approached his daughters carefully. True to form, Penny was more reserved than Patsy, who wholeheartedly welcomed her new family. She seemed to understand something of the longing Karl had endured for his children, and when he bent down to greet her in her wheelchair, she hugged him warmly. Penny simply offered her hand to her aunts and her father, watching them warily as if unsure that all this was real. The revelation that they were adopted and had "another" father had been very hard for both girls to accept, causing the reticence that had given John and Louise some concern.

However, her bonding with Polly was instantaneous as they both remembered meeting at Grandmother Christy's luncheon and how they had been drawn to each other. She had missed her companionship with Eleanor, and Patsy's closeness with Kent in recent months had given her the feeling of being left out. She seemed to sense in Polly a kindred spirit that reached out to her and gave her comfort.

So Polly was greeted with a hug by her younger sister, who jumped up immediately upon seeing her alight from the car, and ran to meet her.

"Oh, Polly, I can't imagine anyone whom I would rather have for another sister! I just couldn't believe it when Dad and Mom told us about you!" Stopping to take a breath, she rushed on, "Did you know who I was when we met at Eleanor's party?"

"No, Penny. I had no idea that we were sisters – or even related. This was just as big a surprise to me as it was to you. We have lots to talk about, but I want to meet my other sister first." Polly looked about her, before turning again to Penny, who had taken her hand and was pulling her toward the house.

"She's in here, Polly. You know she's in a wheelchair, and she can't wait to see you." As they reached the door, Penny paused and looked at Polly uncertainly. "You know about her accident, don't you?"

Polly nodded. "I heard Dad and Aunt Rosi talking about it, but I don't know details. All I know is that she's in a wheelchair."

"Well, we'll tell you all about it. Come on, she's waiting for you."

Ushered in by her newly found younger sister, Polly found herself looking at "another Penny", who was leaning forward eagerly, and reaching out to her sisters.

"Polly, this is my twin, Patsy. Patsy, I told you about meeting Polly at the luncheon, but I didn't have a clue then that we were sisters!" Patsy reached up and Polly leaned down to give her a long hug. Then she looked at the two sisters, now sitting beside each other with their gaze turned on the sister who had fought so hard to keep them many years ago.

"Why, you two are as alike as two peas in a pod!" she exclaimed.

The twins burst into laughter. "People used to always say that about us," Patsy finally managed to explain to their mystified sister. "That's why we were laughing so hard. But that was a long time ago, and it was funny to have you say those exact words the first time you saw us together!"

Now Polly was laughing, too. "Well, they were right! And do we have other brothers and sisters?" Penny's eyes were as big as the proverbial saucers.

"Yes, you do. We're really quite a big family, and you've only met a few of us. And you not only have brothers and sisters, you have cousins." She reached over and pulled Bardy into the circle. "You know Josh and Celee. Well, this is Celee's little sister, Aunt Rosi's younger daughter. And of course now Josh is your cousin, too."

Bardy broke in. "And don't forget Marty and Margaret. They belong to Aunt Babette and Uncle Jesse," she explained to the now bewildered twins.

Polly grinned mischievously. "I told you there were a bunch of us! Let's see, I have pictures here in my purse. You have no idea how excited they are at the prospect of seeing you." Then she held out a picture of a dark haired, handsome young man. "This is your brother, Karl Jr., and he's just two years older than you are." She paused and her face grew sad. "You had another brother, too. A very special brother. He was the oldest, about two years older than me, and we were great pals. Peter loved to go out on his boat, but one day a storm came up quickly on the lake, and he didn't make it back to shore. That was a long time ago, but I still miss him. He used to take care of me when I was little. He thought that I was his special responsibility, and I loved him dearly." She held a dog-eared picture in her hand, and gazed at it as she spoke. Tears were in her voice, and Penny put a sympathetic arm around her shoulders.

"I think I know kind of how you feel, Polly. When Patsy had her accident and we thought she might die, I wanted to die, too."

Having introduced her siblings to her new sisters, Polly realized that they had been huddling around Patsy's chair, and that she had monopolized their attention. Quickly she turned toward the others, now sitting nearby and seemingly all talking at once.

Polly was very emotional at meeting her younger sisters, but was trying hard not to embarrass them by showing her feelings. But, as a matter of fact, emotions were so obviously on the surface with everyone involved, that the embarrassment would hardly have been noticed. Tears of joy flowed from Babette's eyes, and Rosi watched the drama surrounding her with wet eyes and a heart full of praise. How good God had been to reunite her family in such a wonderful way.

Penny and Patsy were trying hard to comprehend their new relationships, each in her own way. Penny had at first been somewhat resentful of the intrusion into their lives. However, as she learned about her new siblings and saw the pictures Polly had brought, the reality had to be acknowledged. She began to realize that this was not an intrusion. Instead, it was an exciting gift – still unbelievable but with great promise. The future would be full of new experiences as they met their family, and if the others were anything like Polly, she was ready and willing to meet them

Penny studied Karl with narrowed eyes. He was the most difficult for her to accept. Her birth father would not replace John in any way, she was sure of that. After all, John was really their father. He had given them his love, cared for them in sickness and in health, put up with their shenanigans as they grew up, and showered on them all the good things that a father could give his children. However, she regarded Karl with interest. Maybe he would be like an uncle – which would be a new experience for the girls.

And the aunts would take some getting used to. She of course knew that Aunt Rosi was a very important person, and someone to be admired. Babette she studied carefully. Perhaps here was still another grandmother. Penny still missed her Grandmother Katherine, whom she had loved dearly. Maybe this new family was going to be interesting!

Patsy accepted them all without question and with open arms. She, too, loved her mother and father, and would allow no one to replace them. But this invasion of relatives was exciting and having a large family would be something new and different. And to think there were more of them that she hadn't even met yet! She could hardly wait to write to Kent! She knew that he would be just as excited as she.

John was relating the story of the accident now, and everyone was listening. Louise was wiping tears from her eyes – tears of relief that this reunion had come off with love all around instead of blame and resentment. And the tears always came whenever she was reminded of that horrible night when they thought they might lose Patsy forever. Of course the part that Pastor Sig and Julie Anderson had played in the rescue came into the account, and at that point John made a surprising statement.

"You know, I didn't realize it then, but now I see that God had a hand in everything that happened that night. I've done a lot of thinking since then, and I've come to understand that He protected Patsy from what could have been a fatal accident." He was quiet for a moment, then slowly admitted, "For a long time I blamed Him for letting it happen at all. But I've seen that He used that reckless young boy to bring Pastor and Mrs. Anderson into our lives, and then He used the Andersons to bring about this reunion." Again he paused and everyone was quiet – almost breathless, awaiting his next words. He reached out to Louise, who was sitting beside him on the sofa, pulled her close to him, and put his face close to hers.

"But I guess the most important thing is that, through all of this, He brought us to our senses, and made us realize how far away from Him we had gotten, since we started living this selfish and cruel lie. For the first time in years, we both have peace (Louise nodded as she continued to dab at her eyes) and we have the privilege of seeing our entire family again and of being able to enjoy just being with them." He looked around at his listeners.

"You know, it was awfully lonesome without all of you. We lost many years – Louise and I and the girls – many years of happiness in sharing love with brothers and sisters, of watching cousins grow up playing together and loving one another, of helping each other over tough places, and of just knowing we were there for each other, no matter what happened – good or bad.

"So I guess I owe all of you, not just Karl, an apology. But believe me, we cheated ourselves as much or more than we cheated you! As I told Rosi, if you can all forgive us, we will be forever grateful!"

This was the signal for everyone to again reassure each other, for hugging and more tears, and for a bonding that had been delayed for so long. There was a period of almost eighteen years to catch up, there were other members of the family to be inquired about, and still others for Penny and Patsy to hear about for the first time. Wistful, nostalgic anecdotes were told about Grossmutter and Little Mutter, and tales (once aggravating, now affectionately laughable) about irascible Vater. The twins learned that they had still another uncle, Ferdinand, who lived in Brutus near Aunt Babette, who was famous for his beautiful gardens.

Finally Patsy, confused with the torrent of new names, asked, "How many more are there that we still don't know about?" Her question brought laughter, but it was the kind of amusement that felt like loving arms about her, and she didn't mind at all.

Aunt Rosi was the one to answer. "Some are not blood relatives, but so special that they might as well be. One, for instance, has been sitting here as quiet as a mouse, and listening to the rest of us jabber our heads off. Patsy and Penny, Beth here is truly one of the family. Celee, Bardy and I couldn't get along without her, and Babette and Jesse claim her as their adopted daughter. Then of course, there's your Uncle Jesse, Aunt Babette's husband, who's been like a father to all of us."

Bardy broke in. "Mom, don't forget Celia and Court, and Grandma and Grandpa Wheaton, and the Marlowes…"

"Okay, okay – no more – at least not right now!" Patsy and Penny were both laughing now. "We have some more to add, too, like Kent and Aunt Mary Ann and Uncle Gordon – Wow, what a family! Just think what Christmas is going to be like! Dad, do we have room for them all?"

John laughed too. "Maybe not in the dining room, but we sure have room for all of them in our hearts."

Again there was a silence, but this time it was a comfortable, dreamy quiet as everyone contemplated the miracle that had taken place here. As Sig had reminded him, John looked about him and thanked God for the extended family from which he had been alienated for so long.

Chapter 26

*T*he four sitting around the kitchen table at the Anderson home had much to talk about. Josh and Celee had returned just two days before from their Florida honeymoon, and one of their first visits was to see Uncle Sig and Aunt Julie. A long telephone conversation with her mother had brought Celee up to date on the recent events.

"I hear you had some real excitement around here while we were gone." Josh reached for another cookie. It was always hard to make the coffee and cookie come out even, and Josh could usually manage to stretch the cup of coffee so as to prove that he really needed that extra cookie!

"I've never seen a more amazing – or a more satisfying series of events in my life," Sig returned. "From the time we first met that trio of kids on the Little River Road, until the actual reunion took place, it appears that seemingly unrelated events were all working in harmony to bring this family together."

Julie put in, "Sig, you know all those things didn't 'just happen'. It was in God's plan for those precious twins and their family. The Lord was working it all out. He just didn't find it necessary to tell us what He was doing!"

"You're right, Honey, and I haven't forgotten that for a minute. You know, Josh, you kept talking about the twins and Polly reminding you of someone. I think they were reminding you of each other – with probably a faint family resemblance to Celee. It was just enough to nag at you and drive you crazy when you couldn't identify it, but looking at it with hindsight, it was a clue – if we could have just recognized it."

"And my passenger's story of Karl and the twins!" marveled Josh. "To think they were right here in Little Rapids all the time, and the rest of the family had no idea who - or where - they were!"

Celee commented thoughtfully, "Well, Uncle Kuno – or John – had made them promise never to try to make contact with them, and he even changed his name to keep them apart! When Aunt Rosi recognized him she was too honorable to give away his secret, but seeing her at least shocked Uncle Ku-John into realizing how much he missed his own family."

Josh was laughing at the difficulty she was having with her uncle's name. "Go ahead and call him whatever you please, Honey. We know who you're talking about. And I couldn't get a thing out of Mom, either. She absolutely refused to even discuss it for fear she would say something she shouldn't!"

Celee grinned. "If I'm having that much trouble with just one name, imagine what it must be like for the twins, all of a sudden having a huge family to get acquainted with! I can't wait to go and visit them. Do you think we could do it tomorrow, Josh?"

"I don't see why not. After all, we are cousins, aren't *we*?" he reached over and hugged her as he emphasized the "we". "And I can't wait to see Kent. We talked a lot about the fact that God has a plan for every person's life – a concept that was totally new to him. I'm wondering what he thinks about this new large family that has materialized so suddenly and the way the 'plan' is working out in his life. He and the twins were always a very private 'threesome', and they were very reluctant to let anyone else in."

Uncle Sig nodded. "I'm looking forward to having Kent home again, too. You know he and his roommate were here just a couple of weeks ago. You two were so busy with your wedding that there wasn't any chance of getting you together. However, Kent and Patsy attended a couple of my youth Bible classes, and they brought Penny and Kent's roommate, Roger, along. That's the first time Penny has ever attended, and according to Eleanor, Penny doesn't have any more use for 'religion' than Eleanor did for so long. Kent told me later that Penny scoffed at the teaching of the Rapture, but he was sure she had been deeply impressed. He and Patsy – and now Roger, too – are praying that Penny will accept Christ."

Sig hitched his chair around to a more comfortable position. "You know, that boy, Kent, has had a remarkable witness back at school, and even his former science teacher has shown an interest in the debates the boys have started in the dorm. They debate a variety of issues, but I guess the Scopes trial comes into the limelight quite frequently. It's still fresh enough in everyone's mind to trigger a lot of controversy." He smiled at Josh and added, "I get some very interesting letters from him, and I marvel at how much he has grown spiritually since the day he asked you if you believed all that stuff I preached!"

"That's great to hear, Uncle Sig. I'm going to be watching Kent, and hopefully I'll be able to see a lot of him. I think there's something pretty special about that boy. As to God's plan for us, Celee and I have seen such wonderful things happen in our lives that we're just waiting – almost breathlessly, I guess - to see what comes next!"

Sig looked serious. "We're *all* wondering what's coming next, with all that's going on in Europe. I have the horrible feeling that history may be repeating itself and that our 'war to end wars' didn't! Julie and I tremble for all you youngsters. However, we know that nothing in this world can destroy whatever plan God has for you – or for Kent or Karl Jr., or for any other young person who belongs to Him."

Very soberly Celee offered, "You know when Polly came back from her last trip to Europe, she said she wasn't sure if it would be safe to go again. That man Hitler has things terribly stirred up in Germany, and she didn't feel real safe in Italy, either. I don't know what it all means, but it makes me feel very uncomfortable."

Julie decided it was time to take things into her own hands. She stood up, began to pick up the coffee cups, and handed the plate of cookies to Josh. "Let's go into the den and make ourselves more comfortable. Josh, I don't mean for you to eat *all* of the cookies, just take them into the den so we can munch on them. Then I want to hear all about Florida. That's a place Sig and I have never had the privilege of visiting."

Grinning sheepishly but nevertheless relishing a quickly disappearing cookie, Josh led the way into the comfortable and familiar room. "Well, Aunt Julie, if you want to stay up all night, Celee and I can guarantee the entertainment. Florida and our trip south just happens to be one of our favorite subjects."

Later, in the privacy of their bedroom, Josh took Celee into his arms and whispered, "Honey, the conversation tonight got pretty heavy, but I'm sure of one thing. Whatever the future holds, I'm not afraid, and I don't believe you are either. And the way things have worked out for your family to be reunited has been a miracle. So no matter what may happen in the coming years, we can trust and not be afraid. We have the promise of God's plan, not for us only, but for the whole world. And God always keeps His promises!"

Also by Evelyn Wheeler Towler

Under Sheltering Wings

The Road to Home

About the Author

After 38 years working in the field of education, Evelyn Wheeler Towler is now retired and lives in Dunedin, Florida, the city in which she grew up. During her career she was involved in the founding of a Christian school in Lakeland, Florida. While teaching in public school, she received awards in 1971 and 1973 as a 'Leader in American Elementary Education' and as 'An Outstanding Elementary Teacher'. In 2005 she was named in 'Who's Who in America' and in 2006 in 'Who's Who of American Women' and 'Who's Who in American Education'.

During her teaching career, her first concern was always the individual student, whether child, teen-ager, or young adult. As she counseled with them over the years, she came to identify three main areas of confusion with which they struggled:

1. making good choices in life and understanding the consequences of bad choices
2. seeking the will of God for their lives, and
3. surviving the pitfalls of modern dating, and of finding the right life partner.

"I was born into a Christian family," recalls Evelyn, "but I remember experiencing the same uncertainties. However, I found many of my answers in the Christian fiction books by Grace Livingston Hill, and I read every one of them that I could get my hands on."

She continued, "I not only loved to read, I also loved to write, and the desire grew in me to also write Christian fiction at some point in my life. Retirement has given me the opportunity to do just that.

"It is my prayer that in reading my story, some will choose to follow Solomon's advice and allow God to direct their lives."